Knight of Light

By

Annette Louise

Ink & Quill Publishers
Henderson, Nevada
2014

Annette Louise

Knight of Light

Annette Louise

Line/Content Editor: Denice Whitmore
Cover: Maxwell Alexander Drake
Interior Design: Jo A. Wilkins & Audrey Balzart

ISBN: 978-1-934051-77-1/Paperback
ISBN: 978-1-934051-80-1/E-Pub

Ink & Quill

www.iqpublishers.com

Published and printed in the United States of America

To my amazing children: Patrick, Mandy and Annamarie. I am so very proud to be able to call myself your mother. You guys are living proof that the good in the world has a chance of winning.

I love you guys!

Knight of Light

Chapter One

"I *need* chocolate!" Miranda flattened her back against the cool white wall of the restaurant's serving station.

The only other waitress in the sterile room looked away from the dessert plates she'd arranged on a shiny serving tray and gave her an appraising look. "You mean, you *want* chocolate?"

Miranda blew out a pent-up breath and glanced back at the still swaying service door. "Nope, definitely need it."

Shara raised a well-tweezed brow. "And why is that?"

"Table seven," Miranda answered, her gaze pinned to the door as if she could see through it. The disturbing energy she'd felt since the occupant of table seven first entered the dining room had not lessened even with a wall separating them.

"Tough customer?" Her friend nodded sympathetically and added another piece of pie to her tray.

"Not…so much." She hadn't even spoken to him yet. A shiver tickled its way down her spine and she straightened away from the wall. Taking a deep breath, she turned her back on the door and totaled the ticket for table number five using the touch screen register. She shook her head at the outrageous amount. It still amazed her that people would spend enough on one meal to pay her rent for a month.

Finished at the register, she moved to the side to allow Shara to complete her work.

"Then, what's the problem?" Shara tallied her own ticket, her fingers flying over the screen, quick and efficient.

"The guy is creeping me out." Miranda felt her gaze drawn back to the door. She tried to suppress the goose bumps that threatened to cover her arms.

Shara eyed her with concern. "What's wrong with him?"

Miranda pocketed the receipt for table five and rubbed her fingers along her long white sleeves. Could she be overreacting from the strange feelings of anticipation this man produced? Will these feelings go away? She shrugged. She couldn't explain. She grabbed a crystal water carafe from the shelf above the prep-counter and placed it on a small tray.

Shara's brows drew together. She slipped over to the swinging door. With one last confused look at Miranda, she pushed it open an inch and peeked out at the man seated at table seven. "Oh, my ..."

"Yeah, tell me about it." Miranda joined Shara at the door. She couldn't help but look. She felt drawn to this man in a way that unnerved her.

"Girl, a guy like that is gonna *melt* your chocolate!" Eyes still glued to the dark handsome man, Shara fanned herself with her free hand. "Scratch that. If you had a man like that, you'd never need chocolate again!"

On tiptoes, Miranda stared over Shara's shoulder. His strong, classical features made her mouth water. Not only was he gorgeous, but the man oozed power, authority, and raw animal sexuality. "Sure you don't have a candy bar in your purse?" Chocolate was by far the safer option.

Shara let the door slip shut, blocking their view. "I don't see the problem here. If a man that hot eyed me, I'd be ecstatic!"

Miranda assessed her friend. Shara stood there tall, busty, and blonde. "Hmm...well, men like that do watch you. Guys like that do not look at me. It's weird."

Shara gave her a quick hug and hurried back to get her tray. "You underestimate your appeal to the opposite sex." She smiled, gracefully hefted her full tray to shoulder level and disappeared into the soft candlelight of the dining room.

Miranda snorted at the empty room. She was short, thin, and her chest wasn't even worth mentioning. Her two redeeming qualities were her big blue-grey eyes and long, brown hair. In the City of Sin, this was *not* enough to generate attention from men like table seven. In her small hometown, her looks were sufficient and she hadn't lacked for dates, but in Las Vegas there was an abundance of extremely beautiful women who made her feel like she blended in with the wallpaper. This suited her fine. Her most fervent hope, to be invisible here, had succeeded a little too well.

Shara blew back through the service door with her empty tray. "You're still in here? If you don't get your butt back out there and flirt with him, at least a little bit, I'm going to cut you off chocolate forever!"

Miranda stepped to the side as a willowy red-headed waitress hurried through the doors and bee-lined it down the short hall to the pickup window. Miranda shot Shara a look that said— *drop dead—I'll find my own damn chocolate.* She took a deep breath of the exquisite aromas wafting from the kitchen, feeling the strange calming effect that food always gave her, and backed through the door with her tray.

She entered the dining room and once again felt his slow appraising stare watching her every move. She couldn't help but look down at herself. What could he possibly be looking at? All the buttons on the white tuxedo style shirt were done up. Her black slacks were not tucked into her socks. Her shoes matched.

Miranda looked back up, straight into his exotic green eyes. The way they stared so deeply into her own was mesmerizing. Everything about him was compelling. His tanned skin and dark hair combined with solid muscles and chiseled features made for an attractive package of pure maleness. She had to be imagining it, but even her fingers seemed to be tingling with the tangible energy building between them. The electricity in the air drew her thoughts toward him. When she realized she was walking toward him, she swallowed hard and nearly choked on her own spit, breaking the spell. At least she hadn't drooled—not noticeably anyway.

She detoured to table five.

"Gentlemen, I hope you enjoyed your meal." Miranda slipped the black leather folder containing their bill onto the edge of the table. The men didn't even hear her. It was as if she didn't exist. She snuck a peak back to table seven. So why was he so aware of her?

She exhaled and lifted her tray up above her shoulder and turned toward him. The energy in the room shifted. She glanced around in surprise. No one else noticed the change. She looked at the big leafy plants, the marble statuary, and the almost half full room of Vegas' social elite. The high dollar restaurant was far from The Strip. No tourist would stumble upon this establishment. It was for the select few who were either born into money or had made enough of their own to be accepted. She shrugged off the unsettling feeling of unease. Nothing would happen to her here. She was safe in a place like this.

Please, oh please don't let me trip over my own feet and drench the divine being with my newfound clumsiness. This awkwardness is his fault. I'm normally very graceful. Most of the time. Okay, at least half of the time. She gave herself a mental shake and put a stop to the silent dialogue in her head.

"Water?" she asked with a low, husky voice. Where did that voice come from? She cleared her throat.

He smiled a slow, brilliant, white smile. His eyes searched hers. "Worked here long?" His deep, smooth, accented voice reverberated through her like a lingering caress.

She closed her eyes. She must be dreaming.

"I've been looking for you, Miranda."

Her eyes flew open. "Wh-what?"

"We were supposed to connect years ago. Although I must admit, I'm curious as to how you've managed for so long. I can't tell you how displeased I am that you have put us nearly two years behind schedule. We must educate you as quickly as possible. Shall we go?"

Miranda took a step back and her eyes widened with a new wariness. "I'm sorry. Did I miss something?"

The handsome man grinned. "Yes, you did."

"Wh-what?" She had to get away from him before her newly acquired speech impediment became permanent.

Again, he lavished her with his devastating smile and said

simply, "Me, *Love*. You missed me."

"*Whuh?*" The air left her lungs in a rush. That was the most intimate thing anyone had ever said to her. Pathetic as that may be. Said with a very British-sounding accent from a man who could have easily been the cover model for GQ. It was a fair assessment to say his one little statement topped her limited experiences in the romance department. And she wasn't even certain it was meant to be romantic.

"I believe you have already been activated, although I'm not sure how that happened without me." He looked perplexed. A small crease appeared between his brows, but only for a moment. He was apparently too self-possessed to doubt himself for long. "However, our connection is strong, our bond remarkably solid." Again, his darkly lashed eyes studied her. "Perhaps I have the power to increase your natural abilities. Interesting possibility."

The intensity of his gaze seemed to suck the remaining air from her lungs. Lightheaded, she forced herself to inhale and find her voice. "I...I think you must have me confused with someone else."

"Miranda—" he leaned forward—"I am not confused. I do not make mistakes. Come here, I will show you."

She couldn't imagine why the physical attraction drew her to him, because if any other man had said those same words to her, she would've run screaming in the opposite direction. She felt an invisible pull from him that she couldn't resist. She shook her head. Her parents had raised her to think with her brain, not her libido. She could resist the attraction for the sake of her safety. "I think I need to finish with table five…"

Without breaking eye contact, he informed her, "They are gone."

She looked over her shoulder—sure enough, she hadn't even noticed them leave.

"Come here." His demanding voice held the promise of reward if obeyed.

She backed up one small step.

"There is no reason to fear me. I am not the one who means you harm. Come with me and I will teach you what you need to know."

"Of course you will," she said in a voice meant to placate the mentally disturbed hottie. He was way too perfect in the looks department...and this was Vegas. Most of the good looking guys were gay. Did that make all the *really* good looking ones psychotic? "I had teachers in school. Got plenty of education there, so I think I'll pass on the whole teaching thing, but thanks for the offer."

"Do you fear me? I assure you, I have much to offer you."

I just bet you do. "Tempting—" heaven only knew how tempting— "But no."

He inhaled a deep breath, then exhaled slowly through his long aristocratic nose. "Look, *Love,* we don't have a lot of time. We must get started. I know you haven't had a chance to adjust to the idea of me as your trainer, but it is imperative we do not waste what time we have left."

"Yeah...see, about that," his having a deranged mind did help to make the temptation a little easier to resist. "I have no idea who you are, or what you're talking about. So, if you're ready to place your order, I would be happy to help you. But if you need more time to decide what you'd like for dinner, I'd be happy to check back in a little while." Like next year. I'm so outta here. She would plead a sudden case of nausea and run for home.

His disturbing smile said he knew her thoughts.

"My mistake," he said. His words surprised her. Didn't Mr. Perfect just say he didn't make mistakes? "I gave you more information than you were ready for. Perhaps you will teach me as well…patience."

She snorted. "Good luck with that. I can't even wait for Christmas to open the presents."

One corner of his lips lifted in what appeared to be an involuntary smile. A new sparkle lit up his eyes.

She felt the heat creep up her neck. Quite possibly the most attractive guy in all of Las Vegas sat before her and she had made a very unladylike noise and said something childish. No wonder she was still single, she thought with a sigh.

"I'm gonna…" she motioned somewhere behind her. "I should…" When words failed her, she turned to go.

"Wait."

The command had her turning back to face him.

Again with the slight wrinkle between his brows, he regarded her and she had the sensation of being examined on a deeper level. "I will have the house special, medium rare, with the Caesar Salad. Water with lemon to drink." He held out the black and gold menu to her.

Now he wanted food? She stood stunned at how fast he changed his direction.

With one more reassuring look at the security of the restaurant's clientele, she gave a mental shrug. So what if this gorgeous piece of eye-candy is a little deranged? Most people are to some extent. She felt flattered he had chosen to flirt with her—she could daydream about him for months. All she had to do was serve him his meal and get him out of here before she caved in to the desire to cuddle up next to him and never leave his side. She could do it.

He moved the menu an inch closer to her and lifted his brow at her reluctance to take it.

She looked at his long, tanned fingers that held the menu and wondered about her sanity. She took a small step toward him and felt the hairs on her arms raise. She took another step and could actually feel the energy around them increase. One more involuntary shuffle and she was standing much closer than necessary to take the menu. She reached her hand forward and he shifted just enough for their fingers to brush. An electric shock went through her. An energy current traveled up her arm, branched out and spread to the tip of her head, all the way down to the end of her toes. She blinked at the shimmering white particles gathering in the air around them. Shocked, she yanked her hand back and her gaze flew to his.

He acknowledged nothing.

All the white energy in the room gathered closer to her. It came faster and stronger than she could ever have created on her own. She tried to repel it, but it amassed too quickly. "Can they see it?" she whispered in a panic, motioning with her head to the other guests in the room.

"Not yet," his response soft. "But I can."

"No, no, no! Not here. I can't control it like this!" she hissed between clenched teeth before turning on her heel and hurrying back to the safety of the serving station.

The swinging door opened by itself when her hand neared it. She hoped her fingers were close enough to the black metal panel that no one noticed she hadn't actually touched it.

She set the water tray on the counter and leaned against the wall. Her heart pounded in her ears and she placed a hand on her chest trying to stop the frantic beating. She closed her eyes, she didn't have to see to know the glittering white filled the air. More than she had ever seen before. She needed to disperse the accumulated energy back to the surroundings before she did something bad.

A few years ago, she started to see the sparkles in the air. At first she thought her vision was playing tricks on her. When she mentioned it to her mom, she earned a trip to the eye doctor. He explained some people could see 'floaters' in the air and believed glasses would help. They didn't.

It wasn't long before she realized she saw something no one else could, and sometimes, she could control it. On a very small scale. The light shimmered everywhere. Some people attracted it. Some people repelled it. No one else seemed to know it was there.

But she knew. And if she didn't do something in a hurry, the diners in the restaurant were going to know. A heavy dread settled over her. She tried to feel the comfort of the glittering energy, to let it wash through her body and pass on through to her surroundings. Closing her eyes she tried to calm herself. She couldn't relax enough to let it through. There was too much power and she couldn't disperse enough of it.

Being alone in the room wouldn't last. She looked around, anxious. She'd never experienced this much of the energy, somehow she needed to discharge some of it to lessen the force. She hesitated, then reached her hand forward and allowed a spark to flow from her fingers. She intended for it to bounce harmlessly across the white tile floor then fizzle into nothingness, but what shot out of her fingers had more power than she could've imagined.

The blast cracked three of the large tiles before zinging down the short hall where the order pick-up counter and her boss's office were located.

"Holy crap!" How do you explain broken tiles to a power-hungry boss? Her eyes settled on the serving tray and she stretched her hand forward and let a smaller, more controlled zap knock the crystal carafe to the floor. It would cost more than she made in a night to replace the pitcher, but what choice did she have?

She did a quick mental inventory of the energy. Satisfied she could control it now, she stooped down to pick up the broken glass shards and the swinging service door opened.

"Uh-oh. Thought I heard glass." Shara bent down to help. "Would you look at that?" she exclaimed. "It broke the tiles! How did the pitcher manage that?"

The side door down the hallway opened and they both held their breath. The night manager stalked toward them. "What's going on out here?"

Miranda stood up and dropped some of the larger pieces of glass into the trash can. "Sorry, John. I came through the door and slipped. The carafe fell. I'll pay for it."

The manager did a quick inventory of the floor and did a double take. "How in the hell did you break the tiles?"

"They cracked when the carafe hit. Sorry." She hoped she sounded more convincing to John than she did to her own ears. She would have to practice lying, or her explanations of the strange things that sometimes happened around her, would not be plausible.

"Three of them broke when one pitcher fell?" His expression was dubious.

She shrugged with her hands in the air. It was the best she could think of.

John was getting worked up. "We should take the cost of replacing them out of your check as well."

Shara stood up. "Oh no, you won't. It's not Miranda's fault the tiles broke that easily. And don't you dare charge her for the carafe either. You're lucky she doesn't sue you for slipping. She could've been hurt."

True friends are beautiful. Miranda concentrated hard and funneled a small amount of the excess 'light' still in the room to Shara. In small doses, it felt wonderful.

John's face flickered with emotion. She directed a small amount of the shimmers away from him—let the all-powerful boss struggle a little.

Shara patted her on the arm and smiled at John. "Aren't you going to ask Miranda if she's all right?"

John glared at Shara and remained silent.

"John, I think I pulled something in my back when I slipped. I really need to go home for the rest of the night." A half lie, half-truth.

His face went red and she channeled a little of the light back to him. She had to get out of here, even if it meant making him feel good.

"I don't know..."

She directed a little more his way.

"Of course. Go home, get some rest. Call if you aren't well enough to come in tomorrow." He patted her awkwardly on the shoulder and returned to his office.

"Huh. Didn't think Mr. Control Freak had it in him to be nice," Shara said in surprise before whirling back to Miranda. "You okay? How's your back?"

"I'm fine. I think taking the rest of the night off would be a good idea though. It's slow tonight. Would you mind finishing my tables?"

"Course I will. You go home and take it easy." Shara wasn't stupid. "Table Seven?"

Miranda ducked her head and avoided the real question. "Table seven has just ordered." She scribbled the man's order onto the order sheet and handed the pad to Shara. "Five has already left and my other tables are empty. The rush is over, so it shouldn't be too hard."

Shara shook a finger at her. "Did you at least give him your number?"

"This is Vegas, you don't go giving your number out to strangers. Not safe. Didn't your parents teach you anything?"

Shara crossed her arms. "Not kidding. That man is hot and you need to date more."

Miranda grabbed a broom and swept up the smaller pieces of glass. "*More* would indicate that I date at all."

"Exactly my point. You should give him a try."

"Not this one. He's hot, but he's not playing with a full box of crayons, if you know what I mean."

Shara laughed and grabbed the metal dustpan off the wall hook. "A guy that perfect doesn't need any crayons! He can draw a colorful picture with just his body language. You can't leave without giving him your number."

"Yes, I can," she mumbled to herself.

"If you're not going to do it, then I'm gonna give your number to him." Shara positioned the dustpan flat on the floor.

Miranda's heart skipped a beat. "No! Please don't." The words came out in a rush.

Shara did a double take. "Honey, are you scared of him?"

"No, no. Nothing like that…I'm just not sure if I want to go down that road." She swept the glass into the pan. Was she afraid of him? No. Even now, she felt the tempting pull to go back into the dining room and be near him, but given what he'd just done to her, she was going to use the intelligence she'd been blessed with and run straight out the back door and pray he never came here to eat again.

Shara dumped the glass from the pan into the trash and stood up. Another waitress entered the room. Shara ignored her, but lowered her own voice. "It's time you joined the rest of the world. If you don't want him to have your number, I'm gonna set you up with one of my friends."

Miranda rolled her eyes. "You mean one of your old boyfriends?"

"Yep. Don't worry, I'll pick you a good one."

"If he's such a good one, why aren't you keeping him for yourself?"

Shara smiled. "I'm not ready to settle down. Good or bad, I don't get serious with any of them. Not yet. Don't worry, we'll have fun. You go on home before I change my mind about covering for you. It's gonna be a boring night without you."

Miranda gave her a grateful hug before running down the short hallway. She detoured into the small break room, grabbed her purse from her locker, then went left out the back door to the rear parking lot. She pushed through the door, seeing that the sun had set and was relieved to find the night air warm instead of scorching. She hoped John wasn't looking out his office window, because she wasn't moving like someone with an injured back. She needed to hurry. She wanted to be long gone before Table Seven realized she wasn't there anymore.

She crossed the large parking lot. She was almost to her car when she realized that he already knew she had gone. Her steps faltered as she saw Table Seven leaning against her car, his long legs stretched out in front of him and his impressive arms folded across his broad chest. His thick, dark hair, short and off his forehead, left his face easy to read. His expression and body language appeared calm, patient. But his energy pattern radiated irritation, frustration, impatience and…power.

Power contained in such an impressive package had never been so seductive.

Chapter Two

"Have the Arbiters tried to contact you yet?"

"Whaaat?" Was she ever going to understand this man? She shook her head. "Never mind. How did you know I was leaving?"

He raised one brow.

"Okay, how'd you know which car was mine?" she demanded.

His brow lowered and he reached his hands out, almost reverently, to touch the side of her car. "I can feel you here."

She threw her hands up in disbelief. "You can feel me in my Honda Accord?"

"Not your physical body, your energy signature." His explanation was patient, as though it made perfect sense to everyone else on the planet except her.

"Oh, of course. Why didn't I think of that?" She wished she had the little pink canister of mace her dad had given her when she moved to the city. But no, it was sitting at home on her nightstand so that it couldn't accidentally go off in her purse and get her by mistake. She gave a small sigh. Didn't really matter, she wouldn't spray him anyway. She doubted he could do anything that would truly break through the sense of security she felt when he was near. Did serial killers make their victims feel this safe? Is that how they were successful over and over again?

"Miranda, try to have an open mind. Your energy drew me to you. I am your activator. Your teacher. We are bonded. I will always be able to feel you. This is the way of the Salutari."

"You know," she crossed her arms, intrigued with the possibility that although what he said didn't make sense, he *might* actually know something interesting. "I only understand less than half of what you say. And the small amount I do understand makes me think you're a little...woo-hoo." She twirled one finger near her temple.

His lip twitched. "I assure you, my mental facilities are in perfect working order." He looked up at the stars in the clear, warm, night sky and spoke aloud. "This would be much easier had she been allowed to retain her knowledge."

Miranda looked up, saw no one, and narrowed one eye at him. "Who are you speaking to?"

His gaze returned to her as he straightened away from her car and the old, blue automobile rose at the release of pressure against the metal. "I think we should take my car."

She clenched her fists at her sides. "Hate to tell you this, but I'm not going anywhere with you. And what's wrong with my ride?"

He flicked a disparaging glance at the car. Employees parked at the back of the lot, far away from the valet parking area. The soft light way back here flattered her poor old car.

"Hey, don't knock it. It has AC and a sunroof," she said with pride.

"The thing is ancient and too small. I do not believe I would fit well inside it." His tone didn't sound condescending—more like—stating facts.

She eyed his tall frame. Powerful muscles shaped his broad shoulders and his short sleeved, dark blue, knit shirt strained over bulging biceps. Standing half in the shadows, he again reminded her of the knight on the cover of the last romance book she read. He was right, it would be a tight fit for him in her little blue car. She couldn't even promise it would go with his added weight inside it. "I do not believe," she said mimicking part of his words and his accent too, "that I bought it for your riding enjoyment."

"Which is why we shall take mine." He took a step toward her and reached for her arm.

"Oh, no, you don't!" She jumped back from his touch. "I don't know what it is you do, but you are not allowed to touch me in public again."

The wicked gleam in his eyes made her heart start to pound. "Or in private either. You are not allowed to touch me at all."

This time, his lips did more than a twitch, but the smile didn't reach his eyes. "Then, please, walk this way." He gestured two spaces over, where a shiny, silver Dodge Challenger rested. It was one of the new ones—the expensive ones—with the fast motor. She moved toward it in a trance. As she neared the passenger door she heard the alarm disable. The click and beep brought her back to her senses.

"I can't go with you!" She backed up from the muscle car as though it were a snake.

"Why not?" he said.

She held up her hand and ticked off the reasons for him. "One. Because I don't know you. Two. Because...you are either crazy or I am, because I have no idea what you are talking about. And three, the shimmering energy thingy, I don't know how you did it, but I am not going to repeat it." She pushed her hand forward and held up her fourth and final finger. "Because, I am going home."

"Then I shall accompany you there."

"No, you shall not. I need peace and quiet. You're neither of those things."

He gave her a sinful grin. "You are correct. We will be anything but restful together. We are warriors."

She used her whole hand and pointed at him. "See, there you go again."

His hand snaked out lightning fast and grabbed hers. Her brain couldn't process the speed with which it happened.

"No, no! Don't do that!" she said, trying to pull away from him.

He released her hand, but not before the shimmers from the entire parking lot assembled around her. She pulled her hand to her chest and backed away from him. She froze, her eyes wide with wonder. In slow motion, she lifted the hand he had touched in front of her face and watched as the thick air around it sparkled and glowed. "Can others see this?" Even to her own ears, her voice sounded dazed and confused.

"Most cannot. Those that can you need to run from until you

have learned all I have to teach you."

"Why would I possibly need to run when I have this?" she whispered, in awe. She knew the amount of energy she gathered with his brief touch would be enough to do major damage if she wasn't careful. There weren't enough glass carafes inside the restaurant to cover the crack this energy could make into the asphalt of the parking lot.

"Concentrate, and disperse the overload of power until you can control it. Eventually, you will learn to control it all." He stood next to her, but didn't try to touch her again.

Smart man. "I tried that inside, it didn't work. Can you see how beautiful this is?" She twisted her hands in front of her in wonderment, admiring the beauty of the sparkling light.

"Miranda, *Love,* you need to concentrate. The energy is continuing to gather. If you don't disperse it, you will destroy the entire parking lot and possibly the restaurant at the rate the power is amassing."

She looked around. The air was filled with white. "Where did it all come from?"

"Miranda! Concentrate!" The order came out sharp.

She looked at her hand a moment longer before she closed her eyes and tried to funnel the energy through.

"Don't close your eyes!" he said.

She opened one eye. "Why not? It helps me focus."

He exhaled, and she heard the *why me* tone in his voice. "Because you leave yourself vulnerable to attack if you do that."

"Is that going to happen often?" she asked. "I'm going to get attacked?"

"Yes."

She opened the other eye. "Well, don't sugarcoat it for me, okay?"

"Miranda concentrate or I will have to help you to disperse the excess before you hurt yourself."

She had both hands raised in front of her, marveling at the feeling of power that flowed through her. Every cell in her body felt energized. She could feel the light in every pore, every nerve, and in every pulse. How could others not see it?

"Miranda!"

She turned around in a daze. White floated everywhere. If the small amount of energy they had generated inside cracked tiles, this was going to take out a city block. She had no idea how to control this. It was too much. People were going to get hurt… because of her. The surreal feeling faded.

She turned back to face him. "Please, help." The plea came out no more than a whisper, fear causing the sound to lodge in her throat.

He closed the space between them in three purposeful strides and held his hand out for hers.

She hesitated. "Isn't that how this all started?"

"Trust me." His voice came in a low, soothing rumble.

Did she dare? Her instincts said yes, but her brain said no. She looked at the white again. What choice did she have? She slid her hand inside his much larger one. Eyes locked with his, she felt him raise her small hand and placed it over his heart. She could feel the strong, steady rhythm through the thin material of his shirt and her body relaxed. He drew her in and enveloped her in his warmth. His jaw grazed against her ear—thank the stars for high heels—and his free hand cupped her chin, tipping her face to meet his.

She closed her eyes and he lowered his head. His demanding lips met hers. There was no hesitation in his taking. She was lost in the heat of his kiss. This man, crazy or not, knew how to entice a woman. He created a safe haven within his arms for her. He coaxed all thought of resistance from her. He took control from her. The bright light surrounding them now flowed through them both. Lightheaded from the energy surging through her, her last coherent thought before losing consciousness was that this kiss just might cause a massive explosion after all…of desire. She hoped she would live to tell about it.

Chapter Three

She would be furious when she woke up, but he had no choice. He had to drain the energy from her, or let her destroy several city blocks. Her power was much greater than any other protégé he ever trained.

He looked at the small form lying peacefully on his large bed. She was slender, yet pleasantly curved. Her features delicate, her dark hair thick and lustrous. Her lack of height and fragile appearance made her seem very young. Had he not witnessed her awesome power himself, he never would have believed it possible from one so small and unaware.

His grin went unchecked as he looked at her innocent features. She looked too lovely, too pure, and too simple to be the one to contain so much power. But she did, and she had a sharp mind to go with it. She had absolutely no clue, thanks to the Higher Powers, why she was able to do the things she could. He would have his hands full with her training and her stubborn resistance to the whole idea. But this didn't bother him. He actually looked forward to his time with this one.

For the first time in a very long time, he felt hope.

She mumbled and rolled to her side, curled into the perfect image of sleeping innocence—the disaster she already made of his bed proved that picture wrong. He had never seen anyone destroy a perfectly made bed in such a short time. She had a surplus of energy running through her system. Yet, somehow, he imagined this had always been the norm for her.

That brought him back to the most puzzling question about

her. The power in a warrior always remained dormant until activated by the Salutari. They had all been bonded in the pre-existence, each warrior matched to the activator best suited to teach what was needed. Had someone else activated her—which should not have even been possible—there could be no bond existing between Miranda and himself. And yet, there was. A very strong one. There was no denying she belonged to him. This was why she was drawn to him, trusted him, even though he was a stranger.

He sighed. Perhaps she should not put her faith in him. His attraction to her was against the rules, and yet, his body acted of its own accord. For the first time, he was tempted to break the strict laws that had governed his long life.

She mumbled a soft murmur that was indecipherable, and rolled onto her back. She would awaken much sooner than he expected. Her recovery time was amazing. He filed that bit of information away in his head with all the other unusual facts he had gathered about her.

She shifted again and he turned away. Food was necessary to fuel the energy, but he knew it helped to keep her calm. He headed for his well-stocked kitchen. He had better begin cooking or he was afraid there would be no reasoning with her once she awakened.

Chapter Four

Something was wrong. Her sleep-drugged mind couldn't quite pin it down. Too tired to open her eyes, Miranda took mental stock of her surroundings. She was lying down. She smelled food. The bed felt soft, cushiony, like the memory foam mattresses advertised on TV. She smelled bacon. Definitely not her own bed. She smelled eggs. She sensed the presence of another person close by. Potatoes, onions and toast. Where was she? Her stomach grumbled in response to the heavenly smells.

"Food," Miranda whispered with a sleep husky voice. Her eyes popped open and stared at a high ceiling she had never seen before. The last memories from the parking lot came rushing back. What had Table Seven done when he kissed her that made her forget how she got here? Panic tensed her muscles. Miranda bolted up. The room tilted and she fell back into the soft pillows again.

"Head rush," Miranda groaned, raising one hand to her forehead. Still reclining on the pillows, she inhaled the scrumptious scents. Her mouth watered. Danger or food, which was most pressing at the moment? Her stomach rumbled again in response to her silent question.

"It is the after effects of an energy drain," said a familiar, deep, masculine voice. "Not a head rush."

She closed her eyes, blocking the view of the sexy man sitting next to her thigh. His presence eased the fear which had developed. She should hold onto her anxiety, but couldn't help it. Just as she had trusted him in the parking lot, she was comfortable with him now. The man affected her like food. He had a strange calming effect on her—minus the whole hormone thing. Besides, he was the first person ever to claim any knowledge of her strange ability. What choice did she have but to trust him and find out all she could?

Her eyes popped open again. "Hey, this memory foam mattress works pretty good. Just like in the commercials. I'm not even rolling toward your weight. Cool."

He raised one dark eyebrow.

She moved her hand from her forehead to cover her mouth. Not that what she said was all that bad, but sometimes words just popped right on out of her mouth before she had time to think about them.

Her stomach rumbled again.

Miranda jerked her hand down. "Food? You have food?"

He held the plate out to her.

"I'm starved!" She scrambled into a sitting position and all but yanked the plate from his hands.

"This is normal after such an incident," he said.

"Oh yeah?" She shoveled a fork full of eggs into her mouth.

She felt his smirk. He watched her devour the entire plate of food. It was enough for two grown men and yet she managed to eat the whole thing in record time. She licked the fork clean and was debating whether to lick the plate, when he spoke again.

"Would you like more?" His voice sounded flat, but his beautiful, intense, green eyes blazed. Was he laughing at her, or did he actually desire her? It had to be the first, he was just too much male perfection to be attracted to someone who looked like she did. Men of his class dated international models who were fabulously wealthy. These men didn't associate with an average looking, small town girl who was far from perfect. She wasn't even the kind of girl who would try to improve on those imperfections even if she *could* afford it. Though she had been tempted more than once to get a larger chest…

She lowered her fork to the plate as her gaze dropped to the dark green comforter she sat on. The very large bed was framed by a tall, dark, wooden headboard. "I'm good, thank you." She kept her eyes down, but asked in a whisper, "Am I in your bed?"

"Yes."

She looked down at her clothing, the only thing missing were her heeled shoes. Great, now she would be short again compared to his six foot plus height when she stood up. "How did I get here?"

"I brought you here." His words came even, controlled.

She wished she felt in control. Calm, composed, relaxed. Any of the above would be nice. Good grief, given her agitated state, at this point she would settle for feeling plain old nervous. She had to ask the next question, but couldn't bring herself to look at him as she did so. "Did we do anything I should know about?"

He remained silent.

She shot him a quick glance, then dropped her eyes to his chest. It was so much easier to talk to his broad shoulders, muscled pecs and large biceps. She swallowed before she started drooling. What had she asked him? She cleared her throat and raised her eyes back up to his. "I mean, I don't seem to remember anything after the parking lot. We were talking, there was a... light, and then I'm here." Was it possible she imagined it all? She fervently hoped so, but since Table Seven sat next to her on an unfamiliar bed, she was afraid her memory was correct.

"And you were starving."

She felt the heat rising up her neck. "I can't seem to help it. My mom said I have a very high metabolism. I'm always hungry and no matter how much I eat, I don't get fat. Although—" she rambled on—"Mom says to enjoy it because family genetics are only good until I hit about thirty, then the calories will go straight to my butt."

The sound started deep in his chest, then rumbled out of him in a low, throaty, laugh. He was having a good time at her expense. Hope he enjoyed it.

She looked away in disgust and examined her surroundings. The room was large and spacious with a high ceiling, cream walls and dark brown trim. Her entire apartment could almost fit inside his bedroom. She noticed the furniture, large, dark, wooden, masculine, and sparse. Definitely a man's room.

She looked at him again. "Not kidding. I can't help it. I keep thinking I should really learn to control this hunger thing so that I won't get fat when I turn thirty, but I just don't seem to have that little voice inside of me that tells me when to stop eating." She also lacked the little voice that told her when to stop talking. This man was a complete stranger—a man whom she had *kissed*, and whose bed she now rested on. She shouldn't be sharing such personal information with him.

The chuckling stopped, but the same full lips that had been hard and demanding when he kissed her, were still smiling. "Don't worry about the food. It is fuel for the body. The body requires much after an energy load."

"Um, yeah. About that." She swallowed hard. "What exactly is going on here?"

The laughter left his face. "Ask me questions. Specific questions and I will do my best to answer them."

She looked the magnificent man over from top to bottom. Every delicious inch. A perfect male in every way possible. He made her aware of a hunger other than for food. She really had to get a grip on this attraction thing.

"Are you gay?" Her hand flew to her mouth and her eyes locked with his. When he remained silent, she lowered her hand and added hastily, "I'm sooo sorry! You don't have to answer that."

His brows knit together in a dark downward slash. "What have I done to give you that impression?"

She shrugged, embarrassed. "Nothing. I'm sorry. It's just that all the *really* good looking guys are not interested in women for anything more than friendship. Not that friendship is bad. I believe successful romances should start out as friends. But eventually, they have to develop into more than that. Don't they? That's what my brothers say." She ran out of air and took a deep breath. She was out of control with the rambling thing. Again.

A muscle in his strong jaw worked and his eyes bore into hers.

He regarded her in silence until she was too uneasy to remain quiet. "Forget I asked. It's truly none of my business. Besides, it's okay if you are. Nothing wrong with it. Really, it's your choice."

The clenching of his jaw relaxed and his eyes lit up with a devilish light. "I am only attracted to women. I would be happy to prove it to you, *Love*, if that was an invitation."

She swallowed, then coughed. Her throat didn't seem to be working properly.

"Nooo. No, that was not what I meant to ask. Not at all. Can we please start the questions over?" Miranda shifted her position on the comfy bed. The less lounging she did in this man's presence, the better.

"You wish to start over? Do you believe that is wise? I gave you the opportunity to learn the answers to all your questions, and that was the best you could come up with?"

She knew her cheeks were flaming, but decided it was best to just ignore the past two minutes. "You claim you've been looking for me. Why?"

The look in his eyes said he debated whether to follow up on the invitation idea, but he answered her question anyway. "You are an energy warrior and it is my job to train you."

"Warrior?" she snorted. "I don't know karate or anything like that. I'm no warrior."

"An energy warrior does not fight like the combatants you have seen on TV. This is a fight that happens with your mind."

"Then I am in big trouble," she said with a half-grin.

"You underestimate yourself. You are very powerful."

"You know, Shara told me something similar to that tonight and I hate to disappoint you both, but I have a pretty good grasp on reality and what I am capable of."

"You now believe you have a good grasp on reality and your abilities?" He looked pointedly at her as he took her empty plate from her lap—an innocent gesture, except he let his fingers brush against her thigh as he did so—and set the dish on the nightstand.

She jerked back as the white sparkles began to gather. "Okay, okay. I get your point. Now make it go away."

A smile of pure masculine pleasure spread across his face as he leaned toward her, his hands braced on the headboard behind her. "I thought you'd never ask," he breathed into her lips just before claiming them in a searing kiss.

She would have struggled, most likely, had she not felt the gathered energy recede. The power that had started to build from his touch was now a manageable haze. It had the overwhelming good feel she was sometimes able to project with it…or maybe that was just the kiss itself? It was marvelous. She wanted to stretch like a cat and have him continue doing just as he was for a *very* long time.

Before it could get really interesting he broke the contact and, hands still braced on either side of her, his lips still close to her own, he asked in a low voice, "Should we continue until you are drained enough to sleep again, or would you like to finish your questions?"

"Continue," she whispered breathlessly. As a slow smile spread across his lips, she blinked and added, "With the questions."

"Are you certain, *Love*? A good night's sleep would certainly be beneficial to you."

And what a way to be put to sleep. "Hold on a minute. You mean when you kiss me it drains my energy?"

He lowered his head and pressed his lips into the sensitive curve of her neck and shoulder. "Yes."

She couldn't help but arch her neck, giving him better access, as she felt herself relax even further. She'd never felt this wonderful in her entire life. If she truly were a cat, she'd be purring. But she wasn't. "Then back off, *Loverboy*." It took a lot of effort to get those words to come out—she wished they sounded more like she meant them. "I have some questions you still haven't answered."

He straightened, his eyes searching hers before he returned to his sitting position at her side. "That is because you still haven't asked them."

"We got sidetracked. Okay, so you've found me. Why am I the 'chosen one' to be an energy warrior?" She held her breath in anticipation. She had wondered about the shimmers for so long, never believing she would ever understand, that the suspense was killing her.

"It was preordained before you came to this earth."

Her brows drew together and she released the breath. "This earth?"

He shrugged one muscular shoulder. "As opposed to the above."

"Above, like as in Heaven?"

"Yes. Most humans call it that."

"Most humans," she muttered, her eyes widening. "Are you not human?" That would explain a lot.

"Yes, I am human."

Her eyes widened further. "Am *I* not human?"

His lips twitched. "You are human."

She threw a pillow at him. "This isn't funny."

He caught, then tossed the pillow to the side. "Listen and I will teach you." He turned to face her. "In Heaven, as you call it, before humans came to earth there was a war. There were two sides to this war. Good and evil. Do you understand this?"

Her attention was riveted. "Go on, go on."

"Two-thirds of the hosts of Heaven chose to go with the Salutari—which is Latin for The Saviors. One-third chose to go with the Arbiters—or The Controllers."

This was getting heavy. "Hosts of Heaven? Were they the angels?"

He frowned a little. "You could call them that, but they were more of a spirit. A living being, without a physical body."

"So we were spirits in this war?"

"Correct. You and I chose the side of the Salutari."

She nodded, encouraging him to continue.

"In Heaven, we were warriors in this battle. Some of the more valiant warriors were chosen to continue the fight on earth. We were chosen."

Her jaw dropped. "Are we Angels?"

He smiled. "We are humans. We were spirits above and when we came to earth we gained a body. We are human. Human... with a little extra."

Her voice was nothing more than an awed whisper, "How long has this war been taking place?"

"Since the beginning of time. There will always be a struggle between the good and the evil."

"Always? It will never end?"

He shook his head. "Without misery, there could be no joy.

But if the Arbiters should win, there would only be darkness."

She sat up straighter. "But if two-thirds chose the Salutari, the Arbiters are outnumbered. Surely we can win with those odds."

"Your optimism is good, but evil is powerful. Slowly they have been taking over our planet. Their powers are causing the murders, the wars, the destruction. Humans are more wicked now than they have ever been in the history of the planet. The number of Salutari warriors is dwindling fast. If the shift of power doesn't change soon, the war may end…and with it, life as we know it."

She slumped back against the headboard again. "You're kidding, right?"

He shook his head.

"Hey—" she sat forward again—"how come you know all this and I don't?"

"Agency. It was promised to all but the generals. Two generals had the knowledge. One from each side. No one who comes to earth, except for the generals, is allowed to remember the previous existence."

"Are you a general?"

"Hardly."

"So, if the generals know, they tell their warriors and the fight continues. Where is the agency in that?"

He took a deep breath. "Not everyone chooses to believe, and those that do believe do not always choose to fight. And sometimes, they choose to fight for the other side. That is their agency."

She sat quietly for a moment. If it weren't for the shimmers she could see, would she choose to believe it? "Well, I guess that evens things out a little, right?"

"No."

"Why not?"

A muscle near his temple ticked. "Evil cheats."

She raised her knees to her chest, hugged them and rested her chin on top of them. "The all-mighty and powerful general cheats?"

"Yes, he lies. He lies and makes promises, knowing he will never keep them."

She raised her head. "That's not fair."

"It is war."

"And 'all is fair in love and war'?" she said.

He leaned forward, his forearms resting on his knees, his body angled so he was still looking at her. "No, nothing in this war is fair. We cannot win, but we certainly cannot allow them to win."

"What could they possibly gain if they win the war on earth? Won't it be the end? Where's the victory in that?"

She heard the rasp of his five o'clock shadow against his palm as he ran his hand down his face in frustration. "We cannot let them win, or they will control everything."

"If we're dead, what does it matter?"

He sat up straight and she saw the proud, fierce warrior within. "Our bodies die. Our spirits do not. The Arbiters would control all of eternity."

Chapter Five

"You are my most favored warrior. You must hunt down this new power I have sensed this night."

The warrior stood proud. "Yes, General."

"This one is different," the mighty General paced before him, his long, rich robes fluttering with the movement. "You must use cunning and wisdom. Do not underestimate the power this one wields."

It was always an honor to be singled out by the General. He would do whatever the General wished of him.

"If you can persuade this one to our side, it would change the entire course of the battle." They were alone, yet the General's powerful voice echoed throughout the large and opulent assembly room.

"With respect, General, we are already winning. Should we not just eliminate the threat?"

The formidable General stopped pacing across the marble floor. "No."

"As you wish," he mumbled.

"I want this one's power on our side. Do everything you can to convince it to change. Eliminate it only as a final alternative."

He stood straight and tall. "Yes, General."

With a flick of his wrist, the General shot a flash of energy at the warrior. It came on so strong it nearly brought him to his knees—and yet, he knew it was only a small taste of the energy signature the General wanted him to track. No wonder the General wanted this one's power.

The General turned away from the warrior in dismissal, then the always confident General, spoke with his back still to him. "Do not disappoint me, my warrior. I will not take failure in this matter lightly."

The warrior was very much aware of this fact. He didn't become the favored one by disappointing the General and he would not fail him now. "Yes, my General."

Chapter Six

"Wow. Eternity, that's a long time," Miranda blew a stray hair from her face and slumped down into the pillows propped behind her.

"This surprises you?" He studied her with interest.

Her silvery-blue eyes were vibrant and direct as she answered him. "Yes. I never gave it much thought as to what would happen when we passed on." She shrugged her delicate shoulders. "I thought it'd be better than here. A good place. Maybe a place of light."

"It is. If we are successful, it will stay that way."

"No pressure, huh?"

She reached up and released the hold the clip held on her long hair. He inhaled as the thick chocolate brown strands tumble across her shoulders and halfway down her back. His heartbeat quickened when she sighed in pleasure and dug her fingers into her hair to massage her scalp.

"I hate wearing my hair up for too long, makes my head hurt. Guess it's the weight. I have to keep it back for work though. Probably ought to just cut it short."

"No." The word came out much sharper than he intended it too, but it would be a shame to destroy such beauty. "Leave it. We have much work to do. There is not time to worry about hair. Long is good as it can easily be pulled out of the way."

"Out of the way for what? What am I supposed to do?"

"You are supposed to learn. Together, we can do much." Now that he had sampled her power, he didn't doubt this.

"Together?" Her eyes went wide.

"Yes. Your power is substantial, but together, I believe your ability is multiplied exponentially."

Miranda caught the end of a lock of hair and twisted it around her finger. Rather than a coy or seductive move, it seemed an unconscious habit. Her hand stilled. "So it won't always be as strong as it is when you touch me?"

"No. At least, I do not believe so. An activator has the ability to begin the power, and to drain or modulate the energy when needed. We don't generally increase the power as in your situation."

"But at the restaurant, you knew that touching me would make me lose control of it. Didn't you?"

"Yes."

She narrowed her gaze. "How?"

"I could feel it. Your spirit was drawn to mine. I could feel the power building the minute I pulled into the parking lot."

"And yet, you did it anyway," she said in disgust.

"Of course—" he knew she didn't understand, but how could she not? "It was the only way to get your attention. You thought I was..." he twirled a finger near his temple.

"Woo-hoo," she said. "Still not sure on that one."

"Why did this make you angry? When I touched you in the restaurant?"

Miranda shot him a look of disbelief. "I've been trying to hide what I can do for years. I left my hometown and came to Vegas before I could screw up and embarrass my family. I've done pretty good at hiding this *thing* and five minutes after meeting you, I nearly expose myself to an entire restaurant full of the social elite. How did you think I was going to explain a..." she paused, looking for an adequate description, "an *indoor snow and lightning storm* to all of those people?"

"The room was less than half full. There had been nothing to worry about."

"*That's beside the point!* I would've still had to give some kind of explanation." She crossed her arms in front of her as if taking a stand.

"They could not see your 'shimmers,' or the power you

release." He looked at her curiously. "You think it is better to be in Las Vegas than your hometown if you should expose yourself? Why do you believe that to be true?"

"This is *Vegas*—" she waved her hand in the air—"anything can happen here. I would've said something about practicing magic to get my own show."

"Interesting. What do you think may have happened had they not believed you?"

She glared at him. "Then they probably would've burned me at the stake for being a witch and my family would be humiliated for generations to come."

"Then it is good you were able to discharge some of the energy in the serving room."

"That didn't go so well either." Her cheeks were flushed a darker shade than usual and her eyes flashed, though her tone remained steady—if perhaps a bit sarcastic. "It's gonna cost me a night's worth of tips to cover that stupid carafe."

There would be no time for her to continue to work as a lowly waitress earning tips. She was a warrior. Her time should be spent training. He wondered if she would fight him on this as well. Her stubbornness was a good thing. The Arbiters would not easily sway her to their side.

"So, how come you didn't just wait until I got off work instead of risking my lack of control in public?"

He stared at the beautiful woman next to him. "I spent two years looking for you. I was not about to wait any longer."

She rolled her eyes. "Another couple of hours wouldn't have killed you."

"There was no reason to try my patience with a further delay. The sooner we move forward with your training, the better." In truth, he hadn't even considered waiting. The bond had physically drawn him forward into the restaurant and only due to the public nature of the situation had he waited to speak to her until she approached him at his table.

"You keep saying you were supposed to activate me?" She sighed. "How exactly were you supposed to do that?"

His mind pictured the kiss he would've given her to activate her power and electricity coursed through him at the thought.

He had never been attracted to one of his students before. It unsettled him, but it seemed even more uncomfortable to her. For some reason, he enjoyed provoking her in this way. He focused his gaze onto her lips and waited for her to catch on. She did.

"Ohhh."

For the first time she had nothing to say. It didn't last.

"Hey, wait," She leaned forward a little. "I thought that was how you diffused the power. Not how you started it."

He shrugged. "It works both ways. I can activate it or diffuse it. In your case I can increase it. Whichever I choose."

"So you can control it?"

"Yes."

"How come I can't?" Her lips closed in a pout.

"You will, once I train you."

"So are there other 'activators' out there?" she gestured about.

"Yes."

He watched her mull it over for a moment. "Are they all male?"

"Yes. There are very few of us left." He had to push down the anger this made him feel before he caused the energy in the room to shift to a darker power.

"Are all of the Salutari warriors—the ones who need to be activated—women?"

"Yes."

"Huh." Her look was thoughtful. "Why do you suppose that is?"

"It was the Creators plan that men and women would work together to form a united front against the Arbiters."

Her delicate brows rose. "Are we—" she gestured between them—"to form a united front together?"

He smiled. "Yes. I am an activator. I am your teacher. When we are done with our work together, I will move on to the next student and you will continue fighting." With any luck, that would be the truth. Not enough past students were still fighting. Most had either not survived the fight, turned to the other side, or even worse, they had given up. To stop trying to win was an admission of defeat.

"You look so serious," she whispered.

He studied her features. Would she survive this fight? If she did, how would she look when the innocence was gone from her expression?

"What's wrong?"

"Everything...and nothing." It had been a long time since he felt sure he knew the answers to this war. "You have asked your questions, now it is time for mine. How did you avoid me for these past years?"

She tipped her head to the side. "I wasn't avoiding you."

"Where have you been living, that I was unable to find you? I have searched all of Las Vegas, many times, and was unable to find you."

"I only recently moved to Vegas." She smiled. "Before that I lived in a little town called Overton."

Her smile lightened his mood. It may have been the energy she exuded, but he doubted it. She made him feel the end was not near. Perhaps there was hope when innocence still existed. "Overton? I have never heard of Overton."

"Most people haven't heard of it." She chuckled. "Overton's very small— by Lake Mead, about sixty miles north of here. At least I think its north. Are we still in Vegas?"

"Yes." He answered her question, but had more of his own. "You have been living sixty miles from here?"

"Till about three weeks ago, yes."

"Three weeks?" He was stunned. "Sixty miles? I felt your energy signature from *sixty miles* away?"

She raised her hands in uncertainty. "Is that not normal?"

He searched her face intently. She was indeed special. "No. That is not normal."

"Is that good or bad?"

"Both." He had never had a connection this strong, or this physical to a student before. "The Arbiters have no doubt known of your power, but like me, couldn't find you. They must have sent many to search for you, but obviously, they were misled like me. Eventually, we would all have found you. It is good I located you first."

"So we're safe. The scary bad guys don't know where we are?" she asked hopefully.

"I was able to shield your energy, so they are unaware of the power surge at the restaurant and because of the energy drain, they won't be able to track you."

"So we're gonna have to... You're gonna have to...drain me of energy all the time so they can't find me?"

"Only when it builds too strong. Then, yes, I will have to... *drain* your energy to a more manageable level." That, or shield it. The draining would definitely be more enjoyable.

She hesitated, "I guess if you're going to keep draining my energy, I should probably know your name?"

"Braedan."

She studied him. Her big, dark lashed eyes taking in every detail. "Braedan. Unique. I guess it fits you—one of a kind and sort of stiff."

"I am not stiff," he said, affronted.

"Formal. Your speech is so proper—my English teacher in high school would've swooned. You need to lighten up a little."

He knew what he was, an activator, a teacher, a warrior. "I do not need to 'lighten up.' My speech is unlike yours, because I come from an old family. From a different country than America. I have an accent too, you forgot to mention that."

"Nah, didn't forget it, Danny. It works for you. Bet the girls love it."

"Danny? You will not call me that. My name is Braedan."

She grinned and her eyes sparkled.

"I forbid it. You will not call me that name."

"Whatever you say."

"Why do I not believe you will behave on this issue?"

"Because you have no faith in me." Her eyes were full of humor.

"I think perhaps you are correct."

She hit him in the shoulder with a pillow. He grabbed the pillow still in her grasp and leaned in close to her. "You will have to learn control or we will spend much of our time draining energy from you. I do believe I will enjoy the process."

He could feel the power gathering around them just from being near her. She glared at him and he could actually feel some of the energy drain from him. He grinned at her feeble attempt to make him feel bad. She failed to realize there was currently more shimmering energy flowing around and through him than he had ever experienced in his life before meeting her.

"Did you enjoy draining your other students?"

He heard the jealousy in her voice and loved it. "Not as much as I enjoy doing it for you," he answered honestly. He leaned in closer, keeping the pillow between their bodies so that they would not touch. "Are you feeling too much energy, *Love*?" He let his breath whisper over her neck and inhaled her sweet fragrance.

"Yes. I mean, no." She looked down, refusing to make eye contact.

"Would you like me to drain just a small amount to make you more comfortable?" he offered fanning his hot breath across her neck and ear.

"Hmmmm." Her head tipped, giving him better access to the vulnerable skin of her neck.

If she was going to be so obliging, how could he resist? He lowered his head and nuzzled her ear. A jolt of power ran from her body into his. Interesting. Perhaps he should research a little further. After all, as her instructor it was beneficial for him to learn all that she was capable of. Perhaps, if an explanation was needed, she would believe that excuse. He knew better. He placed a light kiss on her neck and the light gathering around them shimmered. Intriguing.

He traced the sensitive line of her neck with his tongue and he felt the energy in the room vibrate. Remarkable.

She pushed her arms past the pillow and entwined her fingers in his hair, drawing his mouth to hers. As their lips connected, the energy in the room throbbed. Fascinating.

His lips pressed against hers again and again, until he licked at her lips to gain entrance to her mouth and the energy pulsed through the room in waves. He forced himself to concentrate and sensed her energy signature extending as far as three blocks away. It was like nothing he had ever felt before. She radiated the kind of energy that made one feel happy and energized and she didn't even appear to know she was doing it. His neighbors would smile for days.

As much as he wanted to send this good will to the whole world, he knew it was time to rein it in before the Arbiters tracked her through it.

He placed his large hands on either side of her face as he deepened the kiss. He forced himself to open to the power and shield the energy around them, containing the waves emanating from her. The pulsing stopped as the energy outside of the shield dissipated. The energy inside of the shield was a different matter.

He pulled back and waited for her to open her eyes. For the first time ever, he had a student he couldn't fully control.

"Wow," she said, breathing hard.

He couldn't help but grin, in fact, he couldn't help but chuckle, which soon turned into a hearty laugh. He felt good. No, he felt great. She must have felt it too, for she soon joined in.

Braedan felt the energy filter through them with their laughter, controlled, and he dropped the shield. The room still vibrated with light, but it posed no danger.

The joy radiating from her mesmerized him. She was so very tempting. How could this be? She was his student, yet the attraction remained. He was not supposed to increase her energy. He was not supposed to have lost hope. And yet, thanks to his new student, he felt more alive than he had in years.

She said he was unique, but she was more so than he. She was the first student, ever, to teach a teacher.

Chapter Seven

This one's energy signature was vaguely familiar. He felt it as he walked down the dim lit, empty hallway. Perhaps it came from the blast the General had given him? Maybe, but something tickled at the back of his mind. He felt he should know this particular signature.

He slowed near her door. The light radiating from inside said she must be at home. He had hoped to find her apartment empty so he could search and get a feel for her before he attempted to sway her. Not a problem. He had found her. His first goal achieved.

Secure in his powers of persuasion, he could afford to be patient.

He turned away from the light reluctantly—she had a strong pull. Already he could feel the light penetrating his shield. It felt good…like warm sunshine after a long, cold winter. He increased the strength of his shield to block the warmth and retraced his steps to the ground floor of the apartment building.

Why would someone with so much power live in a place like this? The building wasn't old, but it was not a place where the powerful and wealthy would reside. Perhaps she wasn't fully aware of the perks of being a powerful warrior?

He left the building and circled around until he could see the rear of the apartment. Both of her second floor windows radiated light. The light beckoned him. His pace slowed as he climbed up the fire-escape that went past her unit.

Outside her window he relaxed and let a small amount of

the power flow through him. He absorbed more light than was comfortable as he tried—and failed—to pinpoint the location of her inside her apartment. He paused, then focused again, and still couldn't feel the center of the power. He gasped in surprise. She wasn't there. The residual power alone inside her apartment was stronger than what most warriors possessed on a good day. The General was right. This one would change the entire course of the battle. It was up to him to make certain they control this power on their side.

He touched his hand to the glass of the window and the latch on the inside unlocked. He slid it open and slipped inside.

Not bothering to close the window behind him, he looked around. He didn't need to turn on any lights, not with such a bright energy lighting the room. To his eyes the place shined as bright as high noon on the ocean with it's light reflecting off the water.

Her residence was small—a studio apartment. The single room was homey and comfortable. She had decorated the walls and shelves with pictures and plants. The colors were soft and light. A short couch sat in front of an equally small entertainment center, a table meant for two, a desk, two tall wooden book shelves, and a large closet. Her twin sized bed told him she lived alone. She lived simply. She lived without luxury. Perhaps she could be easily swayed by the riches he could promise her.

He walked forward, running his hand along the back of the short beige couch as he passed by it. He could feel the energy race up his arm just from making contact with something she had touched. He grinned and planted both hands on the soft suede fabric. The energy rush was incredible—almost better than sex.

He allowed himself to absorb the power only until the painful brightness in the room dimmed enough that he no longer needed to squint against the glare. He moved away from the couch and studied the pictures on the wall and desk.

These were interesting. The resemblance of the people could have only meant siblings and parents. She appeared to have a strong family connection. He studied the pictures carefully as he tried to single out which one the general had sent him after. Not one person stood out to him as the one with all the power, but it was difficult to see a light signature in a photograph.

Each picture showed a different family outing. Most were centered around outdoor activities. Perhaps the lure of riches would not be as successful as he had originally thought. Nature types were rarely influenced by monetary possessions. Someone with strong family ties would also be difficult to persuade. He would have his work cut out for him with this one.

He rifled through the mail and papers on her desk. An insurance bill, a letter from her mom stating she was due home for a visit, a pay-check stub from a restaurant called Cheri.

He moved to the only door in the apartment other than the front entrance and looked inside. He had discovered the bathroom and it smelled like a woman. He inhaled deeply and grinned—he loved that particular smell. The tub was large for a small apartment and was jetted. There were all kinds of scented bottles and candles lining the edges. A narrow bookcase resided next to the tub. A quick scan of titles revealed a collection of romance novels to be read while relaxing in the hot scented water of the massaging jets. This was a room for pampering. Perhaps riches would work on her after all.

He returned to the main room and opened her closet. Her clothes were hung neatly and for a woman, there were few of them. There appeared to be a varied collection between casual and dressy and the garments hung without being crushed together. He couldn't help but touch the glowing fabrics, which had all touched her skin at some point. They shimmered on their hangers. His thoughts drifted to what it would be like to touch her. Would she feel as good in person as her energy signature, or would it be too strong and therefore, painful? He looked again at the clothing. She did not appear to be a big shopper—was this due to lack of funds or lack of interest in materialistic objects?

Always thorough, he glanced down. The floor was covered with shoes—she had more footwear than clothing. She obviously had an obsession for shoes, particularly high-heeled ones. He squatted down and picked up a delicate, pale pink, stiletto heel. He smiled as he placed it on the flat of his hand. The shoe was so small that it didn't even reach from the tips of his fingers to the base of his palm. He wrapped his fingers around the tiny shoe and slowly put it back exactly where he'd found it. These sexy beauties were definitely a sign of worldliness.

He closed the closet door and inspected the double set of bookcases that lined most of one wall. This woman liked to read. He read the names of a few obvious romance titles before pulling one off the shelf. The book was called *Knight Games* and had a picture of a muscular man without a shirt holding a woman whose dress had slipped off one shoulder. He admired the woman's luscious body before returning the book and grabbing another. This one had a highlander he guessed—because of the tartan that barely covered the man's brawny chest—and had yet another well proportioned, scantily dressed damsel draped across the hero's body. The woman he was seeking may be a powerful warrior, but she was a romantic at heart.

He returned the books to the shelf and took the two steps necessary to reach her bed. It was topped with a light pink, thickly cushioned, down comforter and a *lot* of pillows. This was where she spent the most time while in the apartment—her signature was strongest here. He gave into temptation and laid down on the glowing softness. It would have been a ceaseless, divine rush of white...if he had fit. As it was, he rested his arms behind his head and left one leg off the bed, bent at the knee to help balance him and let the other leg hang off the end from the calf down. She was tiny. Tiny, but powerful.

He could feel the strength of her light as he lay on her bed. He closed his eyes and gave in to the temptation to absorb the power into his body. It bordered on a pleasure/pain as the dark was being pushed aside by the light. The darkness was strong and refused to be overcome. He sighed and allowed the darkness to shadow the light.

He opened his eyes and stared at the ceiling. The pleasure of the light was gone now, but the power of the darkness pulsed through his veins in triumph as he thought about the warrior woman whose bed he lay upon.

She was family oriented. She liked the outdoors. She liked to be pampered. She shopped, but not excessively. She lived alone, and with a bed this size, she didn't bring many men home with her. She was an intriguing mix of personalities, but as he looked at the light colors, felt the soft bed, and recalled the beautiful women and muscled men of her massive romance collection, he smiled. Because he knew exactly how he was going to sway this one to the General's side.

Chapter Eight

"It's not going to happen, so you can just get that thought right out of your head," she informed him.

Braedan slanted a look at her as he drove the powerful car in the still busy traffic. "I fail to see the problem here. We need to train and it is the most logical solution."

"Logical? Who are you, Spock from *Star Trek?*" She knew she was overreacting, but the man had *informed* her that she was moving in with him. He didn't ask, just told her he wasn't returning her to her home to stay, but to collect her things for her to move in with him. Even if she was tempted—which she was almost sure she wasn't—she wouldn't do it.

"You are being unreasonable." His voice was calm.

"Me?" she said, her voice squeaking. "I have known you less than one night and you want me to move in with you—"

"For training purposes."

She snorted. "Yeah, training…with perks."

He looked at her again in obvious confusion.

"Watch the road," she said. 'The City That Never Sleeps,' was an apt name for Las Vegas. Four in the morning and traffic was still heavy. Back home, they literally rolled up the sidewalks when the clock struck midnight.

His gaze returned to the street in front of him. "I would never force you to do anything you didn't want to do—other than train."

She stared at the lights whizzing past the passenger window. That was the problem, he wouldn't force her…he wouldn't have to. "I'm sorry," she apologized. "But I just can't."

"Why?"

One simple word, but many reasons why. "I have a lease on my apartment."

"I will pay the fee to break it."

"I like living alone." She really did. After living in a crowded house with her parents, three brothers and a sister, it was refreshing not to worry about what anyone may accidentally see if she wasn't in complete control at all times.

"You are no longer safe on your own."

She watched his chiseled features and wondered about this man. Could he really keep her safe? He claimed earlier to be her trainer, not her protector. She looked at the bulging muscles of his arms as he drove the car. Judging from the size and condition of his body, he could certainly keep her safe from normal thugs and gangsters, but what about all the weird warrior stuff? "Just how much danger am I in?"

She saw his hands tighten on the steering wheel, but his face remained impassive as he continued to drive. "I doubt they have found you yet, but I am certain they are looking."

She shook her head. "My family would never understand."

Again, he looked away from the road and straight at her. "Do not tell them."

She choked on a laugh. "They only live sixty miles away. They'll figure it out."

"Then you shall keep your apartment and live with me."

"It's not that simple." She sighed. "I would know. And I would have to lie to my parents. I can't do that."

"Do not lie. Only avoid telling them the whole truth."

"Wow. I bet you gave your mom grey hair at a young age." She leaned her head against the headrest. She had napped in his bed, but still felt exhausted. "Turn left at the next stoplight," she directed him as her eyes drooped closed.

"Look, *Love,* you need to be safe and we need to train. I cannot do that with you in your apartment."

"Why not?" She didn't try to hide the yawn. She was so tired.

"Because, I'm afraid your apartment is like your car," he said.

She turned her head toward him and opened one eye. "What's

that supposed to mean?"

"That your apartment is small and lacking in comfort. Am I correct?"

She closed the eye, but still managed to sound indignant. "It's a studio, but it's a nice one. We can't all live in big houses and drive expensive cars. Turn right at the stop sign."

"Just tell your family you answered an ad for a house-sitter position for a wealthy businessman who is rarely in residence and needs his plants watered."

Too worn-out to argue, she just shook her head against the headrest.

"Would it help if I placed an actual ad? The rest is true."

She felt the car slow for the speed bump at the entrance to the apartment complex she lived in and pointed. "Last building on the left, far left door."

The car stopped and the ignition turned off. "Miranda?"

"Mmmm."

"Miranda, *Love,* we are here." His soft voice comforted her.

She tried to open her eyes, but they wouldn't budge. She heard his door open and close, and a moment later her door opened to the warm night air.

"Come on, *Love,*" he whispered. He undid her seatbelt, dug in her purse until she heard the jingle of keys, then he scooped her into his arms.

"I can walk," she mumbled into his neck as his long strides reached the door.

She felt the deep rumble in his chest, which pressed against her body. "You cannot walk if you cannot open your eyes to see."

She felt safe. She felt relaxed. She felt the soft cushion of her bed beneath her and the downy comforter as he tucked it around her. She sighed in contentment and slipped deep into oblivion.

She was too stubborn for her own good. He pulled the covers up and around her, and she snuggled in. She was exhausted. Perhaps tomorrow, after she ate, she would be more reasonable.

He looked around the much too small apartment. What was that old saying about the bull in a china shop? All her things were little and fragile. He looked at the small bed she lay on and the even smaller couch. He should've just taken her back to his own house where there were many guest rooms for her to choose from and he could have slept comfortably in his own large bed.

He locked the front door, checked the windows and the bathroom. Everything appeared secure, but he couldn't shake the feeling something was off. His warrior instincts had kicked in. He didn't feel the immediate need to do battle, but he didn't like the low power signature in the room.

He expected the light to be stronger here. Her car had been so bright he had seen it from six blocks away and she spent much more time here than in her car.

He looked at the small bed again in disgust and sat on the even smaller couch. He groaned. He would never get any sleep on either one. It would be the hard floor for him tonight.

He sat and watched her sleep. She was beautiful. Not in an obvious, flamboyant way, but in a graceful, delicate, strong inner beauty kind of way. Her thick dark tresses were spread over the pale pink pillow, the light color accentuating the darkness of her silky long locks. Her cheek bones were high and slightly pronounced, her nose thin and straight, her lips full. Those eyes, when opened, were amazing—they were big, wide, silvery-blue, and thick lashed—making it difficult to think straight when she focused them on him. Her chin defined—she would never sport a double-chin in her older years. Her neck long and elegant, her collar bone pronounced—the two combined giving the false impression of frailty. Her small body had long legs for such a short height and she had the tiniest feet he had seen on an adult, he knew this as he had removed her shoes for her twice now. He did not know it was possible to buy high heels for feet so small. They were cute and sexy at the same time.

The overall package was deceiving. At first glance, she looked pleasing. At second glance, her beauty surprising. Third glance, and she took your breath away.

His protégé. He was not supposed to find her attractive. How would he train her with his mind busy elsewhere every time he looked at her?

He groaned again. He would have to fight the attraction he had for her. It had been so long since he felt any desire for a woman. It disturbed him that the one he wanted above all else should be off limits to him. Not for the first time, he wished he could change his profession. But he wouldn't. Humanity must survive and he would do whatever necessary to make it so. Including the discomfort he would bring himself by denying the obvious link he shared with the sleeping beauty on the pink bed.

The couch was uncomfortable for one his size. He got up in agitation and walked the short distance to the fridge where he scanned its contents. It was surprisingly well stocked for one person. Then again, he had seen the way she ate. He smiled thinking of her nervous rambling. Her mother was wrong, her bottom would never get large, not even when she got older. The massive calories were required for someone using so much power.

He closed the door, satisfied there were enough ingredients for a good breakfast. Food was a definite necessity to get her to see reason in the morning. Braedan turned back to the small living area and sighed. He shoved the couch against the table to clear a spot large enough for him to lie down. He tossed the small square pillow and light weight blanket from the couch onto the floor and settled in for the night. He listened to her even breathing and decided it would be wise to wait until she had a very large breakfast to tell her not only would she be moving in with him, but she would also be quitting her job.

Chapter Nine

Food. Her eyes popped open. She was hungry and something smelled fantastic.

"Good morning, *Love,*" came the now familiar accented voice.

Mmmm. Man. Food. She turned her head toward the sound and saw Braedan pouring thick maple syrup on a tall stack of French toast. The perfect golden color made her mouth water... or was it the man?

"Are you hungry?"

At the heavy lidded look in his eyes, she wondered whether he referred to himself or the food. Tough choice.

She stretched and sat up, feeling refreshed and absolutely starved. The food won.

He set the plate of French toast on the table with a second plate of eggs and bacon. "Protein to go with the carbs."

She couldn't care less about nutrition, but was desperate to eat. "Thanks." She threw the covers off and made a bee-line for the table.

She made good progress through the mountain of food. He joined her with his own plate heaped high. "Do you get hungry like I do?" she asked around an indecent mouthful.

He grinned. "I'm not certain anyone gets hungry quite like you do, but yes, I eat more than the normal man would eat."

She smiled in relief as she chewed. After swallowing she said, "I'm glad. I won't have to be embarrassed around you."

"Agreed. At least not until you turn thirty and the calories start to stick to your—"

"Shut up."

He grinned and took another bite.

She closed her eyes in pure pleasure as the warm French toast seemed to practically dissolve in her mouth. "Where did you learn to cook like this?" She opened her eyes to take another large bite.

"I can do many things well," his low voice sent shivers down her spine.

She swallowed without chewing and almost choked.

"You will learn much about me as we spend time together training."

She took a drink from the tall glass of orange juice and thought about the drive home. "I can't move in with you, but I'm willing to train with you every day until I go to work. I'm an early riser and I don't have to leave for work until four, so we can spend the days training." She watched for his reaction to her compromise and she took another bite.

His expression remained calm. "No."

"What do you mean, *no*? I'm trying to be reasonable and work a deal with you. Can't you meet me half-way?"

"No."

"Well, why not?" She was irritated by his refusal to negotiate.

"Because I will not compromise with your safety. I will not bargain with the welfare of man-kind, and I will not negotiate the fate of our souls for eternity."

Wow. When he put it like that, she sounded petty and selfish. She took another bite.

"Do you not understand what is at stake here?" His eyes bore into hers.

She chewed before nodding. "I think so."

"Good. When you are done eating, you will call your boss and let him know you are quitting. You will then pack your belongings and we will return to my house to begin your training. We have much to do."

There it was again, that arrogant ordering around of her personal life. He might be right, but it was still her life. She took her time chewing the bite of food in her mouth giving her time to think. "Where's my agency?"

His jaw locked.

"Where's my choice in all of this?"

The muscle near his temple twitched.

"Look, I promised my parents that I wouldn't disappoint them when I moved to town—"

"There is nothing a parent would be more proud of than a Light Warrior who saves the souls of mankind."

She ignored him. "They were worried I'd be corrupted if I moved to the *City of Sin*—"

"This city needs you more than any other. It is most corrupt. They will be proud of your decision to help fix it."

She continued. "I've only been here for three weeks. I cannot, and will not, call them up and say 'Hey mom and dad, guess what? Remember how you thought I'd go off the deep end if I was exposed to so much corruption? Well, I made it a whole three weeks before shacking-up with some guy. We aren't having sex yet, but I sure want to! So, don't worry, I'll be a sinner before you know it!'"

His eyes went dark with a seductive visual caress. "Care to repeat that last part again, *Love*?"

She slapped her hand over her mouth and closed her eyes, wishing she could take back the words she blurted out. When would she learn to control what came out of her mouth?

"Miranda," he said in that low rumble of his.

She kept her eyes closed hoping her face wasn't as red as she knew it was.

"Miranda, *Love*, pack your bags. We are going home."

Home? Home was here. She took a deep breath and let her hand drop into her lap. It took her a moment longer to open her eyes.

"Come on, *Love*, it's time we were going."

She wished he would pick another nickname for her. She couldn't think when he called her that. "I can't."

"Yes, you can."

She shook her head. "No. I will train, but I'm keeping my job and living here."

He slapped his hand down on the table, making her jump. "Why are you so stubborn?"

"It's who I am. Perhaps I wouldn't be the warrior you think I can be, if I was that other kind of a person."

He took a deep breath. "Moving in with me will not make you immoral. I have trained many Light Warriors and have never compromised their virtue."

"Really?" Her brows rose in surprise. He was highly sexual, how had he been able to resist them? For that matter, he was so masculine, so sensual and so very...tempting. How had the other women managed to resist him?

She straightened in her chair. "I will train with you...all day, every day. I will fight with you to save mankind. But I'll do it while I live in my own place, paid for with my own money."

Their eyes locked in a battle of wills. She was calm and determined. She realized his idea was probably the safest and most logical way to go, but she couldn't do that to her family. She couldn't hold her head up in pride, knowing she had disappointed them. And she would disappoint them. She was attracted to this man and for some reason, he was willing to lower his standards for her. If they were together twenty-four/seven she wouldn't be able to resist.

"Fine. Change your clothing and we will leave for the day." He wasn't happy with her, but he wasn't pouting.

She looked down at her clothes. She still wore her work uniform. Ugh. She probably had mascara under her eyes and hair sticking up in all directions. She raised one hand to the top of her head. Yep. It was. He, however, looked magnificent. The only sign of sleeping—*just where had he slept*—was that dark stubble on his jaw. It made him look even more desirable, just like the sexy men on the covers of her beloved romance books.

She jumped up from the table and hurried to the bathroom. Closing the door she leaned against it. He may look a lot like the knight on the cover of her favorite book, but as she stared at her reflection in the mirror above the sink, she knew she looked *nothing* like the beautiful, voluptuous woman the hero held passionately in his arms.

Chapter Ten

"Ouch!" Miranda rubbed her temples. "That hurts."

"Not if you focus."

She glared at him and continued to massage the sides of her head. "I am focusing!" Her voice echoed in the large, high ceilinged basement.

"No, you are not."

She dropped her hands to her waist. "Just what do you think I've been doing for the past five hours?"

"Playing and eating."

Was he serious? *Big jerk.* She folded her arms across her pink t-shirt and wished, not for the first time, she had something in this big empty room to throw at him. "I can't believe you just said that."

He raised a brow.

"Okay, maybe I can," she said in disgust. It wasn't nice of him to rub her nose in her inabilities and her hunger. But after today, she wasn't at all sure he fit into the 'nice' category.

"Let's do it again, only this time focus."

"I still don't understand how this is supposed to work," she said, grumbling.

"When the white energy is unfocused it is very dangerous. You cannot control the amount, or strength, or even how or when it is discharged."

"Like when I annihilated the tiles at work?"

"Yes. That was an uncontrolled release. Once you learn to focus the light, you will be able to use it as a weapon. Then you will be able to train in the art of war."

She frowned. "I don't like the sound of that."

"Why not? It is an honor to fight as a Light Warrior for the Salutari."

She wrapped her arms around herself. "Death, destruction, innocent people dying. War is terrible."

His demeanor softened. "This war is not as the government wars. Innocents are rarely harmed, unless influenced to do wrong by the Arbiters. This is a war to push the darkness back. The only humans to be fought with are the dark ones, and they are not innocents."

A chill ran down her spine. "You said the Arbiter General cheats, that he lies. What if his warriors believe they're on the right side? We'd be killing innocent people then."

Braedan scowled. "There is no disguising darkness as anything but darkness. The Arbiter General seduces his followers with lies—mixed with small amounts of truth—and offers them power and wealth beyond their wildest dreams. He convinces them they are meant to rule mankind. He tells them mankind is not capable of handling the responsibility of choice—that man needs to be controlled. He promises positions of gods and kings over humanity when the battle is over."

She stared at Braedan. This was all so unreal. Two years ago she was nothing but a small town girl with no worries in the world. Life was great. It was fun. The evil of the outside world rarely stretched into the peaceful existence of her life. How did things get so mixed up?

Braedan must have sensed her struggle. "Not all of the battles you will fight will be hard or dangerous."

She was confused again. "They won't?"

He smiled. "The largest part of the war is in shifting the darkness to light. That part will be easy for you and will bring you great joy."

"In that case, how about we skip the hard stuff and go straight to the fun part?"

He ignored her comment. "We are behind schedule and must not only push the dark back, but prepare you for battle."

"So how long does a student usually have to prepare for the Arbiters?"

"Two years."

She swallowed, afraid to ask. "How long do I have?"

His eyes turned hard. "Today. Try it again."

"Today?"

He sighed. The all-patient Braedan was losing patience. "I do not know when they will attempt to sway you, but it will not be long. Focus. Try to find your center."

She brightened. "They'll try to convince me to switch to their side? They're not gonna try to kill me?"

"Once they realize they cannot turn you, they will destroy you. For this, we must train." His words were hard, the tone of his voice deep and angry.

"I'm nobody. Why would they even bother with me?" This was starting to scare her.

His eyes locked with hers. His face composed, but his body tensed and his eyes burned. "They will come for you because you have the strength to push the darkness back. You can save humanity or destroy it."

She felt a little overwhelmed. "What if I don't want that kind of responsibility?"

His jaw stiffened. "It is your choice."

"What kind of a choice is that?"

"You must either fight for the light or join with the darkness. If you ignore the battle and do nothing, you choose the darkness. There is no in-between."

Now she was a *lot* overwhelmed. "Look, Danny, I didn't ask for any of this. If you really think I can make a difference, I'll give it a shot, but I don't think I'm the person you think I am. I'm no warrior."

He crossed his muscled arms over his bare chest. "I do not make mistakes," he repeated the words he had spoken to her last night. "You are a Light Warrior. This is to be treated with reverence and respect. Do not mock this gift." He straightened and clapped his hands together. "Enough time wasted. Let's begin again."

She glared at him, but nodded. She'd agreed to train, and train she would.

Braedan took her hand in his and the white gathered. "Concentrate. Relax. Let the energy flow through you."

She shook her head. "There's too much, it won't let me relax. It makes me feel tense, agitated."

"Focus." The word came as a sharp command. "You are a warrior. You can do anything you put your mind to."

She shook her head in denial. "I'm not a warrior. I'm a waitress from a small town...and I can't relax!"

He released her hand and moved behind her, his large hands began massaging her neck and shoulders. "Calm. Find your center focus."

Her head dropped back in bliss. She could feel the soothing heat of his hands through the thin material of her top as his fingers worked the knotted muscles in her shoulders and neck. She'd chosen a soft cotton t-shirt and shorts since she had no idea what a student should wear to train. For that matter, she'd no idea what a Light Warrior *did* to train. "I have no center focus."

"Yes, you do. Once you find it, you will have better control."

"Fine," she said snapping at him. "How do I find it?"

His voice when he spoke sounded annoyed. "It is *your* center. You have to find it."

"Great. What does it look like?"

He snorted. "In your case, it probably looks like a big cheesy pizza."

"Very funny," she said through clenched teeth. The air was thick with white. It was so bright it should've hurt her eyes, but strangely, it didn't. She guessed the dark walls and flooring helped. "Look, Danny, I'm losing control here again and I need your help."

"Do not call me that."

She'd hit a nerve. Good. "Then help me."

"You enjoy my kisses that much, do you?"

"Big deal. It's just to discharge the power," she fired back, turning her head to look at him. But—wow!—what a way to release it!

"Unless you plan on sharing more than kisses with me, you had better plan on finding your focus soon." The heat in his eyes made this a warning.

Whuh? Her breath left her in a rush and she looked forward again. The image that statement invoked was better left alone. "This isn't funny!" she said through gritted teeth. "If you don't want me to blast a big hole in your fancy house, you'd better do something quick."

He dropped his hands from her shoulders and moved back in front of her. Where he stood, the air was clear around him. "I told you, this room is protected. It is shielded. You cannot hurt it. But you need to focus before you hurt yourself."

He had warned her not to close her eyes, but she couldn't focus while looking at him. So she settled on a point past his shoulder on the wall where the dark paint swirled into what looked amazingly like a large, round pizza, and imagined finding her center. No good. She had no idea what she was looking for. She took a deep breath and tried to let the energy flow through her. Focus. Her stomach growled. How was she expected to concentrate when she was hungry?

Focus. Pizza. Concentrate. Spaghetti. Find your center. Steak with mashed potatoes and gravy. Relax. Angel Food Cake. Let it flow through you. Strawberry sauce with whip cream. Control the power. Strawberry sauce with whip cream and a hot trainer. A shirtless trainer. With ripped abs. And bulging biceps. Karate pants. Barefoot. Ooooh, yeah!

"That is it!" Braedan exclaimed joyously and clapped his hands once before raising them above his head in victory.

"What?" Startled, her gaze reverted back to him. Which was a mistake. His body was glorious with its rippling muscles. The exercise session they began with had his muscles absolutely bulging. Her mouth watered. White fluffy whipped cream against his hard and tanned skin…

"You did it! You have found your center!"

"I did?" Confused, she looked away from her imagined

whipped cream dessert and noticed the white was...controlled. It no longer amassed in a fury around her. It flowed through her, dispersing harmlessly back into the surroundings. She could feel the additional power the control provided. Power she could draw upon and use at will. Power she could wield as a weapon. This power was what made a warrior real.

He grabbed her hands. "You did it." There was a look of pride on his face. "Where did you find your center?"

Oh, no. No way. She tried to pull her hands out of his grasp, but he held tight and she could feel the added strength his touch gave her. She shook her head in silent denial. Her center was food. Food and...oh, crap. She'd take her center to the grave with her.

"Miranda?" His brow furrowed at her silence.

"I just focused, and there it was!"

Braedan looked at her in curiosity.

As far as she was concerned, he could wonder until he turned grey, because she wasn't going to tell him a thing.

Her stomach rumbled again. "Food?" she asked hopefully. The white was wavering. She was losing her focus.

"Make it all go away and I will feed you." It was a blatant bribe.

"I don't think I can—"

"Of course you can. You have found your center. Go to it, and release all of the excess energy."

She felt the heat crawling up her neck.

"Miranda? What is wrong?" He was confused.

"Nothing," she mumbled. She looked at him, then embarrassed, looked away. She could do this. This time, she'd only focus on the food.

Pork chops. Tacos. Lasagna.

The white wasn't going away.

"Concentrate. Go back to your center." The words were half encouragement and half demand.

She cleared her throat and tried again, staring hard at the pizza looking paint blob. Lobster. Crab. Salmon in lemon sauce. Her stomach growled.

"Miranda, go to your center."

"It's not working!"

"Focus as you did last time."

"I can't." It was too embarrassing. She would not, could not, admit—not even to herself—that he might be her center. Especially not with six-pack molded abs and sweet whipped cream.

"Yes. You can."

"I'm too hungry, and I'm tired. I'm done for today." Like a coward, she gave up.

He threw his hands into the air, turned around and walked a few steps away.

"I promise to train again tomorrow," she tried for a compromise.

He remained silent, his lean and muscled back to her. It was all she could do not to drool. Since when had a man's *back* become sexy?

"Tomorrow. All right?" She was pleading with him now.

"Agreed." His voice was strong as he turned to face her again. The devilish look that lit his eyes, made them impossible to look away from.

She blinked in confusion as he ruthlessly strode toward her, the light in his eyes getting brighter with each step. Her eyes were drawn to his well-muscled form moving with the grace of a jungle cat stalking its prey. He was a force of nature, she thought in helpless fascination. She was both drawn to him and yet, almost afraid of him at the same time. She moved backward matching each step he moved forward.

He backed her across the room until her spine rested flush against the cool wall. His body close, his eyes burned into hers. He planted his hands, palms flat, on either side of her head. "I will help you drain the energy—" he offered in a low, velvety rumble—"since you refuse to do it yourself."

"Ohh," she whispered, unalble to utter anything more.

He looked directly into her eyes with such a promise of passion that she nearly whimpered.

Inch by inch, he purposefully lowered his head to hers.

Her subconscious had been waiting all day for this, not the chaste kisses he used to drain the excess energy while training, but the fiery, passion-filled, kisses she remembered so well from last night. She tipped her head up to meet his. Their lips met in a dazzling shock of white light that she felt clear to her toes. Her mind went blank and her knees were weak. His mouth demanded, but gave much in return. Her body responded of its own accord.

Long before she was ready to be done, he pulled back, but only with his lips. His body, his hands on the wall on either side of her head, the incredible heat, it all remained. She exhaled as she forced her eyes to open. He stared down at her with smoldering intensity.

"Food, or continue?" The soft air from his husky voice a caress against her sensitized lips.

She closed her eyes and felt the energy. He'd done his job well—it was low enough for her to control now. Too bad. "Food?" she whispered and opened her eyes again.

A crooked smile tilted his lips. "Upstairs on the table. If you choose to work in your little restaurant today, you had better get moving or you will be late."

"What time is it?" She ducked under his arm, leaving the heat of his body, and took off running for the stairs—she needed space to clear her head and there was food up there!

"Two-thirty. If you choose to shower and change and be to work by four, you had better eat quickly."

"Not a problem," she said, calling back and taking the stairs two at a time.

Chapter Eleven

"Girl, where you been? I've been calling you all day!" Shara had a knowing grin on her face.

"Why?" Had Shara seen her leave last night with Braedan?

"I called you!" Shara grabbed Miranda by the sleeve and pulled her to the side of the serving station counter and away from the gossip hearing ears of the other servers.

"So?" Miranda fiddled with her apron ties.

"I called to see how you were feeling, and guess what?" Shara's eyes were wide in excitement.

"You called? I didn't know you called."

Shara looked like she was ready to burst. "*He* didn't tell you I called?"

He. Crap. "Um, did you call the right number?"

"Oh, yeah." Shara smiled. "I called early, and guess what? This deep, sleepy voice answered and said *you* were still *sleeping*." Shara tapped her own chin with a long manicured nail. "Now I ask myself, who would be answering your phone while you were sleeping?"

Miranda raised her hands in surrender.

"So, I'm thinking, Miranda's not dating anyone right now. Her family's not in town. Hmmm. Where did Table Seven disappear to last night, I wonder?"

Miranda swatted her on the sleeve. "It's not what you think."

"Yeah? And just what am I thinking?"

Miranda rolled her eyes.

Shara chuckled. "You two positively sparked off of each other."

She had that right.

"Give me details!"

Miranda breathed a small sigh of relief and they both straightened away from the wall when John's door opened and he strode purposefully into the center of the serving room.

"I have an announcement. Everyone gather around." John demanded. He loved attention and he often called meetings that allowed him to be the main focus.

"What now?" Shara whispered from the side of her mouth, before pulling Miranda closer with her to hear his news.

John cleared his throat. "Before we begin the evening crowd, I wanted to let you all know that today the *Cheri* has changed owners. The new owner is expecting the very best from his employees, should he decide to keep you all on."

The room buzzed with the concern of lost jobs before Shara spoke up. "Is there talk that some of us will be fired?"

John took his time answering. "Not at this time, but new owners will often make changes when they acquire a business."

Shara leaned closer to Miranda and whispered, "Yeah, to management."

Miranda grinned. "We can hope, right?"

"There will be no one getting fired with the change of ownership," a strong, new voice said as the swinging door opened wide and an unknown man entered the room.

Miranda felt an immediate energy shift in the room and heard Shara's surprised gasp. She turned to look at the owner of the new voice and was astounded by what she saw.

"I am Andrade," the angelic vision before them introduced himself. Tall, blonde, he was California surfer tanned and muscled, wearing black slacks and an expensive white dress shirt with the top two buttons undone and the sleeves rolled up. "I purchased the *Cheri* today, because it is a high-class dining establishment that has fantastic employees keeping things running smoothly. I don't wish to change something that's working so well." His smile nearly made the women in the room swoon. "However, I find myself interested in the running of such an establishment and you may see quite a bit of me."

Some of the waitresses twittered over this, obviously not disappointed over the idea of seeing more of their handsome new boss. This man exuded such a level of charismatic power, Miranda knew women weren't drawn to him just because of his wealth.

She held her breath as he looked at her and her brain confirmed her first impression. Miranda had met her new boss before. Several years ago, in fact. She slowly released the air in her lungs—there was no way he would remember the encounter, although it was etched permanently in her memory.

Andrade looked away from her as he stepped forward and offered his hand to the waitress nearest him. "Your name?"

"Paula," the attractive, mature woman answered with a girlish giggle.

"Very nice to meet you, Paula." He shook her hand professionally, then released it and turned to the next server, offering his hand again.

"Stephanie." The well-endowed, platinum blonde purred and placed her hand in his. She fluttered her lashes at him.

"Stephanie, nice to meet you." Again, professional. He ignored the obvious silent invitation she offered and turned to the next one.

"I'm Katherine," the statuesque red-head said, leaning toward him.

Miranda rolled her eyes. These women were used to rich, handsome men—they worked at the *Cheri* after all—and yet, here they were, making fools of themselves over the newest one. She silently prayed she wouldn't make a complete idiot of herself when it was her turn. After all, unbelievably gorgeous men appeared to be the new norm around the *Cheri*.

"Shara, nice to meet you." Shara was also professional as she shook his hand.

Miranda blinked. Shara had handled that well. She didn't appear to be impressed with his looks and money. It felt almost as though Shara didn't like him.

"Nice to meet you too, Shara," he replied with a sincere smile, unaware of her coolness.

Then Andrade turned to Miranda. She was the last one in the room to be met and everyone was staring.

"And you are?" His eyes searched hers as he extended his hand to her.

"Miranda," she managed to say in what she hoped was a nice and even tone as she reached to take his hand.

"Nice to meet you, Miranda." His large hand engulfed hers.

The shock that ran through her arm was nothing compared to the energy she felt gathering around them. Her eyes flew to his in surprise and she pulled at her hand to break the contact.

His hand tightened on hers, and did not release. His brows were drawn together. "Pardon me, but have we met before?"

She tugged at her hand, not wanting to make a scene in front of the others watching, but he held tight. The white was gathering. She focused on the wall behind him and thought of Braedan. She tried to ignore the women staring at her and the new boss. Concentrate. Braedan would tell her to find her center. Not food...Braedan. Braedan training her. Braedan feeding her. Braedan kissing her. Braedan and whipped topping. She could feel the energy start to flow and disperse. She could feel the eyes of the women in the room burn into her. She could feel the intense look of Andrade as he waited for her reply. The light started to gather again, she was losing her center and control of the energy.

"I-I don't think we've met before," she said a little desperately. She needed to leave before the light grew out of control.

Andrade would not release his hold on her hand. "I am certain we've met before. Are you from Vegas?"

She shook her head and tugged a little harder. She knew the others were staring. She needed to leave. "No, I'm from a small town north of here."

He smiled and clasped his other hand on top of hers, a casual move to the onlookers, but deftly securing her hand in his. "The name of this town? Perhaps we met there?"

Concentrate. Find your center. Let the power flow through and disperse back to the surroundings. "Overton."

He closed his eyes in apparent thought. When he opened them again, they seemed bright and his smile was contagious to those around him. "I've never heard of it. Is it near?"

Focus. "Yes. Most people haven't. It's very small."

"How can it be close and yet, I haven't heard of it?" he wondered aloud.

Braedan. "It's on the north end of Lake Mead."

"Now, I've heard of Lake Mead. In fact, I like to go boating there. Did we perhaps meet there?"

She needed to leave before something bad happened. Now was not the time to remind him of their chance encounter. It was years ago and he had been with some perfectly shaped, flawless woman. A man like him, with a woman like that hanging on him, wouldn't remember someone as insignificant as herself anyway.

The air was starting to get thick with white. What had Braedan done to her? She never had problems like this with the white energy before meeting him. She pulled at her hand.

"It is hard on my ego, that a beautiful woman like you wouldn't remember meeting me. Let me think, perhaps I can remember and refresh your memory as well." The look he gave her before he closed his eyes was direct and probing...sensual. Miranda stared at him, wondering if she imagined the whole situation. The new boss had been so professional with everyone else, why would he single her out? The other women here tonight were much more attractive than she was. She shook her head once. This man belonged on the cover of GQ, he wouldn't have given her a look like that.

She looked around the room at everyone smiling. The white energy had affected them all. She tugged at her hand again.

His eyes opened and he grinned. "Perhaps it will come to me another time," he said. He patted her hand and finally released it.

She blinked in surprise. The white had dimmed and no longer gathered like a storm in the small room.

He turned back to the rest of the staff. "I know you're all busy and I will allow you to return to work. It was a pleasure meeting all of you and I look forward to spending my time here. John?" He gestured with one hand for John to lead the way to his office and they both disappeared into John's room, without so much as a backward glance.

"Wow!"

"Did you see—"

"I want a piece of that!"

Miranda turned away from the giddy women and tied her apron around her waist.

"What was that all about?" Shara asked her in a whisper.

Miranda glanced at her, then away. "What are you talking about?"

"Ohhh, no you don't! I've known you your whole life, you can't hide something like that from me." Her look was direct while she tied her apron strings.

"Something like what?" Miranda said, trying to look innocent.

"Miranda! That man knows you! How can you have met a man like that living in Overton and me not know about it?" Shara was digging.

"Okay, okay. I met him out at the lake once. Two years ago. He rocked my world, but I didn't even think he noticed me."

"Obviously, he did! Why didn't you say something when he asked?"

"I was flustered."

Shara laughed. "Weren't we all?"

Miranda smiled.

"That man is amazing!" Shara placed a hand on her heart. "Between Table Seven and Andrade, I'm beginning to think we work in heaven!"

Miranda laughed. "Heaven for you, maybe. I'm thinking closer to hell."

Shara's look became thoughtful and she leaned one hip against the counter. "Did you say out at the lake? Two years ago?"

Miranda tucked a loose strand of hair back into her ponytail and nodded once.

Shara's eyes rounded. *"He's the one?"*

Miranda couldn't help laughing.

"He's the no talk, kiss and leave, guy?" Shara's eyes were huge.

"Yeah."

"No way! No wonder you fantasized over him for so long. The guy is hot—if you like the All-American stud look!" Shara planted her hands on her hips. "You know, I always believed you—even though things like that don't happen in real life to people like us—but didn't think it was possible the guy was as incredible as you made him out to be. I apologize."

Miranda grabbed a tray from the clean stack on the counter. "Don't feel bad. I wondered if I had imagined him myself."

"Wow! Some girls have all the luck!" Shara grinned.

Miranda reached for a water carafe. "I got the impression you weren't impressed with him."

"Oh, nooo. Didn't say that." Shara clicked her pen open and closed. "Liked him well enough—he's about the hottest thing I've seen in my life—but, there's just something about him...I can't put my finger on it. He was perfectly mannered and didn't flirt with the hired help—except for you, but…" She shrugged. "Guess if he's attracted to you that would explain it. However, I can still appreciate his beauty...and girl, that man is drool worthy!"

"He is kinda...yummy."

Shara laughed. "Trust you to compare him to food!"

Shara didn't know anything about the white energy, but she knew all about Miranda's high metabolism.

"Still, you should'a told him where you met."

"Come on. He was with *Barbie*. He couldn't have even noticed me."

"He noticed you enough to *kiss* you and two years later you stirred his memory," Shara said, pointing out the obvious.

"It was an 'in the moment thing.' He would've reacted the same way to anyone in the same situation."

Shara cocked her head to the side. "Do you think he'll remember?"

Miranda lifted one shoulder.

"Want me to help him remember?" Shara wiggled her brows.

"No! Promise me you won't say anything. He's our new boss. It would be awkward."

Shara smiled mysteriously—without agreeing to anything—and changed the subject. "Ooooh, that reminds me!" She slapped one hand to her forehead. "Table Seven spent the night with you!"

Miranda groaned. Of course Shara wouldn't forget. "It's not what you think."

"Oh, yeah? Then tell me what it is?"

Miranda opened her mouth to explain, then closed it. *What was he*? She pulled a face. "He's my...trainer?"

"You're what?" Shara laughed in surprise.

"He's my trainer. I wanted to get in shape and learn self-protection and he offered to teach me." It sounded lame even to her own ears.

"You know, I might fall for that, except trainers can't afford to eat here. You don't make enough money to afford one, and they don't usually spend the night at their client's home."

"He didn't actually eat here…"

Shara regarded her quizzically. "But he did spend the night at your apartment?"

Miranda stared at her in frustration. She hadn't had time to think of a better story and now she was stuck with a lame version of the truth. "He is my trainer." She held up her hand before Shara could say more. "He's not doing it for sex. I have no idea why he's bothering with me, but I'm glad he's willing to do it. I'm not sleeping with him. I'm not living with him. I'm only training with him. Happy?"

"No." Shara eyed her shrewdly. "I was hoping you'd finally met a man you at least *wanted* to sleep with. It's time for you to date."

Oh, she *did* want to sleep with him, but she wasn't ready to admit that to Shara. Probably because it wasn't really an option. He only kissed her to diffuse the energy overloads, not because he was hot for her body and couldn't help himself.

"So, Friday night, after work, don't make any plans...we're going out." Shara grabbed a tray from the stack.

"Going where? That's too late to start a night out."

"We're going on a double date—don't worry, I'll line you up with someone good—and it won't be too late at night to start. The night life here doesn't even begin until after eleven o'clock!"

Was he watching her, or was she just being paranoid? The hair on the back of her neck was tingling, but every time she looked at Andrade, he was otherwise occupied.

Disgusted with herself for even thinking he might have any kind of an interest in her, Miranda lifted the now empty tray to shoulder level and turned back to the serving room to get the next order of food that was surely up by now.

As she turned the corner, she collided with Andrade.

"Whoa, there." He steadied her with a hand on each shoulder.

He had crystal clear blue eyes. Two years ago, when she first saw those unusual eyes, she knew she would never forget them, and so far, she hadn't.

He ducked a little to her eye level. "You okay?"

The white swirled around them, like a light snow flurry, and she shook her head in confusion. What had Braedan done to her that every man could now start the light in motion? Was it only men, or would women set it off too? Great, he turned her into a leper and she would never be able to touch anyone again.

"You're not okay?" Concern was present in his voice.

She shrugged and slipped out of his grasp as she headed for the serving station. "I'm fine, just busy." She gave a poor attempt at a smile.

She ducked into the room that was full of bustling people trying to get their work done. No privacy. What would she do if the energy didn't disperse? She stopped short and looked around in surprise, the white was barely above normal. No massive overload of light. Where had it gone?

Chapter Twelve

Where is she? He should have gone with her and protected her. Stubborn student. He had been too easy on her today. She was stronger than the others he'd trained and instead of being exhausted when the training session was over, she had been energized. Tomorrow, he would push her harder. Perhaps if she was tired she wouldn't run off to work in her restaurant.

How was he supposed to protect her if she wouldn't stay with him? He had no choice, but to let her go. Whose bright idea was it to give them their agency?

Feeling out of options, he commandeered the apartment at the end of the hall, next door and to the left of hers so he could be nearby in case she needed him. This meant they shared a common wall, which was good as he would be able to feel her through that thin wall. He looked around at the small apartment. At least it was bigger than hers, but not by much.

He paced the living room, waiting for her to return. His senses were in tune to every sound, and should her soft footsteps tread down the hallway, he would hear them. He inched toward the door and listened. Nothing. Perhaps she was so slight of build his warrior senses may not hear her? He cracked the door open and then resumed his restless prowl around his too small apartment.

Thank the stars he would only have to sleep here. They would train at his much larger, much more comfortable, much safer house. Then he would become a dinner-time regular at her restaurant where he could keep an eye on her.

His frustration built, seething to get out. This was ridiculous.

He was a seasoned warrior. A revered trainer. He should not be reduced to this status—physically and mentally—simply because a small slip of a girl had over-developed morals.

He heard light footsteps on the stairs that clicked as only high-heeled women's shoes could do. The steps were quick and almost noiseless. He looked at his watch…eleven-thirty. Didn't the restaurant close at ten on weeknights?

He opened the door and leaned against the frame waiting for her to reach the end of the hall.

He watched as her walk down the dim-lit hallway. The horrible outfit she was required to wear as a uniform left too little, and yet, too much to the imagination. The pants were snug on her small waist and backside, but they draped down her well-toned legs and partially covered her high heeled sandals. How could anyone wear such instruments of torture for a whole night? The shirt was high-collard and long sleeved, yet form-fitting. Again it showed too much, while making men wish to see more and forcing them to imagine the rest. The imagination could be a very powerful thing.

Worse for him, since he had an eyeful of her body today while training. She hadn't dressed immodestly, yet he'd seen most of what the uniform covered. Shorts and a t-shirt had left little to the imagination. For being so slender, she was shaped nicely. She had great muscle tone and long legs. Her body was trim and tight. No jiggle on this girl when she moved.

He gripped the door frame on both sides while he waited for her to realize she wasn't alone.

She let out a startled little squeak when she was nearly level with him.

"Had I been the enemy, you would have been dead by now," he said through tight lips.

Her eyes were round. "What are you doing here?" She peered at the doorway he was lounging in and a frown creased her brow. "Why are you in Mr. William's apartment?"

He stood straight and folded his arms across his polo shirted chest. "Mr. Williams moved out and I am now your new neighbor."

"You moved in next door to me?" Her expression was incredulous. "What about your house?"

"We will still go there to train." But not to sleep in the big, comfortable bed. Not to cook in the well-stocked kitchen that had room to move about comfortably. Not to enjoy the privacy its high-walled isolation provided.

She looked like she had something more to say, but instead held up one hand as though to stop him from saying anything further and with a shake of her head, unlocked her front door and went inside closing it firmly behind her.

"Damn." He was all worked up. He realized he had been looking forward to a nice little fight with her to blow off steam. He glared at her door. Now the only option to get the additional energy out would be to train. To physically exhaust himself. Fighting with her would have been much more enjoyable.

Chapter Thirteen

"Yes, General. I have found the power source." Andrade spoke into the special cell phone that was a secure line to the General. The General had all kinds of interesting toys the rest of the world didn't have yet.

"Well done my warrior. Have you made contact?"

"Yes, General. I have made contact and she is magnificent." He didn't hide the pride in his voice.

"There is satisfaction in this for you?"

You couldn't hide anything from the General. "Yes, General. This one belongs to me. I was the one to activate her."

"Excellent." There was a note of exhilaration in the General's voice. "This will give you a bond that she will not break easily. When did you activate her?"

"Two years ago. She was one of my first. I do not know if she remembers me, but the connection is still there. I have felt it." Andrade picked up an apple from the fruit bowl his maid had left on the kitchen table.

"She remembers you," the General said.

"Perhaps," he said, conceding the point. He tossed the apple in the air and caught it before placing it back in the bowl. He was puzzled as to why she refused to acknowledge their meeting.

"Tell me your plan." The ever present command filled the General's voice.

"I have searched her apartment. I have learned of her interests. I have imprinted her signature. This one will not be easily swayed. She will require some time to win over, but with my skills it can be done." He moved from his dining area into the dark living room.

"Your strategy?"

"She is a romantic, she will need to be seduced." This would be a challenge he would enjoy as much as any battle, he thought as he wandered around the room.

"Do not forget to shield your darkness from this one until she is ready. If you truly share a bond, she will sense it."

"Of course, my General. I will not fail you."

The General sounded irritated. "Do it quickly. I want this power."

"Yes, General. I understand, but I do not believe it would be wise to act hastily." He paused at the large windowed wall and looked out at the lights of the city below him. In the distance, he could almost pin-point the area of man-made lights her apartment building was in. "You are correct, her power can win this battle for us, but it will have to be done with patience. It would not be wise to rush her."

He could feel the General's rage at the delay through the phone, although the General remained quiet.

"She will not be easily swayed by riches," he explained, as he touched the cool glass in front of him with his fingertips. "She loves nature and cares not for most worldly things." He hesitated, knowing the General would not like the next bit of information. "She has a strong bond with her family."

The General was incensed. Andrade did not have to see the General to know this. He could feel it. Not through the phone line, but through the power the General wielded over his subjects.

"However—" he interrupted the General's tirade before it could even begin—"she is a romantic. And with the right *hero*—" he placed his hand flat on the glass—"she can be won."

"Make it so." The demand was issued and the call disconnected.

"Of course, my General," he concurred, although the line was already dead. "It will be my pleasure."

Chapter Fourteen

Miranda stared at the door. She could feel him on the other side, waiting for her to let him in. She rested her forehead against the cream colored wood. Was she up for this? Evidently, humanity needed her. She snorted. Boy, were they all in trouble. She straightened her spine and opened the door.

"Are you ready to go?" Braedan asked.

Her stomach did a funny little flip-flop at the sight of him. No single male should've been given so much in the looks department. It wasn't fair to the rest of mankind.

She motioned him in and walked back to her kitchen. She hadn't slept well last night, thinking of the new developments in her life, and now she was more confused than ever. She picked at the breakfast burrito on her plate and pointed him to the full plate of them sitting on the counter. He grinned and helped himself to one. Her chewing stopped as she watched him. He was so darkly handsome, where Andrade was so blond and sinfully wholesome.

"I just don't get it," she said, blurting the words. "What do you see in me? I mean, why would you waste your time on me?" Why would Andrade look at her twice? These men were wealthy, powerful, cultured…and way out of her league.

Braedan stared at her, his gaze level and deep with something she didn't understand. Several long heartbeats thudded in her chest before he turned away and walked around the small room.

He picked up a framed picture sitting on her desk. It was a photo of her family hiking in the Valley of Fire. He held it up for her to see.

"You love your family, you have strong moral values, you are a good person." He ignored her protest and continued. "You are not only beautiful outside, but inside as well." He placed the photo back in its place. "Because you have always possessed such a strong spirit, you were gifted with the ability to control the white energy. The beauty on the inside shines through and overpowers the beauty on the outside. This is why the white energy is drawn to you. This is why I willingly choose to 'waste my time on you.' Because I feel it is a gift to be chosen to train you."

She wished she had a witness to those astonishing words. Even if she could remember them all, her brothers would never believe someone had said them about her.

His eyes were dark as they burned into hers. "Beauty is in the eye of the beholder. I believe you to be a very beautiful woman."

She was not only speechless, she was breathless.

"With a little work, you will make a fine warrior." He held his head high and continued to pace the room. He stopped a moment in front of the double bookcase and pulled one of her favorite books from the shelf. He raised one brow and held it up for her to see. There was a knight on a white stallion, holding a beautiful woman in his lap. "Perhaps you would prefer to be a knight instead of a warrior?"

She felt the heat in her cheeks. "Put it back."

He looked closer at the cover. "Perhaps *I* would like to be a knight," he said with a chuckle.

She groaned. "I never wanted to be a warrior or a knight. I wanted to be the *woman* in those pictures. The one that was rescued and got swept off her feet by the knight in shining armor." She grimaced and placed her empty plate into the sink before turning back to him. "The man is supposed to save the woman, not the other way around."

He lifted his brows and opened the book to the center.

"No!" She rushed toward him. "You can't read from the middle."

"Why not?" He raised the book above his head and out of her

reach. "His silken lips brushed against hers—" he read aloud.

"Give it back!" She tugged at the arm holding the book.

"Her body melted into his—"

"Why do men always do that? It sounds corny if you don't read it with the whole story," she fumed.

"She had never felt desire such as she did in his arms—"

"Oh, for crying out loud!" she muttered as she jumped for the book.

Braedan moved it higher and turned away from her. "This is interesting. No wonder women read these books all the time."

She snorted in disgust. "The sex stuff is the only part a man would enjoy and those sections are few and far between, so give it back." She held out her hand.

He read on silently for a moment more, before making eye contact again. "Women really like the whole knight idea?"

She rolled her eyes. "Yes."

"Why?"

"Why?" She threw her hands up. "I guess because life is hard. The idea of a handsome man who is strong enough to come in and sweep you off your feet, to take care of everything, to protect you...it's all very tempting."

"Really? I thought women wanted to be strong and independent?"

Miranda shrugged. "Some do. Since romance books sell more than any other kind of book, I'd guess it's fair to say most women secretly still want the whole romance thing."

"Why would women hide such a desire? There is nothing wrong with being treated properly."

"Yeah, well—" she searched for the right words—"most men don't really deliver in the romance department any more. Romance has been forgotten. If you even kiss a man, he wants to jump straight to sex. Don't even get me started on Valentine's Day. Modern man has forgotten about the whole courting idea. They make fun of women who want to be wooed."

"Wooed?"

"You know—" again she struggled to find the right words—"... leisurely romanced."

He looked back up at the book he still held out of her reach and read on, "His hands were hot as they traveled slowly over her supple curves..."

She reached for the book again.

His eyes met hers as his arm closed around her waist and pulled her up close against his own warm body in an effort to stop her quest of retrieving the book. "Yes, I can see why women would want to be 'slowly' romanced."

She pushed against his chest and glared up at him. "Are you done making fun of me yet?"

He looked surprised. "I'm not making fun of you. I'm making fun of your book."

It happened to be one of her favorites. She glared at him and reached for the book again. She could almost reach it since she was so much closer to him now than she had been before.

He tightened his grip on her waist, securing her body snug against his and effectively keeping the book from her grasp. "Yes, I do believe I would like to borrow this book. May I?"

She could feel the hard muscles of his body against her own. What had he asked her? "That's not fair."

He looked puzzled. "Borrowing a book is not fair?"

"No," she clarified, "you can't come in here and tell me I'm wonderful, flirt with me, romance me, and then make me go train until I'm exhausted. That's cheating!"

"I never cheat. We train because we are honor bound. There is nothing unfair about it." He nuzzled her neck and softly rumbled the next words in her ear. "I flirt and romance you because I cannot seem to help myself."

"Oh," she said as a shiver ran down her spine. "Well, in that case..."

"Yes, in that case." He kissed his way up her neck and across her jaw.

"Definitely, we should..." She lost her train of thought as she turned her head to meet his lips.

"Yes," he whispered as he covered her lips with his own. His were insatiable, taking all she chose to give.

She returned his kiss, rising up on tiptoe to better meet his demands. Her head spun and her ears rang. Her ears were ringing? Correction, her phone was ringing.

Braedan stopped, but didn't release her.

"I, uh, better get that." She couldn't look away from his eyes.

"Why?" His gaze continued to hold hers.

"Um," she couldn't remember why. "Because?"

His smile tilted one side of his lips into a sexy grin and he loosened his hold on her. "In that case, you had better answer it."

"Yes," she said, still dazed. The phone continued to ring and she forced herself to pull away. She fumbled with her cell until she found the start button. "Hello?"

"Hi, honey, it's Mom."

"Mom?" she said.

"Were you still sleeping? I'm sorry, did you work late last night?"

"Uh-huh." Miranda looked at Braedan.

"I'll keep it short and let you get some rest, but I just wanted to make sure you were still coming home on Saturday?"

"Saturday?" Miranda looked away from Braedan so she could think.

"Yes, honey. It's Mother's Day and everyone is getting together for a family dinner. Remember?"

"Of course I remember, Mom. Wouldn't miss it for the world, but you remember I have to leave early Sunday, right? New job and all, can't get the holiday afternoon off."

"But you do have all day Saturday?" The hope in her mom's voice could be heard through the phone line.

Miranda looked at Braedan. There was no doubt he could hear the entire conversation, but his expression remained impassive. If he minded her missing training that day, it would be too bad.

"Sure do."

"Good!" Her mom sounded happy. "See you Saturday!"

"Love ya." Miranda hung up the phone and looked up to see Braedan watching her.

He cleared his throat. "We are going to meet your family on Saturday?"

Oh, boy. "I don't know about that."

He cocked his head and crossed his arms. "You are in training. It is not safe to go away on your own."

She picked up a shoe that hadn't made it to the closet last night and put it away. "I'm just going to Overton. Believe me, I'll be safe there."

"Consider this, what if your family is not safe with you there?"

The blood left her head in a rush and she turned quickly away from the closet. "My family?" Her voice came out higher pitched than normal. "They could be in danger because of me?"

He hastened to reassure her, "I will protect them."

She shook her head vehemently. "I'm not going. I won't put my family in danger."

Braedan walked forward and wrapped his arms around her. "You may go, you just have to allow me to accompany you to make certain all is well."

She looked up at him. She was barefoot and had to tip her head at quite an angle. "I thought I was the warrior and you were just the teacher?"

He grinned. "You are the 'knight' of light—" he teased—"and I have a few skills of my own. We will train until Saturday, and then, together we will go to see your family. Your loved ones will be fine."

"Yeah, at least until they see how you help me diffuse the extra energy," she mumbled into his chest.

His laughter rumbled against her cheek.

She smiled, enjoying the feel of his arms around her. He made her feel safe. Her words came back to her mind: Life was getting difficult, and he was handsome, strong enough to come in and sweep her off her feet, he was capable enough to take care of everything, he could protect her...the thought of him as her knight was very tempting.

"Shall we go and find your center?"

She pushed away from his chest, he was *not* a knight in shining armor. No, he was her very own, personal instructor...to a lifetime of hell.

Chapter Fifteen

Miranda breezed through the back door of the *Cheri* prepared for work. She trained all day with Braedan and it had been brutal. He physically exhausted her, then pushed her to mental strain. She was so very grateful—as strange as it might sound—to leave the training behind and go to work. She couldn't quite get the whole center thing figured out. There had to be a focus not related to her trainer. She was determined to find it. She just needed time.

The heavenly smells from the kitchen wafted toward her and she tucked her purse into her locker in the employee break room. Her stomach rumbled. She had been in too big a hurry to get away from Braedan and his incessant pushing to find her center, for her to eat much at his house. Then when she returned home, the delivery of a huge bouquet of flowers had distracted her long enough that she only had time for a quick peanut butter and jelly sandwich eaten on the way.

Looking at her watch confirmed traffic had cooperated nicely and she had fifteen minutes before her shift started. With a grin, she headed to the kitchen. Good thing there was a very nice employee discount, or she would never be able to eat the expensive food here.

The flowers had been costly too. A large spray of mixed white and pale pink blossoms in a crystal vase. They were delicate, fragile, and absolutely romantic. The card had simply read, "For an unforgettable kiss."

"Hey, Miranda," one of the cooks called happily from his work station, bringing her mind back to her hunger issues. "The usual?"

Miranda nodded with a smile. Chris made the best cheese and chicken quesadilla she had ever tasted. It was filled with mushrooms, onions, and red peppers. Chris always made it special just for her—very full, with extra cheese. Funny thing was, it wasn't even offered on the *Cheri's* menu, but he always made it for her anyway. Chris was in his fifties, married, and had two grown children. He claimed she reminded him of his own skinny daughter and was determined to fatten Miranda up, since his daughter lived so far away that he couldn't feed her.

Unforgettable kiss? Her mind wandered as she watched Chris work his culinary magic. She couldn't imagine Braedan sending her the beautiful flowers. He was her trainer. He was strict and disciplined. He kissed her because he had too, not because he chose to. Didn't he?

"You look tired tonight," Chris said as he drizzled olive oil on the grill and placed a wheat tortilla on the sizzling heat.

She watched his efficient hands spread cheese, chopped meat and veggies over the tortilla before covering the mountain of food with a second tortilla. "Yeah, I am. But it's okay. Just had a lot of exercise today."

Chris grinned. "Then you'll need a lot of food to give you energy for tonight." He grabbed a plate and loaded it with fresh fruits, then deftly flipped the full tortilla over to brown the other side.

Her stomach rumbled and she grinned at him. "I could eat an elephant tonight!" She smiled and sent a little of the white in the air toward him.

Chris laughed and the white swirled around him. He was a good man and the white liked him.

But Braedan couldn't have ordered the flowers. They'd been together constantly right up until she entered her apartment to get ready for work. Which is when the flowers had arrived. Besides, he wasn't interested in her *that* way.

Chris swooped the tortilla off the grill and onto a plate and cut the thick round into quarters. He handed her the full plate with a wink. "Enjoy your elephant!"

"I will!" She laughed and headed back to the break room. She sat at the only table in the empty room and grabbed a hot slice of the quesadilla, lifted it, dripping cheese, and took a huge bite.

"Ummmm." She moaned, closing her eyes in absolute bliss. Chris had outdone himself.

"If customers could watch you eat—" a low voice said from the doorway—"I'd have the most successful restaurant in all of Las Vegas."

Miranda jumped and opened her eyes. Andrade stood there, his dark tan set off by the white dress shirt he wore. Again, he had the sleeves rolled and the top two buttons undone, but although he looked similar to the way he looked last night, she could see the subtle differences in the clothing—today the white shirt had a swirled pattern, the slacks, though black, were a different style, and of course the expensive dark leather shoes were different too. It was a good look for him. The businessman style accentuated his good looks, was casually professional, and screamed successful wealth.

Her mouth was too full to talk and she turned away to chew.

She could hear him move quietly into the room. "Mind if I join you?"

Her mouth was still too full to speak and he took advantage of it to settle his impressive frame into a hard plastic chair next to her at the small square table.

"Have you remembered where we met yet?" His eyes were steady on her.

She chewed a few more times and tried to swallow. The food kinda stuck halfway and she drank some water to wash it the rest of the way down.

"I do." His gaze lingered on her face.

"You do?"

"Of course I do," he said. "I would never forget rescuing a beautiful damsel in distress."

She blinked.

He continued. "It was two years ago on Lake Mead. A storm came out of nowhere and the waves were fierce—I've heard tell that particular lake can sink a house boat in a storm—and there you were. You looked magnificent on the Jet Ski, your body wet, long hair loose in the wind, jumping the ferocious waves and laughing."

She swallowed. Audibly.

"I couldn't resist joining you and together we raced for miles in the storm."

She knew she should say something, but was at a loss for words. His memory of the event was every bit as fantasized as her version was.

"The waves got larger and still you laughed. You were young and indestructible, until a giant wave knocked you off your ski. We were headed to the beach when it happened, and I dove in the water after you and helped you to shore. As we reached the beach, I gave you mouth to mouth resuscitation and saved your life."

That got her voice working again. "You did *not* save my life and that was *not* mouth to mouth, that was a kiss!"

He grinned. "Why yes, it was. But I could hardly call it that with your brother watching us from up the beach, now could I?"

She snorted. "It wasn't my brother you were worried about, it was your Barbie girlfriend you were trying to console."

"Brother. Girlfriend. Either way, rescuing was less troublesome than explaining the need to kiss a woman I didn't even know." He winked and relaxed back into the small chair.

"In case you hadn't noticed, you really didn't save me. We were very close to the beach and I'm a good swimmer. I would've made it back on my own just fine without the help."

"But then, I wouldn't have had an excuse to touch you, now would I?"

She rolled her eyes, but couldn't suppress the smile that crept across her lips.

His eyes burned into hers. "Did you really not remember me last evening?"

She fidgeted with her food. "I did, but it had been so long ago, and I was wet, no make-up, and far from here. You were with someone else." She shrugged one shoulder. "I figured you wouldn't remember me."

"I'd never forget a woman I had...saved the life of." There was a teasing light in his eyes.

"Oh, but you might forget one you had kissed, huh?" She fired back with a grin.

"I do not remember Barbie."

"But you remember me?"

His eyes darkened. "In two years, I haven't forgotten that kiss. In twenty years, I will still remember that kiss."

She gulped. Had he just topped her list of romantic things said to her? Braedan would to have to step it up a notch.

The back door opened and they could hear several of the dinner crew coming in for work.

He covered her hand with his and she felt the energy swirl around them. "I hope you will remember it as well," he said softly, and he rose to leave the table.

She most certainly would.

Chapter Sixteen

The *Cheri* was busy for a Wednesday night. Miranda had been so involved with work, she hadn't had time to think about Andrade. She barely even thought of Braedan until she saw him sitting at a table in Katherine's section.

Why would he sit in Katherine's section and not hers? Had he decided red-heads were more his style? When they looked like Katherine, who could blame him?

She saw Andrade one other time during the night as he made the rounds through the restaurant, checking on the guests. When she looked his way, he was staring intently at her. When they made eye contact, one side of his mouth lifted in a crooked grin and he winked.

In that instant, she realized he had been the one to send the flowers. She was sure of it. The card had said, "*For an unforgettable kiss.*" Flustered, she looked away...and ended up making eye contact with Braedan. His look was dark and his jaw tight. His eyes bore into her until she could feel the energy in the room start to shift. He broke the connection first, and his gaze shifted to Andrade.

She raised her tray above her shoulder and headed for the safety of the serving station.

Andrade was flirting with her, no doubt about it. He was discreet, but definitely showing interest. Of course, a man like that couldn't be interested in her for anything more than a light flirtation. While sweet smelling and expensive flowers were a rarity to her, they wouldn't mean anything to a man like him. He probably sent them to women all the time. Hadn't he said he didn't remember Barbie? Barbie looked like a wealthy, international fashion model—perfect face, perfect hair, perfect body. Not only could she not compete with women like that, she didn't even want to try. Too humiliating.

And now, her trainer was acting as if he were jealous of her new boss. Her trainer. The man who was interested in her for her mind—how odd was that?—and although she was attracted to him, he only kissed her to diffuse the excess power she couldn't control.

"Wait a minute," she said aloud to the empty room and set her tray on the counter. Braedan had kissed her this morning in her apartment, and there hadn't been an energy emergency then. He kissed her because...because...she didn't know why he had kissed her. But then, as always, he stopped. The phone had interrupted after a few amazing moments, but she doubted it would have lasted anyway. It was as if he were duty bound to do so and ended the kisses as soon as he could be released from the responsibility.

She leaned against the counter. The kiss two years ago from Andrade had been earth shattering to a young and inexperienced girl. Had it been because of a special bond between them? Because of the rush of the daring ride? Or because she had never in her entire life kissed a complete stranger whom she had never exchanged one word with?

The kisses she exchanged with Braedan were every bit as momentous. The power they generated together—unbelievable. Was the attraction between the two of them so unbelievably strong, or was it just the good feeling the white energy could create? She wondered if she fought the desire to become centered and controlled, because then he wouldn't need to kiss her anymore.

What a tangled mess life was becoming.

The door swung open and Shara entered the room with a groan. "Five more minutes. Didn't think this night was ever going to end. Tips were great though. How 'bout for you?"

Miranda gave a lopsided smile. "Almost made enough to cover the carafe I broke last night!"

"If John deducts that from your check, I'm gonna make that nerd sorry he was ever born!"

Miranda chuckled. "What did I do to get such a good friend like you?"

"You stole my boyfriend in second grade. Made me realize what a creep he really was and you've been stuck with me ever since." Shara grinned and popped a grape in her mouth from the abandoned fruit bowl on the counter.

"Told you years ago to feel free to steal any boyfriend I might get to even the score," Miranda said, reminding her, helping herself to a small handful of the big red grapes.

"Up until recently, you haven't bothered with any worth stealing. Speaking of which, you want to invite *him* to go with us on Friday or do you want to take your chances with one of mine?"

Miranda almost choked on her grape. "Him, who?"

Shara narrowed one eye. "How many gorgeous men do you have hanging on the line to invite Friday?"

"None." Her reply had been a little too quick. She turned her back on Shara and totaled all her tickets from the evening.

"Uh-huh. And your man-candy from two nights ago, who was stalking you all night tonight, won't mind if you go out with someone else?" Shara said, moving next to Miranda and totaling her own stack of tickets.

"No, he won't care." As long as she trained with him first.

"Then the fact that he is outside, waiting for you to get off work, doesn't mean anything?"

Miranda slanted a look at her friend. "He's, uh, giving me a ride home."

"Sure he is," Shara said. "My rides always hang out for my entire shift, rather than come back for me at closing."

Miranda stared at her tickets. He had been here all night? He watched her for a long time from Katherine's section, but she thought he left hours ago.

"He lives in my apartment building, so I'm kinda on his way home." She may as well tell Shara now, she was bound to find out anyway.

"What?" Shara grabbed Miranda's shoulder. "When did that

happen?"

"A few days ago," Miranda hedged. She was hoping Shara would assume he moved there before they met at work. It would be easier than explaining his obsessive need to keep her close.

"Well if that don't beat all!" Shara huffed. "Men like that don't live in my apartment building. I gotta put up with crying babies upstairs all day long and fighting newlyweds downstairs all night while you get Vegas' most delicious man for a neighbor. Life's not fair."

Miranda gave her a half smile and stacked her tickets into a neat pile.

"I noticed he wasn't the only one watching you tonight." Shara continued to add her own tickets as if she hadn't just said something interesting.

"What are you talking about?" Miranda finished with her tickets and started counting her tips.

"Thought I saw the new boss checking you out," Shara said. "More than once."

Miranda lost count.

Paula picked that moment to breeze through the room. "Floor is empty. I'm outta here. Night ladies!"

"Night," Miranda called after her as the fellow waitress headed out the back.

Shara waited for Paula to be out of earshot, before she slapped her tickets on the counter and forced Miranda to face her. "You're killing me here. You gotta tell me what's going on or I'm gonna die of curiosity!"

Miranda sighed. "My trainer, Braedan, I have no idea what to tell you there. Andrade, well, he remembered meeting me at the lake."

"What? When? Give me details!"

Miranda was saved from answering when Katherine came in. "Did you see the hunk that was in my section for so long tonight?"

Shara rolled her eyes. "You mean the short, pudgy, guy with glasses that asked me for your number?"

Katherine gave her a dirty look. "Funny. I was referring to the tall, dark and handsome stud who tipped me so well."

"Hands off," Shara warned. "He belongs to Miranda."

Katherine looked at Miranda in surprise. She gave her a once over, then with a glare at Shara, harrumphed and walked away.

Shara laughed. "Let's get outta here."

Miranda grabbed her tickets and they headed to John's office to drop them off.

John's door was open, but only Andrade sat in the office.

"Dropping off our tickets for the night." Shara reached to place hers on John's desk.

"I'll take those." Andrade took the tickets from her, then turned to Miranda for hers.

Miranda held her stack out and felt the energy grow around them. They hadn't even touched yet.

"Did you have a good night, ladies?"

"Yes, thank you." She was drawn to him. Who was she kidding? She had fantasized about this man for two whole years. Seeing him again in person didn't lesson the memory. If anything, he was better than she remembered—well, sort of. Her memory of him was pretty good...he wore just a pair of swim-shorts and a life jacket, all of his muscles bulging with the exertion of fighting the waves, body glistening with water. That was her past memory. So far she had only seen him fully clothed. His clothing hinted that the muscles below were still impressive, but who knew for sure?

"You ladies go home and get some sleep." He placed his hand on Miranda's lower back and walked them to the door. Just as they reached the door, his hand slid slightly to the side of her waist and gave a slight squeeze. "I look forward to seeing you tomorrow."

Miranda had to clear her throat before she could find the words. "Good night, boss."

"Call me Andrade." He gave a light caress to her back, before lifting his hand in farewell.

Shara fanned herself as they walked out the back door to the parking lot. The door was barely closed before she started, "Ohhh, girl, he's got the hots for you!"

"Knock it off." Miranda laughed at Shara's drama.

Shara's eyes widened and she exhaled in a rush. "Good grief, girl. Must you hog *all* the perfect men for yourself?"

Miranda followed her gaze and felt the sizzle in the air. Braedan leaned against his car, his long legs stretched out in front of him, his arms folded across his chest.

"Hello, Miranda." His low voice vibrated in the air between them.

"If you change your mind about Friday—" Shara said with a nod toward Braedan—"let me know!"

"Sure." Miranda had no idea what she was agreeing to.

"Night," Shara said with a wave and detoured to her own car.

Miranda approached him and the warm night air turned balmy and oppressive. She stopped in front of him and tipped her head to the side. "You waited all night for me?"

"Yes."

"Why?"

"Because you refuse to live with me. I must therefore follow you to make certain you are safe."

The corner of her lip turned down. "Logical." Nothing romantic about that. She moved forward in attempt to open the door.

He didn't move out of her way.

"Excuse me, please." She indicated her need to get to the car door.

"Who was the blond?" His voice sounded harsh, as though he didn't want to ask.

Miranda played dumb. "Shara?"

"No. The man."

"Which one?" She felt an argument coming on and didn't want to participate. "There were quite a few blond men at the *Cheri* tonight."

He crossed his arms and remained silent.

She caved. "He's my boss."

His look was probing.

"That's it. He's my new boss." That much was true. Andrade may have flirted with her, might have even sent her flowers, but he hadn't asked her out. Hadn't so much as asked for her number.

A muscle jerked in his jaw as he ground his teeth. He wasn't buying it. "How come your energy signature is so low?"

"It's low?" She raised her hand. It grew brighter even as she stared at it.

"It was very low when you came out the back door. It is generating again now."

Why did she have to defend herself to him? She had done nothing wrong. "Maybe it's because you worked me so hard today, and I didn't get enough food to eat."

He looked at her as if he didn't believe her excuse. "Then, by all means, we must feed you."

With the mood he was in, she was afraid that for the first time in a long time. She wasn't going to enjoy this meal.

Chapter Seventeen

"Where are we going?" Miranda asked. Braedan down-shifted his powerful car and turned left into a taco/burrito drive-thru.

"Food, then training." His voice was terse.

"What? No, no, no. I already trained today. I worked all evening. Bedtime now," she said.

Braedan's eyes left the menu board and stared hard into hers. He knew it wasn't an offer, but after being forced to sit patiently while the blond had flirted with his protégé all night, he felt an uncontrollable urge to make her aware of him. As a man. She would think only of him for the rest of the night.

She gulped. "Me. Mine. My bed." She adjusted the car's air vents to blow cool air into her face. "Alone. By myself. To get some rest."

His lip twitched. She was doing the ramble thing again. "Yes, alone would be a good idea if you are after rest. We would not rest were we to go there together."

She was speechless. Unusual for her.

He rolled down his window and spoke to the menu board. "I need ten macho tacos and ten deluxe meat burritos."

"Will that be all for you today?" asked the tinny voice coming from the speaker.

He looked at Miranda. Her eyes were unfocused and, guessing from her heightened color, she was picturing what it would be like should they go to bed. Together.

"Miranda?"

She blinked and nodded.

"Yes," he answered the unseen monotone voice.

"Please, pull around to the second window," the voice instructed.

Braedan pulled around and fished his wallet out of his back pocket. The window opened and a bag was thrust out at him. He took the bag and handed the tired teenager a fifty dollar bill.

The girl's eyes widened when she looked at him and she perked up, straightening her spine. "I'll get your change," she said with a lingering look at him.

"Keep it. Have a nice night." His smile, and his money, revived the poor girl.

"Thanks!" she said with a smile, handing him a second white bag.

He handed both bags to Miranda. "Dig in."

She rolled her eyes. "Not until I wipe that girl's drool off the food," she muttered.

He reached over and rubbed the bag against his forearm. "There, think I got it all."

She laughed and slapped at his arm.

He could feel the energy hum inside the car. Even the car motor seemed to gain power.

"That reminds me." She opened the first bag. "What have you done to me that I can't touch anybody without creating a snow storm of energy?"

He looked at her in surprise, but her head was nearly inside the white sack on her lap digging for food. She pulled out a burrito and peeled the wrapper back—licked her lips—and handed it to him, before getting one for herself.

He was hungry, more so than he had thought possible. He watched her absolute enjoyment of the food she was consuming. He had never seen anyone treat food with the reverence and all-encompassing commitment that she did. His grip tightened on the warm food in his hand while his body responded to the pleasure she was receiving. She moaned in unadulterated delight. He knew without doubt, that it was not a burrito that he craved.

He had to force his view back to the road, before he could

continue their conversation. "You are creating energy when you touch someone beside myself?" He took a bite of the cheesy burrito. Perhaps he could feed at least one of his hungers. He looked down at the burrito in his hand. It was a poor substitute.

"Yes." She spoke the one word around the mouthful of food she had just taken. "I swear, I seem to be creating energy from everyone now."

How could this be possible? "Where is this happening?"

"At work." She took another overly large bite. "It's the only place I've been lately."

Braedan pulled into a large parking lot and turned off the motor of his car before facing her. "How do you control this increase when I am not there to help you?"

She chewed for a moment, then swallowed. "I don't know. It just gathers, then seems to disperse all on its own. Weird, huh?"

"Perhaps you have gotten better at finding your center?" That would be good. It often took months, sometimes years, for a student to learn their center.

She shook her head. "No, pretty sure that ain't it."

"Then how are you controlling it?"

She shrugged one shoulder and wadded up the empty wrapper in her hand.

She had made quick work of the burrito. Perhaps she was correct and the low energy signature came from her lack of nourishment. He grabbed the bags off of her lap as she was reaching for another one and exited the car. "Follow me."

"Where we going?" She leaned across his seat and looked up at him—her head was about level with his thigh and she took her own sweet time meeting his gaze with her big, beautiful eyes.

He let the silence stretch before answering. "To eat at a table."

A look of concern crossed her face and she gestured out the front window of the car. "Braedan, we're at a park. In Vegas. At night. Are you crazy?"

He looked around. "I see nothing wrong."

She looked up at him in disgust. "Didn't your mother teach you anything? This is a good way to get mugged, or worse!"

Braedan smiled. "We are warriors. Let them try." When she

still refused to move, he shut his door, walked around to her side of the car and opened her door. He held out his hand to her and when she only stared at it, he leaned down. "Trust me. I will protect you."

"You keep saying that, yet you tell me *I'm* the warrior," she grumbled, accepted his hand and let him pull her out of the car.

The white began to gather in mass the way it always did when they touched.

"The energy is gathering. Do as you do at work to make it dissipate." He waited.

She raised both shoulders helplessly. "I don't do anything at work. It just goes away after a little bit."

He could feel the warrior in him wonder at this unlikelihood. "This is not going to go away after a little time." He raised their joined hands up between them to prove how thick the white was getting.

"I know, I know. I don't know how to explain it." She pulled her hand from his and walked away.

He fell into step with her, shortening his long strides to match hers. "Miranda, *Love*, you can't walk away from it. It is part of you. You must learn to focus it."

She stopped and spun around to face him. "We're in a city park for crying out loud! What am I supposed to do?"

He knew what would be needed when he started this experiment. Part of him had hoped she had a grasp on the control, and part of him was grateful she did not. For now, he had an excuse to help her dissipate the energy.

Her eyes flared wide, but not with fear. "We're in a park!" she hissed. "You can't kiss me here!"

He had a goal in mind and stalked her step-for-step as she backed away. Holding her gaze with mesmerizing force, he gestured around. "There are no children here tonight. The park is nearly empty. We can easily control the energy. Unless you would care to try on your own?"

Unable—or unwilling—to look away, her eyes held his. She slowed her retreat, licking her lips. "I've tried to find my focus again. I don't seem to be able to get it."

He grinned wickedly. *This* was what he fought against doing all night. From the moment he first witnessed the blond womanizer watching *his* student at the *Cheri*, he felt the need to physically claim her as his own. She was *his* to train and some rich surfer-boy from California was not going to touch what belonged to him. "Then I shall help you."

"Then do it already, so I can finish eating," she said, but she didn't look like she was in a hurry to eat.

"My pleasure." He pulled her into his arms. A moan rumbled deep in his throat and he splayed his hand at the base of her neck as he lowered his lips to hers.

She slid her arms up his chest and wrapped them around his neck, pulling herself deeper into his embrace.

Desire slammed through him. He slanted across her lips with a hunger that caused an increase of light brighter than a new star. His hand at her neck tipped her head until he had full access to her mouth. His hands were restless—one of them was in use as he held her in place for the kiss and the other...held two crinkly white paper bags.

She was hungry. She was his protégé. He had no right to be taking liberties like this with a student. He knew better. He had better control than this. He was a warrior, a trainer. A trainer physically attracted to his student.

A student who had too much white energy. He was so caught up in their kiss he forgot to diffuse some of the excess light. Damn, a trainer did not *ever* forget his duties. Continuing the kiss, he reached out with his senses and shielded the entire park. From there, he slowly, leisurely, kissed the excess energy away. He was no longer unaware, although it took a great strength of will to remain focused.

He needed to get control of his attraction to her. He believed he had worked it all out in his mind today, yet when he saw her boss flirting with her, he had been unable to control the primitive need to stamp his claim on her. If she was too busy enjoying his own kisses, the California boy would not have a chance.

He lifted his head from hers. Agency. Just as with the choice to choose which side to battle on, she had the choice of which man she wanted.

Her eyes were silvery and dreamy when she opened them. "Hungry?" He moved the bags into her peripheral vision.

She looked at him, her eyes full of questions, before dropping her arms to her sides. "Yes."

He saw the confusion in her eyes at his refusal to push the issue of the attraction, but the decision had to be hers. As her trainer, he could not force this choice on her.

He guided her to a metal picnic table and handed her a taco. They ate in silence. He surveyed the park. There were some lights placed strategically around the main area, but the jogging path was not well lit—the jogging path was why he had chosen this particular park.

The paved trail circled the large park, the center of which was an open grassy area. There was also a large children's play area with a climbing wall and swings. To the sides of the jogging path there were quite a few trees to provide shade during the high heat of summer. Except for a few late-night joggers and one couple making out on a park bench near the parking lot, they would be left alone. It was perfect for the training he had in mind tonight.

He looked sideways at Miranda. Her brain was spinning and she was making short work of the food. She hadn't been kidding, she was hungry. Then again, so was he. He ate another taco. Pulling the last two burritos from the bag, he tossed her one and stood up.

"Come with me." He gathered their trash and threw it into the nearby garbage can.

She followed.

Walking side by side up the jogging trail, he explained, "One of the battles we face is the darkness creeping across humanity. Our job is to hold it at bay and to push it back whenever we can. This brings great joy to both the giver of light and the receiver."

She remained quiet, but listened intently.

"This is best accomplished when control is learned, but is harmless regardless. Since you struggle in this area, I wanted you to feel the peace the white energy can bring you and the happiness it gives to others. This may help you to better find your center."

"You want to do this here? Tonight?" She looked around nervously.

"Do not fear. We are safe at this time." He would let no one harm her.

"Will others see this?" she whispered as a jogger passed them on the trail.

"No. Not unless they are one of the Fallen Ones and I do not believe there are any here tonight." His warrior intellect sensed no impression of danger. "There is not much here for them to play with tonight." Other than her, and he would protect her should any choose to show up.

"So, what do I do?"

"We shall start simple. See the jogger up ahead?"

She nodded.

"You will share some of your light with him. If his spirit chooses to accept, he will fill with light—pushing all darkness within him out—and feel great happiness. If his spirit rejects it, you will try again, a little stronger. If he should still refuse, it is his agency to do so. Then we move on to the next person."

"I think I know just what you are talking about. I have done something like this before." Her face lit with excitement.

"Very good. The jogger approaches. Gather the energy around you, try to run it through your center, feel its comfort and warmth, then share some of the light with him as he passes."

"Okay." She stopped and stared hard at the man approaching.

"Keep moving or he will become suspicious. After all, we are in a park, in Las Vegas, and it is late at night." Braedan propelled her forward by the arm. "We wish it to seem a natural occurrence that he feels the light."

"Oh, of course," she whispered her words as the jogger came abreast of them.

"Now," Braedan instructed in a very low voice.

"Okay." She was excited, energized.

What happened next, he was unprepared for. In all his years of training, he had never seen the equal. The extremely bright flash of light Miranda sent to the poor, unsuspecting jogger was too much. It literally blasted the large man off his feet and sent him sprawling more than ten feet off the jogging trail.

Chapter Eighteen

Braedan watched the jogger sail through the air as though hit by a truck. He snorted on a laugh and grabbed her by the shoulders, planting a kiss on her surprised lips. One, to drain the immense quantity of energy she had amassed and two, to keep the jogger from suspecting them of foul play. Who could accuse a couple locked in a passionate embrace of knocking you ten feet off your path without even touching you?

He watched through narrowed eyes. The pierced and tattooed jogger rose to his feet, looked around in shock, passed over the kissing couple, and started walking away. Not even a limp.

When the man was twenty feet away, Braedan heard him start to chuckle. When he was forty feet away, the chuckle turned into a laugh. When he was one-hundred feet away, the man had to sit down in the grass he was laughing so hard.

Miranda tried to turn her head to see the jogger. Her body tensed in fear. "Did I kill him?"

Braedan grinned. "No."

"Thank goodness!" She sagged against him in relief.

Braedan chuckled. "Were you trying to?"

She frowned. "I was trying to share the light with him."

"I think you shared a little too much."

She rolled her eyes at him. "I didn't want him to reject it and he looked kinda like he might."

Braedan watched the laughing man try to stagger to his feet, before falling back to the grass again. "I don't believe he rejected it after all." He fought to control his own laughter.

She pushed away from him and crossed her arms over her head. "I can't control it. What if I hurt someone?"

"That man is not hurt." He grinned. "It is likely the best day he has had in years."

She stared at the man rolling in the grass. "Do you think he'll be okay?"

"Yes."

She walked around in a circle. "I think I'd better find my center before we try that again."

"Perhaps," he agreed, *almost* with a straight face.

She shot him a disgruntled look. "I hope you're enjoying this."

He looked at the man still snickering on the ground. "I am." He said, giving in to his own chuckle. The park was filled with light. Everyone there must surely be smiling. Too bad there weren't more patrons to enjoy it.

Miranda looked long and hard at the man on the ground. A smile spread across her own face. "It reminds me of little babies laughing. Have you ever heard that deep, belly laugh little babies get sometimes?"

"Yes. It is good."

She turned her smiling face to him and his breath stopped in his chest. She was beautiful.

"Shall we go?" She tipped her chin back indicating the direction of the car.

Braedan placed his hand on her lower back and guided her further down the trail—away from the car. "Let us practice a little more, then we will go before anyone can track the light."

She looked back over her shoulder at the light. "You drained most of it. Can they still track it?"

"Doubtful. Regardless, I have it shielded now. If the Fallen did not see it originally, they will not be able to see it now." He slowed his pace. "I would like you to try again to find your center. It is peaceful here. It is under the stars. See if it is easier for you to find your center in nature than in an underground room."

Miranda looked at him with skepticism. "I don't think it matters where I am, I just don't seem to get it."

"Try." He allowed the connection his hand had on her back to increase the energy she attracted.

She took a deep breath and closed her eyes.

"Open your eyes." Tonight, he vowed to be patient.

She did. Her gaze locked and held with his.

Her blue eyes were more silver than blue when she attracted large amounts of light. Tonight they almost glowed. It was truly an amazing sight to behold.

"Focus." His words were soft. "Find the thing that brought you to your center once before. It is usually an object. Something you desire. A place or a thing that brings you great strength."

Her eyes shined.

"Go to your center. Take strength from it. Embrace it," he coached her in a whisper.

She took a step closer to him, their bodies were touching.

"You are almost there," he murmured in a low, hypnotic tone. "Embrace it. Take it for your own."

Her eyes were blazing as she snaked her arms up his chest.

With her body, flush with his, her eyes and hands pulling his head down to hers, he barely recognized that her center had been reached.

He sealed his lips over hers, taking possession of her. The moment his mouth took hers, he felt the invisible threads that bound them together tighten. The controlled white light flowing through her body coursed through his and he felt the awesome power she possessed become his as well. They were bound as one, the power vividly strong. His subconscious reinforced the shield he already had in place and easily reigned in the energy that was enough to light most of Las Vegas.

"Braedan—" a new voice cautioned from nearby—"she is not yet trained enough to handle the consequences such a release would attract from the Arbiters."

He lifted his head from Miranda's, but kept her in his embrace. Her eyes were starting to lose their glow. The light around them wavered and lost formation. She was losing her focus and the now uncontrolled energy pushed to get past the shield that had been strengthened by their combined power.

"Amazing." The nearby voice held respect.

"How about a little help?" Braedan said through clenched teeth. Without the added power he had received from Miranda, he was starting to break out in a sweat at the effort required to reign in the energy.

"Miranda," the new voice commanded. "Help him."

She looked over her shoulder at the man and shook her head. "I don't know how. I had my center and then I lost it."

"Focus," the newcomer said in a commanding voice.

She turned back to Braedan. He saw the worry in her eyes as she took in his straining muscles. She looked into his eyes and took a deep breath.

"Concentrate—" Braedan forced the words out—"Ignore all else." He could feel the pressure within his skull. The white was too strong. He could not control it without her. "Go back to your center." His breathing was harsh. He must have her help.

She gave him a long searching look.

Her eyes were like nothing he had ever seen before. They burned right into him. "That is it, *Love*, go to your center."

The fury of the uncontrolled light calmed.

"That's it, *Sweetheart,* use your center to place the light back where it belongs," the newcomer whispered.

She blinked. The sound of the unfamiliar voice must have distracted her and, just like that, her concentration was gone. The light swirled around them.

"Shut up, brother," Braedan said, snarling. He tried to help her hang on to her focus.

She looked around at the thick whiteness in the air before her eyes locked with Braedan's. "Help me?"

"Of course." He once again took her lips with his.

He hoped her belief in the kiss would be enough for her to help him get the power back under control. When the kiss became more of a physical desire than a means to an end, he pulled back. Her eyes lost the glow completely, but the flurry was now back within Braedan's control. Barely, but he contained it. Her faith had been enough.

Her large silvery blue eyes searched his. "Brother?" She looked only at Braedan.

He nodded once in answer to her question, not at all pleased with the timing of his brother's interruption.

"He hasn't mentioned me? I'm hurt." The voice sounded anything but hurt.

"Brother?" Miranda turned in his arms to look at the younger, lighter, version of himself. She looked between the two, then held out her hand to the newcomer. "Nice to meet you." As his brother reached for her hand, she gasped and snatched it back to her chest.

Looking at Braedan with apprehension, she asked again, "Brother?"

"Yes." When she continued to stare at him in question, Braedan introduced them. "Miranda, this is Trenton. Trenton, Miranda."

Keeping her hand held to her, she smiled, her face reddening. "Nice to meet you."

"The pleasure is all mine," his younger brother answered, turning to Braedan with a question in his eyes.

"She is afraid you will increase her power if she allows you to touch her."

"Increase?" His brother looked confused.

Braedan only shrugged. After the inconvenience his brother had just caused, he didn't care to elaborate.

At the pause in conversation, Miranda pointed to the children's playground. "I, um, think I need a drink of water." She ducked her head and dashed off down the trail.

Braedan allowed her to go. He could watch her from where he stood. Without looking away from her, he asked, "What brings you here, Trenton?"

His brother turned to watch Miranda walk across the grass. "What do you think?"

Braedan snorted. "The General has never doubted me before."

"He does not doubt you now."

"Then why are you here?"

Trenton glanced from Miranda to Braedan. "So...she believes you must kiss her to drain the excess energy?"

"Yes." He refused to elaborate.

"When are you going to tell her that a kiss is not necessary?"

"I am not."

"That is unethical," his brother pointed out.

"Yes."

"It is underhanded."

"Yes."

"It is abuse of your position."

"Yes."

"It is brilliant. I do believe I'll have to give it a try."

Braedan slanted a look at his brother, then looked back to Miranda. She sat in a child's swing, pushing herself with one foot.

"So—" his brother watched Miranda too—"she is *The One.*"

"*The One*?"

"You know, the one to save us all..." Braedan raised a brow and his brother continued. "We all know the Dark Side is winning. The darkness is swiftly covering the earth."

"There are still some light areas left." Braedan's denial was half-hearted.

"Very few." Trenton slipped his hands in his front pockets and widened his stance. "We are losing. With her power, we can regain the balance that was meant to be."

Braedan agreed, but remained quiet.

"How is it, that you were given this one? Are you back to being the General's favorite again?"

"The General does not have favorites." Braedan glowered at him. "She was my protégé."

Trenton grinned. "Father loves you best. We all know it, even if he tries to hide it."

The light in the park was strong. Braedan felt good. No, he felt great. "How could I not be the favorite? I am the best." He grinned before he lightly punched his brother in the shoulder. He had missed his family. He had not been home in a long time, because he had spent two long and frustrating years, looking for the missing protégé. This lost time had not only frustrated him, but the General hadn't been happy about the delay either.

Trenton laughed. "And the most humble." He stepped forward and gave his brother a bear hug that would've crushed a lesser man.

Braedan felt some of the leftover additional energy he had received from Miranda flow into his brother.

Trenton stepped back in surprise. "Wow!" He looked at Miranda, who now watched them both. "Is she always that amazing?"

Braedan nodded. "Yes. If she can learn to control it, they will not be able to stop her."

"How long ago did you activate her?"

"I did not."

Trenton turned to look at him in surprise. "Someone else activated her?"

Again Braedan nodded.

"Wow. Who?"

"She does not know, nor do I."

Trenton's brows lowered in confusion. "But I saw the bond between you and Miranda. It was incredible."

Braedan ran a hand through his hair. "The bond is there. I do not know how, but it is."

"Interesting," Trenton murmured.

"Yes." Braedan then shocked his brother by admitting, "I can increase her power."

"Increase?" Trenton looked surprised. "How are you able to do that?"

"I do not know."

Trenton crossed his arms across his wide chest. "I witnessed her conduct her power through you just now. I've never seen anything like it. How did she do that?"

"She is unlike any other student I have trained before." Braedan couldn't look away from her.

"Is it possible it has something to do with the physical connection between you?"

Now Braedan glanced away and back to Trenton. "I have never been involved with a student, but you have. Have you ever had a result such as this?"

Trenton shook his head. "I've never experienced anything like this before." He looked between the two. "I think this is something special. Care to test it out?"

Braedan felt his stomach muscles clench involuntarily. "Exactly what did you have in mind?"

Trenton held up his hand in defense and laughed. "Easy, big brother. I already understand she is yours. Since the bond exists with you, and you did not activate her, I simply meant to see if the bond could exist with someone else." He paused for effect. "By a simple, harmless, touch. No lip-lock involved."

Braedan remained quiet. He loved his younger brother, but should Trenton attempt to kiss Miranda, he would not be held responsible for the damage done to him.

Trenton laughed and slapped him on the back. "As tempting as she is, I will not ever try to take what is yours."

"She has her agency. She can choose whoever she pleases." Even to his own ears, his words sounded harsh.

Trenton let out a low whistle. "That serious, huh?"

Braedan ignored the comment and changed the subject. "She has no recollection of having been activated."

"That is not good. How many does that make?"

"Last I spoke with the General, that makes twelve."

Trenton shook his head. "Wrong. Last count was seventeen in Las Vegas alone. We have no idea how many more there may be. That is why Father sent me here. To do damage control."

Braedan ran both hands through his hair. "Do they know who it is yet?"

Trenton's face was grim. "No."

"Does the General think it is possible they have evolved and are activating themselves?"

"No." Trenton shoved his hands into the front pockets of his jeans. "Until your student, we've been unable to bond with any of them. Not even with their preordained Activators."

"No one would dare touch another man's student. It is inconceivable."

"Someone dared," Trenton disagreed. "Many times."

"But to leave an innocent, unprotected and untrained is a punishable offence. The inability to bond with another trainer leaves the student vulnerable to the dark."

Trenton shook his head. "Always so rigid, no wonder you're

father's favorite."

"Rules exist for a reason," Braedan said, chastising him.

"Yes, and sometimes, they are meant to be broken." Trenton's gaze drifted back to Miranda.

"No," Braedan disagreed. "They exist to keep chaos at bay."

Trenton turned to look at him and his eyes were warrior fierce. "It is not working. When the opposition cheats, we must bend the rules, or we will be broken."

Chapter Nineteen

He felt her. The bond was very strong between them and the amount of power she was releasing was incredible. In the darkness of his apartment, Andrade walked to the wall of windows in his living room and looked for her light. The windows were nearly floor to vaulted ceiling and spanned two walls of his top floor, corner penthouse. The view was spectacular. A view like this in Vegas was hard to come by. Money could buy you anything.

He searched the grid of real estate below and in front of him, and saw a flash of light. An entire block was lightened. He gasped. She was powerful. It was hard to wrap his mind around the power this shy little girl wielded.

A mile and a half away, the power she emitted was shaped into a dome and contained. Someone was shielding her. How was that possible?

He watched as the light brightened to an intensity so brilliant it was hard to look at, and then threatened to leave its boundaries. He froze, his body rigid. The shield was not going to hold.

He did the unthinkable and closed his eyes. He focused his entire being and reached out through the distance to her. He used the invisible threads that connected them to slip past the boundaries of the shield.

Once inside, he opened his body to the light. Pain. The absorption of such intense light into the darkness of his soul, created great enough agony to send him to his knees. His hands slammed against the glass wall in front of him to keep him upright. His heart stopped, then started again with a thudding that pounded in his ears. His body was covered with a fine sheen of sweat. The white knifed through him, leaving him gasping for breath. From his kneeling position on the floor, he forced himself to continue to drain from her until he was certain he had absorbed enough energy that the shield would now hold. He could not allow so much light to be released on the city. Such an amount of white energy would change the City of Sin irreparably. Being the most favored warrior, he would not be forgiven the failure that would bring.

His eyes snapped open to see the light, still very bright, contained within the dome. The shield would now hold. The city was safe in its darkness. The shield that blocked the light from his soul slammed back into place.

He dropped his hands from the glass and collapsed back on the thick carpet staring at the ceiling. He was too weak to lift his hands, but knew they would be shaking if he tried.

His mind searched his body for damage. His insides twisted. The light and dark within him warred with each other for supremacy. The excruciating pain robbed him of breath.

He laid there letting time pass and the fight within subside. His heart rate returned to normal. He turned his head to look out the window. He could not see the park from this position, but knew through his connection, she was back under control.

He rolled onto his stomach, and with a mighty heave, rose to his hands and knees. Every inch of his body protested at the move. He pressed his forehead to the cool glass and watched the faint light that was her.

Chapter Twenty

He looked a lot like Braedan, but younger, lighter in coloring, and less serious. He was still handsome as sin, but in a different way than her trainer. She wondered if Braedan ever had that light-hearted look his brother pulled off so well.

Miranda warily watched them approach her. She wasn't sure she was up to another trainer. If Braedan's touch could generate that much power, how would she ever survive the power of two?

"Hello." The smiling brother neared her seat on the swing. "My name is Trenton. I'm this rule-abiding man's younger brother. I am trying to teach him to lighten up," he said with a wink. "Care to help?"

She kinked her neck back and looked up. He was the same height as Braedan. She looked from Braedan's serious face to Trenton's contagious grin. She felt the smile tip the corners of her mouth. "Oh, Danny's not so serious. I think he's savable."

Trenton laughed. "Danny?"

Braedan glared at her, but remained silent.

"It's my little nick-name I use on your brother when he's being difficult." She schooled her features to reflect innocence to Trenton.

Trenton looked at his brother's dark look and hooted with laughter. "You got a nick-name, Danny?"

"Do not use that name with me, Trenton." Braedan's tone was ominous.

Trenton snickered and turned back to Miranda. "I do believe you will be good for my big brother. If you should ever need an ally, I am at your service."

"Why thank you. Don't suppose I could get you to convince him to lighten up a little on the training?" she asked.

Trenton's face became serious. "That is the one thing I cannot do. For your own safety, it must be done. The quicker, the better."

She pushed the ground with the toe of her foot causing her seat to swing gently. "Yeah, I'm sure you're right, but can't say as I'm enjoying it."

"Enjoyment or not, with the power you wield, it is imperative you learn control." Trenton's tone took on a solemn air.

"Let me guess, you're a trainer too?" Her grip tightened on the chains of the swing and she gave another little push.

The seriousness left his face and his grin was captivating. "Yes, I am."

"I would also guess you're a ladies' man as well?" she asked dryly.

"Guilty, as charged."

"At least you can admit it. That's the first step to recovery," she said, managing to keep a straight face.

He chuckled and punched Braedan in the shoulder. "See? There's hope for me yet!"

"Perhaps." Braedan wore a half-smile.

Miranda watched the camaraderie that can only take place with a sibling you care for. She was impressed. She hadn't pictured Braedan as a family man. How could one possibly grow up with siblings and still be so stiff and formal?

"Miranda—" Trenton had shifted back into trainer mode, this couldn't be good. "—we would like to try a small experiment. Braedan was not the one to activate you, and yet, there is a bond that exists between the two of you. This is very unusual. I would like to see if my touch can generate the same power that Braedan's does. Would you allow this?"

She looked between the two brothers. This was something she hoped to avoid. "Are you sure it's necessary?"

Trenton squatted down in front of her so that they spoke at eye level. "I believe it is. There have been others, like yourself, who have been activated by someone other than their trainer. Because there is no bond with a known activator, we are unable to help them control their powers. If you are able to bond with more than your activator, we could learn from you to help save the lives and spirits of the ones who are suffering."

"Crap. Put like that, what choice do I have?" She looked at Braedan and, at his nod, held out her hand.

"Good girl." Trenton smiled. He stretched his hand forward and engulfed her small hand in his much larger one.

Miranda watched the white float around them. It did not gather in a flurry of thick white as it did with Braedan.

"Perhaps if you concentrate and focus to see if your power can be bound with mine," Trenton suggested.

"I'm not sure how that would work." Miranda's eyes darted to Braedan, then back to Trenton.

"How did you bind with Braedan?" he asked, still squatted in front of her.

She shrugged. "I have no idea."

"Can you not feel the bond with Braedan?"

"I feel...something with Braedan, but I don't understand the bond idea."

Trenton covered their clasped hands with his other hand. "The bond is something special. It is a pull you experience with no other. It allows you to feel him without seeing him. It connects you together and allows him to help you guide the energy."

"And I should feel this with you too?" Miranda questioned.

"We don't know."

"Didn't I feel this with you when Braedan was trying to control the shield earlier?" she asked puzzled.

"No, I was only trying to verbally help you control your focus. Without the bond, I can do nothing more than guide. I cannot help to control."

Miranda frowned, she could've sworn she had felt a second presence—although she hadn't known it was a 'bond' she felt at the time.

"Please search in your mind for the connection. If you can feel this with me, you may be able to help those that are suffering."

Miranda closed her eyes. At Braedan's grunt of disapproval, she opened one eye. "Shhh! It helps me concentrate and both you and Trenton are here to protect me should somebody try to sneak up on me while they're shut." She closed her eye again and took a long slow breath. It wasn't fair that people were relying on her to help the ones suffering. How could she possibly help them?

"Anything?" Braedan's low voice asked Trenton.

"Not yet. Focus, Miranda—" Trenton encouraged—"This is important. We cannot afford to lose the seventeen white warriors that are suffering."

"Seventeen?" she whispered in surprise, keeping her eyes shut.

"Yes. Help them." Trenton beseeched her with his words, but not with any formation of a bond.

She didn't hear so much as a rustle of clothing, but felt Braedan as he came up behind her and placed his hands on her shoulders. She knew she shared no bond with Trenton. He didn't increase her power as Braedan did, which surprised her, since it seemed nearly everyone did these days. But perhaps she could still find a way to help these women with the strong power she generated through her bond with Braedan.

"Imagine what you have without anyone to help you control it." Braedan's voice came to her from above her shoulder.

She remembered the confusion she felt when she first started seeing the light. The constant dread of embarrassing her family. The fear of what might happen should the world discover she wasn't normal. She had left her friends, her family, her hometown, all that she cared about the most, because she hadn't had any help in controlling the power. What would she have done if the power had increased and Braedan hadn't been there to help? Could it happen to these women? What if someone unknowingly increased their power and destroyed hundreds or even thousands of lives without the help they needed to control it?

"I thought the light was supposed to be for good?" Miranda murmured.

"It is. When used properly. Remember, the light can be turned to the dark side and used for destruction." Braedan gave a gentle squeeze to her shoulders. "We have already lost several of these warriors. We do not wish to lose anymore."

This was bigger than her and her embarrassment over just what or who happened to be her center. These women needed her help—if she was capable of it. Already, it was too late for some of them. Every day her powers were becoming stronger and her control...well, it was a little better. Could she help these poor women? No one ever need to find out her attractive teacher was her focus. She filled her thoughts with only Braedan. Braedan was hers. Her very own trainer, even if she had been activated without him. She could feel the bond between her and Braedan strengthen and the white began to flow through her, instead of around her. Her mind cleared and she could see things she had never seen before.

She opened her eyes and saw the surprise in Trenton's. "I can help you with these women."

He gulped and nodded. His eyes lifted in wonderment to Braedan's. "I do believe you can."

Chapter Twenty-one

She was different this morning. Miranda stretched and smiled. Physically, her body was the same. Mentally, things were altered.

What she saw last night in her mind was astounding. She had clearly seen the bond that existed between her and Braedan. It was thick and strong. The fibers glittered like diamonds. There was a thin strand leading elsewhere, that she hadn't bothered to follow as it was not what she was looking for, but it did prove that multiple connections could exist simultaneously. What she *had* been looking for was a way to create a new link with Trenton. As she focused on Braedan—her center—she had been able to weave a brand new bond between her and Trenton. Not wanting that connection, she was able to unravel the strands and disconnect the bond. She knew, with Braedan's help, she could create a tie between the trainerless warriors and their teachers.

Today, while she and Braedan trained, Trenton was going to collect one of the poor women who was without help and see if she could create the needed link between himself and the new student.

Miranda smiled. She could do it. She couldn't guarantee she could control all of the white, but she knew she could create the needed bonds.

The doorbell rang and Miranda sighed. She threw off her covers and rolled out of bed, padding to the door in her pajama pants and tank top. Braedan had already seen her at her worst.

If he was going to come over this early, she wasn't going to bother with getting beautiful before opening the door.

"A little early this morning, don't you think?" she said opening the door. When it wasn't Braedan standing there, she nearly slammed it in the poor delivery boy's face.

"Sorry, ma'am." The teenage boy ogled her braless outfit and messy hair. "I was paid to deliver it at eight o'clock sharp."

The boy shoved two large and heavy gift baskets at her and with one last look at her Tinker Bell tank top, gave her a look that was purely male before he turned to leave.

"Um, wait," Miranda said confused. "Do I owe you a tip?"

The boy turned back with a grin and waved, backing down the hall. "Already been tipped. Nicely, too!"

Miranda was still standing there staring after the boy when Braedan's door opened.

The look on his face as he took in the gifts assured her they weren't from him. The dark look on his face made her uncomfortable.

"Early morning visitors?" He leaned against the door frame.

She glared at him. "I didn't do anything wrong." She grumbled and turned. Stepping back inside, she kicked the door closed behind her. Braedan stopped it from closing with his foot and smoothly entered her apartment, closing the door behind him.

She ignored him and placed the baskets on the counter. The first one contained strawberries, oranges, apples, bright yellow bananas and a pineapple. "Ohhh," she said eyeing the box of Godiva chocolates tucked in with the assortment of fruits. She picked up the box and turned it over. She had heard Godiva chocolates were the best, and very expensive. This narrowed out the gift coming from most of the people she knew. She peaked at Braedan and his scowl and was positive she could narrow out him as well.

She put the chocolates back in with the fruit and tossed him an apple. "Quit glaring at me and eat something. It might help improve your poor early morning disposition."

He caught the apple and took a bite, remaining silent. She dug into the next basket.

It had delicious scents wafting out from under a beautiful thick kitchen towel. She peeled the towel back and inhaled deep. "Fooood," she said lovingly.

"Someone knows how to get to you," Braedan said. "What is that saying? 'The way to a man's heart is through his stomach?' I would say in your case, it is correct too."

"Why, yes, I do believe it is. Is that why you're always feeding me?" She batted her lashes at him, before lifting out several warm, expensive, glass lidded dishes.

The first dish contained a large fluffy omelet with colorful chunks of meat and veggies and covered with cheese. "Yum." She inhaled the steam rising off of the food. The second dish contained a tall stack of thick pecan pancakes with melted butter oozing over the top of the stack. She eagerly lifted the third lid to find lemon poppy seed muffins and cheese Danishes inside.

"Here." Braedan thrust a fork into her hand and pulled out the maple syrup from inside the basket.

"Is that real maple syrup?" she asked through a mouthful of omelet.

"Looks like it," Braedan said with a reluctant grin as he took a bite out of her omelet with his own fork.

She took another bite and closed her eyes in ecstasy. "How do you suppose they got this here so fresh?" She opened her eyes to get another forkful.

"I do not know, nor do I care." Braedan poured syrup over the pancakes still in the dish.

"Drown them," she said, taking a bite of muffin.

Braedan tipped the bottle again, drenching the pancakes in syrup.

"Perfect," she said, and cut into them with her fork.

"That remains to be seen." Braedan placed his hand over hers, redirecting her forkful of the drippy pancakes into his own mouth.

"Hey," she laughed and cut into the pancake again.

Braedan chewed, his look thoughtful. "Yes, more syrup was definitely a good idea."

"Uh-huh." She grinned in agreement and leaned forward to

keep the syrup from dripping onto her top when she tasted it for herself.

Braedan helped himself to another bite of omelet as well as a muffin. "So who is the gift from?"

Miranda shrugged and looked first into one basket and then the other. "Ah-hah!" she exclaimed holding up a small white envelope.

"Open it."

She tisked at his demand and opened the envelope. "It says: I hope you enjoy these enough to make me a rich man."

Braedan looked at her expectantly.

She felt a small amount of heat warming her neck. "What?" She questioned Braedan's stern look.

"Enlighten me."

"What is there to explain? That's all it said." She took another very large bite of the cheesy omelet.

Braedan scowled as he ate a strawberry whole. "I am certain you can clarify the meaning of the note."

Miranda grabbed the next strawberry from his hand and popped it into her mouth. She chewed and struggled for the right words. As she swallowed, she realized the right words were not necessary. Braedan hadn't staked any kind of a claim on her. He had never even asked her out on a date. All of the time they spent together was training related in some form or another.

"My boss saw me eating yesterday before my shift began and said if his customers could see my enjoyment of the food, he would be a rich man."

At first Braedan's look was thunderous, then, slowly he nodded in agreement. "He is correct."

"So I like food, sue me." Crankiness was getting the best of her. She grabbed a banana and peeled it down. Why did everyone have to make such a big deal out of such a common event? "Everyone should enjoy food. It's meant to bring gratification."

"Yes," Braedan agreed. "However, your delight with it borders on immoral."

"What?" She almost choked in surprise. "There's nothing

wrong with the way I eat...except for how much I eat. But other than that, it's perfectly normal."

Braedan shook his head, but a smile formed on his lips. "The enjoyment you receive is not common, but please do not deny me the pleasure of feeding you just so you can be average."

"Whatever." With a shake of her head, she took a huge bite of banana.

Braedan grabbed the pineapple and began to slice into it. "Why is your boss giving you gifts? Does he send the other waitresses presents as well?"

"Haven't ever asked him," she said.

Braedan sliced the pineapple into perfect chunks. He paused when he asked the next question. "Do you have a relationship with your boss?"

"No. He has flirted with me a little, but we've never dated."

His dark brows rose. "The flowers mean nothing?"

She forgot about the flowers sitting on her small table. Her eyes darted to them and she couldn't help but appreciate their beauty. However, she was certain they meant a lot more to her than they did to the man who sent them. "No."

"Good." He resumed his carving of the fruit. "Do not spend extra time with him."

"What?" She closed her mouth which had dropped at his command. "Since when do you get to dictate who I can date?"

"Since you will be too busy training to form a serious relationship, I think it is fair to tell you I do not care for the energy pattern I detect from him."

"Is he a Dark Warrior?" Miranda asked in surprise. "Andrade seems so light and wholesome looking."

"And yet, I am dark in coloring." Braedan again paused in his work. "Do not let looks fool you, *Love*. They can be deceiving. Remember, it is what is on the inside that counts."

She pondered for a moment. "Some people attract the light and some people repel it. Andrade doesn't repel it, so he can't be that bad."

"Choose carefully, *Love*. It would be best for a time to only spend your days with me until you are fully trained and capable of protecting yourself."

May as well tell him now. "Yeah, see, that's going to be a bit of a problem."

He gave her his full attention. "Why is that?"

She cleared her throat. "Shara set up a double date for her and I on Friday."

"Tomorrow night?"

"Yeah."

"Cancel it."

"What?" She folded her arms. She knew he wouldn't like the idea, but she didn't think he would command her not to go. "No. I can't do that. Shara's my friend and it would hurt her feelings if I bailed this late. I'll train tomorrow day. I'll work tomorrow night, and I will go on a short date after work with whichever goofball she has lined up for me."

"If you do not believe you will enjoy the man she has picked for you, why waste your time going?"

"Because that's what you do for a friend. She thinks she's helping me out and if I don't go, she'll never forgive me."

"If she is a true friend, she will not hold it against you."

Miranda held up a hand. "I have to go."

His eyes were dark. "I do not like it."

She snorted. "Ya think?"

Braedan took slow deep breaths. She wouldn't have been surprised if he were counting to ten. "Where are you going and when will you return home?"

"I have no idea, *Dad*. But I promise not to be out past curfew." His look became fierce and she tried to reason with him. "Look, Shara and I don't like the same kind of men. Chances are very good the man she hooks me up with won't like me either. I only have to go for a few hours and then I can bail gracefully without hurting Shara's feelings. Why don't you spend a few hours with your brother while I'm out? It sounds like it's been a while since you two have spent time together."

His lips compressed. "I'll take my cell phone with me and if I need help, I promise to call you."

"What if you should have problems controlling your power?"

"I think I can control it well enough when you're not around to make it ultra-modified, extra-turbo—" she waved her hands around in the air for emphasis—"super-wazoolie, strong."

A reluctant smile graced his full lips. He speared a piece of the pineapple with his fork and offered it to her. "Again, always be careful. The dark side cheats."

"I know. But a blind date with Shara is one of Shara's old boyfriends that she dumped a while back and I don't think anyone would go that far just to get to me."

"It doesn't appear your boss is trying to go through Shara to get to you."

"You think the dark side would cheat with two baskets of food?" she asked as she reached for the chocolates.

Braedan caught her wrist just as her hand closed on the Godiva's and his other hand tipped her jaw and forced her to look at him. He dipped his head until they were nose to nose, his look was deadly serious. "Never underestimate the enemy. They will cheat any way they can."

Chapter Twenty-two

Trenton found a terrified and rebellious teenage girl. Miranda could see the white twinkle sporadically around the short thin girl whose wide green eyes darted between the three adults standing in the luxurious living room of Braedan's home. Her powers were weak, but they were activated.

"I'm Miranda." She offered her hand.

The curly-haired girl kept her hands in her pockets and turned around in a circle. "Nice place." Her stance was a curious mix of combative and ready to take flight. "I've stolen from places with lots less than this."

Miranda raised her brows in question to the girl's statement. "Excuse me?"

"Yeah, well, when the weird stuff started happenin' my parents kicked me out. Got to survive somehow." Her defiant look dared Miranda to try to lecture her.

That took the self-righteous attitude right out of Miranda. She looked closer at the small would-be warrior standing in front of her. Short herself, the girl was even shorter. "How old are you?"

Her rebellious attitude was in full force. "Seventeen. What of it?"

Poor thing was so skinny and small she appeared much younger than her seventeen years. She was what Miranda's mother would've called a 'late bloomer.' For a girl, alone, living out on the streets, this would have been a definite protection for her. Miranda looked close, she saw the tell-tell signs of someone struggling to stay clean without the means to do so. "They kicked you out?"

The girl flipped her strawberry-blonde, medium length hair over her shoulder and shrugged. "Course they did. I'm a freak."

Miranda snorted. "No you're not. You are very special and we can help you. If you want us to."

The girl shrugged her bony shoulders again, her angry attitude increasing. "Why should you care?" Her eyes still searched the room as though deciding what she could take with her when she left.

Miranda turned to Braedan. "She's too young for this to be dumped on her shoulders. Her parents have abandoned her, she doesn't understand the gift she's been given, she's stealing to survive. This isn't right!"

"Agreed," he said. "No one is supposed to be activated until they turn twenty. This is when their powers are at the best level to learn. She is too young and unstable. If they become too old, the power is hard to control for a beginner and it is best to leave them inactive."

The new girl was paying no attention to their conversation. She wore a vacant look on her face that Miranda recognized.

Miranda slapped her own forehead. "She's starving! Braedan, she needs food." She turned back to the teenager. The mention of food brought a light to the girl's eyes. Miranda felt anger and compassion for this young warrior. She could barely keep her own hunger appeased and she had the money and ability to do so.

Braedan headed for the kitchen and Miranda grabbed the undernourished girl's arm, pulling her after him. Braedan rummaged in the fridge for something to cook and Miranda shoved a banana at the girl. "Eat."

She didn't have to tell her twice, poor kid had half the banana in her mouth before Miranda could take a breath. Miranda snatched an apple from a bowl and tossed it to the girl. Grabbing the loaf of bread from off the counter top and a jar of peanut butter, Miranda started making a sandwich.

"Trenton, grab some jam from the fridge," she said while slathering the creamy peanut butter on the bread.

"Yes, ma'am." He set the jar on the counter in record time.

Miranda added the thick, chunky strawberry jam and held the sandwich out to the big eyed girl who reached for it greedily. The banana was already consumed and the apple more than half gone.

"The poor kid is starved. Braedan, how's that food coming?" she asked over her shoulder. She watched the girl inhale the food.

"I'm not a kid." Her words were almost unintelligible around a mouthful of the gooey peanut butter.

"Sorry," Miranda said. But in her defense, the half-starved human standing in front of her still looked like one.

"Just need a minute more." Braedan stirred the scrambled eggs with a spatula in one hand and popped toast into the toaster with the other.

A minute would be too long. Miranda started a second sandwich. "What's your name?"

"Kelsy."

Miranda found a plate in the cupboard and put the second sandwich on it. There hadn't been time to worry about dishes for the first one. "Kelsy, you're not a freak. I have the same gift you do and we can help you."

Kelsy's eyes got even bigger. "You do? I'm not the only frea—" she looked at Miranda and changed the words—"I'm not the only one who can see the white stuff floating around?"

"Nope—" Miranda said cheerfully—"there are lots of us."

"No way!" Kelsy finished off the second sandwich. She sat in the closest kitchen chair with her elbows on the table. Miranda watched her study each of them in turn, obviously trying to decide if they were pulling her leg.

"Way," Miranda confirmed. She looked at Trenton, if he hadn't explained anything to Kelsy, just what had he said to this young girl to get her to come with him? Had he simply smiled and the teenage girl's raging hormones had prompted her to follow him anywhere? Miranda gave him a once over and sighed. She couldn't blame the girl.

Braedan gave Kelsy the history lesson she hadn't learned in school while she ate the eggs and toast. She now had a full belly and people who didn't think she was crazy. Miranda watched as her rebellious attitude almost disappeared.

"So someone did this to me on purpose?" The hurt look in her young eyes, came through in her voice.

"I'm afraid so." Trenton didn't even try to hide the anger this caused him. "With Miranda's help, I think we can create a bond between you and I that will allow me to guide you."

"You?" Kelsy's eyes got big again and a smile spread over her face. Miranda could tell Kelsy' hormones were working just fine as she eyed first Trenton and then Braedan with female satisfaction.

"Yes, me. I would become your teacher and train you on how to use the gift you've been given."

The hero-worshipping look disappeared and Kelsy wrinkled her nose in distaste. "Some gift."

Braedan stood. "Shall we go to the basement and see if you are able to bond them?"

"The basement?" Kelsy looked up, the wary look returning to her face.

Trenton smiled. "The basement is the training room and is shielded should the power become unmanageable. You will be safe."

Kelsy looked up at the three adults and threw her hands in the air. "Why not? What've I got to lose?"

"Oh, shiz!" The words slipped out of Kelsy's mouth. She watched the white gather in a thick frenzy.

"It's okay." Miranda's tone was reassuring to the girl, while her concentration was focused on Braedan. She thought only of him and allowed the energy to flow through her. The grip Kelsy had on her hand tightened.

"I've never seen so much of it before." Kelsy looked beyond nervous.

"Miranda is different than most. That's why we believe she can help you," Trenton said.

Kelsy stared at him hard. "You believe? I'm the guinea pig in this experiment?"

Trenton put his arm around her shoulders and gave her a squeeze. "All will be fine."

She looked at him with adoration, but managed to hold on to her attitude as she warned, "It better be."

Miranda took a deep breath and felt the sparkling threads woven between her and Braedan grow stronger. She smiled at Kelsy and turned her thoughts inward.

"Do you see that?" Kelsy whispered to Trenton in awe.

"Yes."

"Is that spider web looking thing between those two the bond?" she whispered.

"Yes." Trenton tightened his arm around her.

"Is it always like that? So thick and glittery?"

"No. What they have is unique. It takes years to grow a strong bond between a teacher and student. Even then, I have never seen one so strong as this."

"How come I can see it now and I couldn't before?" Miranda watched Kelsy lean closer to Trenton but she didn't release her hand.

"Because Miranda is choosing to let us."

"So we can't see other people's bonds?" Kelsey's eyes were curious when she tilted her head toward the web for a better look, but Miranda noticed she stayed firmly within Trenton's protective arm.

"Only your own, and then only if it's a particularly strong one. As I said, what they have is most unusual."

Kelsy cocked her head and looked at Trenton with a wrinkled nose. "You talk kinda funny."

"Shh. Allow her to concentrate." Trenton lifted his chin toward Miranda.

"Sorry," she whispered.

Miranda could feel the weight of Braedan's hands on her shoulders. She drew on the power he alone could give to her.

"Whoa!" Kelsy jerked her hand free of Miranda's and plastered herself to Trenton's side. "Do you see that?" Kelsy's voice was so low, it was barely audible. "Her eyes are *glowing*!"

"Shhh." The warning had come from both males.

Miranda hadn't known her face could reflect what she saw inside, but it didn't surprise her. Something this strong couldn't be contained within a human shell.

Miranda concentrated and slowly wove a many threaded bond between herself and Kelsy. She heard Kelsy's gasp when Kelsy became connected to her and could feel some of the energy that was running through them both.

As the tie became tight and strong, Miranda transferred it thread by thread to Trenton until the connection was completed between teacher and student.

"I feel it!" Awe filled Kelsy's voice.

"Yes," Trenton said reverently. "I feel it as well."

Miranda focused the energy through her center and tried to fortify the tie between the two. She wanted to make it thick and dense like the one connecting her and Braedan.

"The tie is complete, *Love*," Braedan murmured near her ear.

"But it's not enough. I can't seem to get it as strong as ours." Her concentration was so focused on the light, she didn't know if she spoke the words aloud or only thought them in her mind.

"I do not believe you can make it as complete as ours. They will have to do that on their own," his deep baritone filtered through her concentration.

Trenton spoke in wonderment. "It is stronger than any other bond I've formed with a protégé before."

Miranda ignored them all and turned her mind in even further toward her center. The white surrounding them became heavy.

Kelsy raised both her hands in front of her. Her fingers opened and closed in the thick haze. "I've never felt anything like this."

"Neither have I." Trenton looked around in awe.

"Miranda, *Love*—" Braedan's tone was commanding—"that is enough. It is time to filter the energy back."

Miranda was focused inward. "I believe I can do it." Her voice sounded strange even to her own ears, but at least she was certain she'd said the words aloud this time.

Braedan's heavy hands rested on her shoulders and he murmured his next words in a smooth, mesmerizing, old voice spoken directly into her ear. His warm breath served as a needed reminder of the world apart from her inner mental power. "Allow them to build it for themselves, *Love*. That is part of the training process. Do not deny them the gift of growing together."

Miranda nodded once and slowly filtered the energy back into the atmosphere.

The white dispersed and the heavy blanket around them thinned. Kelsy jumped up and threw her arms around Miranda in a hug. "Thank you, thank you, thank you!"

"No!" Braedan and Trenton warned.

Miranda was jolted out of her concentration and the remaining white began to swirl out of control.

"Braedan?" Miranda asked, tranquil in her knowledge that he could fix the problem.

"Of course, *Love*." He moved from behind her to face her.

"Uh," Trenton said, grabbing Kelsy's hand. "Time for us to go."

"Why? What's going on?" Her wide eyes darting between the other pair.

"I will perhaps explain another day." He ushered her up the stairs and out of site.

Braedan placed a hand under Miranda's chin and she rose to stand before him. His eyes bore into hers as luscious anticipation and a slow burn of desire curled through her. Slowly, lazily, as the white swirled around them, he lowered his mouth to hers.

Chapter Twenty-three

"Yes, General," Braedan said into his cell phone. "She is everything Trenton told you."

"I was aware this one was special, which is why I sent you to find her. You, too, are special, *my son*." The General's pride in his offspring was apparent in his voice.

Braedan walked the short distance of his apartment. "I am a valiant warrior and a trained instructor. You have taught me well, Father."

"There is more to you than you know." He waited for his father to continue. "The light has been losing the battle for many years. I believe the Creator wishes to even the score."

"With respect, General, Miranda is the one who can change the course of the war. Once she is trained, I will no longer be necessary for her to bring the balance back into place."

"Remember the Creators plan. We all have to find our place in this world. I can only guide you. It is up to you, *my son*, to learn where that may be."

Braedan turned and paced the span of the room again. "I have had many years to learn where I belong."

"And because of the strength you and Miranda—*together*—bring to the light, you will have many more. We were sent here to learn. You would be wise to remember this," his father said.

"Yes, General."

"My son, I tell you that as your father. As your General, I would like to know how her training is progressing. Trenton tells me she has not yet fully learned to control the tremendous power she can create."

Braedan was glad his father couldn't see him through the phone as he knew the guilt of his deception to Miranda was apparent on his face. No trainer should deceive a student as he had. The trust between a bonded pair was essential. The kissing would have to stop. "She is learning quicker than any other protégé has ever done. Her powers are stronger than any that have come before her. I am training her to the best of my abilities."

"You are correct in your assessment of her power, but as you train your protégé, do as you request of her, and keep an open mind. She has much to teach you as well."

"Agreed." Braedan *was* learning from her. "I did not activate her, yet a bond does exist between us. I do not know how this possible."

"As I said, she has much to share with you. She is yours to learn and grow with. You were destined to be together. Together you may accomplish miracles."

Until Miranda, he had lost his faith in miracles. Was it possible this one small woman could change so much? Braedan ran his hand through his hair in frustration. His father was so wise, yet always made him search out his own answers. He was a warrior who had battled hard and seen much. Could not the man just tell him the answers on occasion?

His father continued. "Miranda was able to create a bond between Trenton and his new protégé?"

Braedan still felt the rush of power flowing through him. His connection with Miranda was getting stronger. So was her power. "Yes, General. She created a very strong link between them. Trenton will now be able to guide this young girl."

"Trenton said that though the bond is stronger than any other he has ever had, it is nothing compared to the one that exists between you and Miranda."

If he focused, Braedan could even now sense the ties that traveled through the air to Miranda's apartment. He no longer needed to see her, or the threads of the bond. He could *feel* her. "The bond we share is exceptional."

"As I said, my son, you are also extraordinary. That is why

the bond is incomparable."

Braedan remained silent to process the information.

"Do you believe she can help the other unbound students?" his father asked into the silence.

"Yes." The word was said without hesitation.

"Then I will send other Activators to you. Trenton cannot train all of the rogue students on his own."

"Yes, General."

"My son?"

"Yes, Father?"

"I am very proud of you. So is your mother. She has ordered me to tell you it is past time for you to come home."

Braedan smiled. It *was* time for a visit home. "Soon, Father."

"Braedan?" his father said. "Be careful. The Fallen Ones want this power. You know what they are capable of. Protect yourself, and above all, protect Miranda. Neither of you will be the same without the other."

Chapter Twenty-four

"What is this?" Miranda asked Shara through the phone.

"Did you get a package, too?" Shara's excitement traveled through the line.

"Yeah," Miranda answered holding up the sexy little black dress. "The note said to please wear for our date tonight. What's going on here?"

She could hear Shara sigh in pleasure. "I have no idea, but isn't it romantic?"

"What are you talking about?" Miranda was distracted. She tossed the dress onto the back of the couch and picked up the second box. She tested the weight in her hands. The box was plain, but from the size and weight, she would bet it contained shoes. She eagerly ripped the lid off and let out a soft, "Oh!" Nestled in the white tissue paper were small, strappy black sandals with spiked heels. She carefully picked one up and examined it. The detail work on the delicate footwear was exquisite. She plopped down on the couch and slipped it on. It fit perfectly.

She held her leg out and admired the added length the high heel gave her. Not bad. The straps made her small foot and ankle look elegant. She grinned and slipped the second one on. She was in love. Didn't matter who the dweeb ended up being, she was gonna enjoy this date if for no other reason than he had excellent taste in shoes. At least they'd have something to talk about.

Shara's voice startled her when she spoke again. "Have you tried it on? Does it fit?"

Miranda reluctantly looked away from the shoes and picked

up the silky black fabric again. "No, and probably no. I have no chest to fill out a dress like this."

"Mine fits perfectly. Try yours on!"

Miranda frowned. "Did you pick this out?"

"No, that's what I'm trying to tell you. The guys must have done it. How cool is that?"

Miranda shook her head. "No man shops for a woman. Who are these guys you've lined us up with?"

Shara squealed in excitement. "I can't tell you! It's a surprise."

Now she was nervous. "I don't like surprises. Who are they?"

"I promised not to tell. Try on the dress! You're killing me. I gotta know if it fits or if he needs to exchange it before tonight."

"I thought you didn't know what was going on?"

"I don't," she said. "But my note said to let him know if either dress needed to be exchanged. Does it fit?"

"Hold on," Miranda said with a reluctant sigh. She stood, slipped off her robe and slipped the dress over her head. The soft fabric slid like a caress over her skin and settled easily into place. She picked the phone up and headed for the bathroom. "It's on. I think it might be okay."

"Tell me about it?"

Miranda closed the bathroom door and looked into the full length mirror that hung on the back of the door. Her eyes widened. The dress was divine. The black fabric accentuated her coloring, making her eyes stand out. The high neckline detracted from the lack of cleavage most dresses tried to flaunt. The wide straps, but lack of sleeves kept the sexy look in place as it gave the impression of lots of skin. The bodice was snug, but not tight, showing curves and flatness of stomach. The skirt was narrow, but the silkiness of the material still allowed for freedom of movement. The skirt stopped a few inches above the knee. With the spiked heels, her legs looked very long. All in all, it was quite simple and modest, yet incredibly sexy.

She ran her hand across the fabric covering her stomach. It felt expensive. Perhaps money could buy clothing stitched so well that it gave the mirage of curves that didn't normally seem to exist?

"Well?" Shara demanded from the other end of the phone

line.

"It's perfect." She turned around to view the back and sucked in her breath. "Except, there's no back to this dress."

"What? I want to see."

"How do they keep it snug in the front and open in the back?" Miranda wondered aloud.

"I'm coming over," Shara said. "I gotta see this!"

Miranda looked at the clock. "Sorry. No can do. Braedan will be knocking on my door any minute now."

"Really?"

Mirada could visualize Shara's face and look of contemplation of what that meant in a romantic sense—all from the way she voiced that one little word. "Yep. Don't get excited, we're just training."

"Okay, if you say so. Someday soon you're gonna have to teach me some of this self-defense stuff he's teaching you. You sure there's not time? I want to see that dress on you!"

"Sorry." Miranda turned from side to side to view the new outfit from every angle.

"It's all right. Bring all your new stuff to work so we can get this party started right after closing." Shara hung up the phone.

Miranda clicked her phone shut and turned a complete circle in front of the mirror and smiled. What would Braedan think if he saw her in this dress? Her smile dimmed. He was her trainer. Doubtful he would even notice the difference.

She turned one last time. She'd never looked better in her life. Someone had gone through a lot of trouble to purchase a dress and shoes in her size. She just might have a fun time tonight after all.

Andrade wasn't at work.

Braedan was. He even sitting in her section tonight—for the first time since they met and he had been glaring at her since he first arrived.

He had been distant all day. More of a teacher, less play. He forced her to focus and control the energy without his help. There hadn't been another bond to create today, but he promised her there would be one in the morning before they left for Overton to see her family.

Braedan had been very stiff when he knocked on her door to program his cell number into her phone. He made her promise to call immediately if she felt any threat at all. She made him promise to spend time with his brother and not worry about her. He silently refused.

Once at work, the night simultaneously flew by because of the normal Friday night high flow of business, yet crawled by at the anticipation of the unknown date, and the discomfort of Braedan's glowering.

Where had Andrade disappeared to? She had almost become accustomed to the nervous adrenaline rush the two gorgeous alpha males provided during her shift. Work at the Cheri was anything but dull.

Miranda set the water glass in front of Braedan and waited to take his order.

He remained quiet, his dark eyes looked steadily into hers.

She cleared her throat. "What would you like tonight?"

Without blinking, he said in his deep baritone, "You, *Love*."

Chills ran up her spine and yet, her body felt warm. "I...I meant what would you like to eat?"

His eyes bore into hers.

"Food?" she squeaked, and cleared her throat again.

"If you insist."

She nodded, not trusting her voice after the last sound that had come out.

He closed the menu he hadn't even looked at. "Surprise me. You have excellent taste in cuisine. I trust you know what I like."

Were they even talking about food?

He held the menu out to her.

She stared at the black menu warily thinking of the first time they met. She felt a low heat in her cheeks at the thought of him helping her to disperse the excess energy at work. *Tempting...*

"This is why I have chosen to sit in other sections than yours this past four days. I did not wish to make you nervous about the white energy while you were at work."

"Oh." She had wondered why he had chosen to sit anywhere but with her.

He looked up at her, his eyes serious. "Please. Do not go on this date tonight. It is unsafe. You should remain with me until you are fully trained."

He almost had her at 'please'. Right up until he mentioned the training. "You know, that just doesn't work for me." She snatched the menu out of his hand, careful not to touch him and turned to leave.

"Miranda," his voice stopped her, "you have gone through many changes this past week. It would be best if you stayed with me until you have full control. If you still choose to go tonight, do not forget that you are important to the well-being of all mankind. Be aware that the Arbiters are looking for you. Do not hesitate to call me if at any time you feel the least bit threatened."

Miranda sighed. He truly did have her best interests at heart, or at least, mankind's best interests at heart. She looked around to make certain no one was close enough to hear before she spoke. "It's just a date. People manage to date all the time. I promise I will call you if I feel even the tiniest bit threatened. I am strong enough now to protect myself." At his look of disbelief, she said, "at least until you could get there to help me."

She headed for the safety of the work station when it looked like he would argue further.

He continued to alternately glower and flirt with her all through the scrumptious meal Chris had prepared special for her new 'friend.'

During his main course, they argued again about where Kelsy was living.

"It's improper for her to be living with your brother."

"My home was built for the purpose of training. She has her own room. You think it would be better if she continued to live on the street, fighting for survival and her virtue, while Trenton trains her in a house that is large, safe, and protected?"

Miranda was taken aback. "Of course not! The streets are no place for a kid. She could move in with me."

Braedan shook his head once. "Who would protect her while you work and go out on dates?"

Miranda glared at him and walked off. Kelsy was better off with Trenton. Trenton would protect her and train her. As young as she was, he wouldn't take advantage of her. That still didn't make it right, but considering her lack of parents, it was the best solution for the time being. But should Kelsy not like the arrangement, Miranda would happily move the young girl in with her. She had siblings, she could handle Kelsy.

Just before closing, Braedan left after one final argument about her date. Miranda had refused to budge. He left angry, leaving three crisp one-hundred dollar bills for her tip, which had angered her further. You don't just leave cash like that lying on a public table.

Finally, the Cheri had closed its doors and Miranda sighed in relief. She totaled her receipts in peace, but the reprieve didn't last long.

John entered the room and paused when he saw her, waiting for her to look at him before speaking. "Do you know what you're doing?"

"I beg your pardon?" she asked, surprised.

He seemed uncomfortable. John was never uncomfortable. It was his life's ambition to make other people uncomfortable. "The new boss. It never works out for an employee when it's over with. A man like that, he's not really your type."

"I...know."

He wasn't done yet. "You'll end up hurt and out of a job. Real life isn't like the fairy tales—there won't be a 'happily ever after.'"

Was he being mean, or was he really concerned about her? "Thanks, I think."

He was done now. "Just be careful."

Little did he know, she already knew everything he just told her. She was very much aware Andrade was only amusing himself. For that matter, he was probably done with her already.

John left the room without another word.

Miranda stared after him. Was it possible John had a heart after all?

Shara breezed into the back room with a single pink rose and a small envelope, thrust them both at Miranda with a grin, and started counting her tips.

"What's this?" Miranda turned the unopened envelope over in her hands.

"Read the note," Shara said in a sing-song voice, counting her tips with a smile.

Miranda sniffed the delicate rose and opened the white and gold trimmed envelope.

The note said: Change and meet me out back. I look forward to our evening together.

Miranda stared at Shara until she looked up.

"Oh, no. My lips are sealed." Shara laughed and grabbed both of their tickets before she started down the hallway. "Let's get changed. You'll find out soon enough."

Miranda followed, her steps slow. With all the unusual things happening lately, her nerves tingled.

"I don't think I'm up for this." Her sheltered life hadn't prepared her for mind-blowingly handsome men, romantic gifts, and activities that would include expensive clothing.

Worse yet, what if her date looked nothing like Braedan or Andrade? It would be a definite let down after all the enchanted storybook adventures she experienced the last few days. Would it be unforgivably rude to just keep the shoes and skip the date?

"Come on." Shara motioned her with one arm to follow.

"Just answer me one question." Miranda took a deep breath. "Is he a toad? A nerd? What's wrong with him that he has agreed to go on a blind date with me?"

Shara shook her head. "Honey, there is nothing wrong with you and I guarantee that you'll like this one."

The transformation from work uniform to date dress didn't happen quickly. Shara pulled out her own supplies and gave Miranda a make-over a professional make-up artist couldn't compete with.

Miranda stood gaping at the beautiful woman who stared back at her in the reflection of the restaurant bathroom mirror. She turned her head from side to side and twirled in a circle while watching the image. She barely recognized the woman as herself.

"Let's go." Shara tossed her brush into her bag and turned to Miranda. She gave Miranda a once over. "I am sooo good!" she said with an enormous grin and pushed Miranda out of the bathroom.

Miranda barely noticed Shara stuffing their belongings into her work locker, but when she heard the click of the lock, Miranda snapped out of her daze with a nervous jerk.

"I don't feel well. I think I should just go home." It wasn't a lie. She reached for her purse and keys. The unknown was unnerving. Why couldn't this date be with Braedan? He was handsome and her time with him was never awkward or boring. Even walking in the park with Braedan was bound to be more fun than whatever her unknown date had planned. For that matter, she was pretty sure even training would be more fun. Shara had set this date up. The man didn't even know her. He probably wouldn't like her. Braedan liked her. Even if he only chose to be with her for training purposes...

Her stomach did a little flip-flop. Yep, definitely didn't feel well.

Shara gave her a funny look and linked arms with her before she pulled Miranda toward the door. "Oh, no, you don't. You are not backing out of this. I promise, you're going to like this guy. You're going to have the time of your life, and you're going to thank me tomorrow."

Miranda nodded—unconvinced—but Shara didn't see it. She plowed ahead, dragging Miranda behind her.

The door to John's office opened as they reached the back door.

"What's going on out here?" John was back to his usual—bossy—self.

Shara turned, her arm still linked with Miranda's, forcing her to turn as well.

"Just leaving work, boss man," Shara said with a sassy smile.

John did a double take at the way the two women looked and gulped. "Uh, next time, you should, uh, get ready at home for these kind of...things."

"And just what kind of things do you think it is we're doing?" Shara raised a brow.

John's eyes traveled over their expensive evening wear. "I don't know, but I'm sure I don't want to know unless it involves work." He went back into his office and shut the door with extra force.

"What is wrong with that man?" Shara said to no one in particular.

Miranda stared at the closed door. Had she just caught a glimpse of...longing? Jealousy?...in John's eyes when he looked at Shara. Could it be, the reason the man gave them such a hard time was because he was secretly attracted to Shara?

"Whatever," Shara muttered, turning back to the door.

Miranda took a deep breath. Shara released her arm and pushed the heavy door open. Miranda walked, head held high, out into the parking lot with Shara. She agreed to this date and to back out now would be rude and ruin Shara's night as well.

Miranda's eyes widened at the shiny white limo parked near the back door of the restaurant. The man leaning casually against the car in the nearly empty parking lot, waiting for her, was one of the most amazing specimens of masculinity she had seen in her lifetime. This couldn't possibly be her date.

She stopped and looked at Shara who was headed to the side of the second man that Miranda had only just noticed. She watched the second man lean down and place a kiss on Shara's cheek. Yep, that one was Shara's date.

Which meant the blond hunk was for her. She looked back at him and saw the look of male appreciation on his face as his eyes leisurely traveled the entire length of her.

He straightened from the car and strode forward. Stopping just in front of her he reached for her hand. "You look absolutely stunning," his deep voice rumbled, sending goose bumps up her arms.

"How...why...?" she couldn't quite form the sentence.

"Because a man never forgets a beautiful woman he has saved the life of." He leaned down and kissed her cheek.

Chapter Twenty-Five

She was spectacular. Money fit her well. Tonight he was going to do as he had been commanded and begin in earnest the battle he already started, using money, power and seduction to win her heart over to his side. Although, somehow, he didn't believe she would truly appreciate the significance of his efforts.

He, however, most assuredly appreciated the opportunity. This stunning creature standing confidently, if a bit confused, before him in the dark sultry night looked exactly like the kind of woman who could control power. In every sense of the word. A woman this beautiful could control men without the white energy.

Keeping his hold on her hand, uncomfortable as it now was after the internal battle he had recently waged, Andrade took a small step back from her, raised their hands above her head and guided her into a slow turn so he could view the full effect of the designer dress. He had been careful in his selection, picturing in his mind the way the midnight hue would accentuate her own coloring, the way her dark hair would cascade down her bare back, caressing her pale skin. The way the silken fabric would cling and drape against her body. He was not disappointed.

His eyes traveled down the length of her body to her long legs. His mind appreciated the way the straps and the spiked heels of the sandals accentuated the delicacy of her bones and made her legs look impossibly long.

He spent much time selecting the correct footwear for the evening. He suspected she may refuse the dress, but knew she wouldn't if he chose the right shoes to complete the outfit. Shoes were her one known vice and they had to be perfect. They appeared to be all that he envisioned. He had removed the twenty-eight-hundred dollar price tag before having them shipped to her. The expense was nothing to him, yet the finer things in life were not what she was accustomed to. Part of his strategy was to let her experience the benefits of wealth, become accustomed to the luxury, enjoy all of its advantages, before she realized what was happening. Should that fail, which he suspected it would, he would rely solely on his powers of seduction.

"I shall be envied by all men tonight." He was amused at the light flush that colored her cheeks. How could a woman this incredible, blush at a simple compliment? The kind of women he dated never blushed. Interesting.

"I bet you say that to all the women you pretend to save." Her smile took his breath away.

"Perhaps. Is it working?"

"Most definitely."

He chuckled. This did not feel like war. "I do believe we shall have a great night together."

A strange look passed over her features.

"What is it?" Andrade asked in concern.

"Just now, you sounded like a friend of mine. Are you not an American?"

Damn, he was slipping. He would press later for the name of this 'friend'. Only one breed of human spoke as he did, and only one breed of human knew how to create the kind of shield that had surrounded her in the park two nights back. This incompetent friend of hers had almost destroyed Andrade's beloved city with his lack of control over his own shield—which he shouldn't have been able to create for her to begin with. Being forced to step in for this friend was what had taken the pleasure out of her touch. Her energy had been like a drug to Andrade, he hadn't been able to get enough of the ecstasy he received in draining small amounts of her power away. Now, it only caused him to suffer. He would kill this friend for that mistake alone. Slowly. Painfully.

"I am. My mother was not. Occasionally, when a beautiful

woman upsets my world—" he flirted shamelessly to distract her—"I might revert into forgotten accents from childhood."

Again, the light color to her high cheekbones. He found this strangely pleasing, rather than annoying.

"Shall we go?" He escorted her to the limousine.

"Where *are* we going?" she asked. He held the door for her and settled her into the plush seat across from Shara and her date.

"It is a surprise," he whispered to her with a wink, before closing her door. He rounded the back end of the car and inhaled deeply at the pain touching her had caused him. He clenched his fists to keep his hands from shaking.

He hadn't expected her touch to stir up the internal battle again. He knew the war between the light and dark still raged inside him, but until now, believed he had it under control. It had taken two full days to get it contained and now, it was beginning once more. Perhaps as long as he was near her, there would be danger to his dark soul. He was not afraid. The darkness inside him was strong. It would conquer the light trying to penetrate his core. He may suffer a little, but this was acceptable. He was a warrior.

As far as war wounds went, the painful touch of the beauty waiting inside the car for him was worth every second.

Chapter Twenty-Six

Miranda swallowed hard and wiped her damp palms on her thighs. She looked at Shara's wide grin as the limousine pulled up to the curb in front of an impressive looking building. A uniformed doorman stepped forward and opened the car door.

Andrade took her arm and escorted her up the wide steps where another doorman held the intricate glass and iron door for them.

"Welcome, Mr. Andrade," the man murmured.

With a small nod of recognition, Andrade guided her into the building, where a maître de showed them the way through the crowd of well dressed people. He led them to a secluded table at the back of the club's dining area.

After they were seated in the private little alcove, lit only by candle light, Miranda turned to Andrade. "Where are we?"

He grinned. "An exclusive club. It's similar to a country club. Kevin and I thought perhaps dinner and dancing?"

The look on Shara's date's face showed he was clearly not a member of this club, but happy to have been included in any plans Andrade had made.

Shara, seated across from Miranda, leaned forward. "Is that Brad Pitt?"

Miranda looked to the left where Shara had indicated with a slight nod of her head. It sure looked like the famous actor. In fact, as she looked around in the dim light, she thought she recognized several of the clubs occupants from the big screen. She also thought she saw the mayor. She looked back at Andrade in surprise. He had been recognized by nearly all the people they passed on their way to the table. The polite head nods and quiet hello's had not passed by her unnoticed.

Miranda looked away from Andrade when he returned her stare. Shara's eyes sparkled with excitement, but Miranda felt tense. She was so out of her league here.

She looked sideways at Andrade and he reached for her hand under the table. At his touch, a small amount of the white light near them gathered around her and a feeling of calm came over her.

"I know you both have access to excellent food at work, but the chef here is incredible—don't tell anyone, it could be bad for business at the *Cheri*," he said with a lopsided grin. "After we eat, the club is famous for its excellent taste in live bands. If you women aren't too tired from working, perhaps we could try out the dance floor."

Shara turned to Kevin. "You had all of this planned and didn't say a word?"

He shrugged. "I was sworn to secrecy."

Shara's tinkling laugh drew several appreciative male stares. "I love surprises!"

Kevin looked at Andrade. "I am deeply in your debt."

Andrade returned the smile, then asked Miranda, "And you? Do you enjoy surprises as well?"

"Not really." She had a few too many of those lately.

"Hmm," he said, giving her hand a gentle squeeze before reaching for his water glass. "What do you enjoy?"

She shook her head. "I'm not sure."

"She really enjoys food," Shara inserted helpfully with a grin.

Miranda shot her a dirty look, then shrugged. Andrade already knew that.

Andrade's look was hot as he smiled at her. "What a lucky man I am. Eating is a pleasure that should be enjoyed by all."

Miranda was tired of people's opinions on her eating habits, so she changed the subject and tried to answer his original question. "I like to do a lot of things. So, I guess it's hard for me to narrow it down. How about you? What do you enjoy?"

His smile was contagious. "Besides rescuing beautiful damsels in distress?"

Miranda rolled her eyes and explained to Kevin. "I was not drowning, he made that up."

"Drowning?" Kevin ignored her protest and looked at Andrade with interest.

Andrade pretended modesty. "The lovely lady was drowning—what's a man supposed to do?—so I gave her mouth to mouth and revived her."

Kevin chuckled as he looked Miranda over. "I'll just bet you did! You just became my new hero."

"Hey!" Shara laughed and gave a playful push to his arm.

Kevin wiggled his eyebrows at Shara. "Anytime you want to drown, I would be more than willing to revive you."

Shara looked at Miranda. "I think they're rubbing off on each other. Should we be scared?"

Miranda looked between the two men wearing innocent expressions. "Definitely."

Andrade draped his arm casually across the back of her chair. "Okay, okay. Besides riding a Jet Ski like a she-devil on the tallest lake waves I've ever seen in my life, what else do you do for fun?"

Miranda took a drink of her lemon water and thought about it. "I guess I'm mostly a small town, desert girl. I enjoy hiking, camping, water sports, trail riding...mostly outdoor activities."

Andrade nodded in approval. "You enjoy danger."

"No, no, no." She shook her head. "I'm no adrenaline junkie. I think a speeding ticket would make me cry. I just like to be outside, I guess."

"This is good to know." Andrade's look promised she would be spending more time with him.

Now she grew nervous again. "I like to be inside sometimes, too. I like to cook and I love to cuddle up with a good book and read for hours. The library is one of my favorite places to hang out. I love going to the movies and I like to play card games with my family. And—" she took a necessary breath—"now I would like to shut up. Please, someone else tell what they like to do."

Shara came to her rescue. "I'm taking a break from small-town life. I like to shop. I like to dance. I like to be around people."

Kevin put his arm around Shara's shoulders and pulled her closer to him. "I like to spend time with Shara, even if it means an occasional dreaded shopping trip."

Everyone looked at Andrade. "I, too, enjoy many things. I enjoy a good book." He stared directly at Miranda. "I love to play games." He glanced back at the couple across the table. "I love to travel. I like to visit exotic places and experience new things. I love chasing wild girls on Jet Ski's over killer waves—" his steady gaze fixed on Miranda again—"and I especially like saving them when they nearly drown." He studied Miranda's face. "I like women who blush...and I like to eat." He looked back at the others. "Shall we order?"

If he had a conscience, he would've felt guilty. He didn't, and therefore, he wouldn't. He always took pleasure in battle—that is why he traded sides—but tonight was more fun than he had experienced during this war. This was not the first time he had been called upon to use his charismatic charm and good looks to tempt light warriors to the dark side, but it was the first time he was drawn into the seduction so completely himself.

The meal was superb—as he had insisted beforehand with the chef that it should be—and the men in the dimly lit restaurant who were lucky enough to notice Miranda's enjoyment of the food had overtly stared in appreciation. He felt no jealousy, only pride that the one they wanted belonged to him.

She *was* his. Almost. He was her activator. They were bonded. He was closer to her than anyone else could possibly be and because of the poor shield incident that changed him internally, she was now a part of him.

He was almost grateful her touch was no longer as pleasant as it had once been. Had it been so, they would've been ending this evening in his bed. The woman stirred his blood and he was confident in his seduction ability. However, this was not the kind of woman who would go to bed easily without regrets. There would be a definite setback to his seduction should he push her that fast.

He had no doubt as to where they would eventually end up. He could bide his time with her, romance her in the way she required and once his internal battle ended, he would bed her with immense enjoyment before turning her over to the General. The wait would make the experience all the more pleasurable.

Andrade participated in the light banter going on around him as they all ate the excellent cuisine. By the time Miranda's plate was clean, the men in the room were openly watching her and had all nearly reached their breaking point of sanity. Food had taken on a new perspective for most of them.

Andrade stood and offered his hand to Miranda. "Please, allow me to escort you to the lower level for dancing."

Miranda looked up at him with her large, luminous eyes and his breath caught in his throat. The heavily lined orbs looked both mysterious and sensual. He slipped her delicate hand into his waiting strong one.

He gently pulled her to stand next to him. Their bodies close, but not touching by anything more than the connection of their hands. His gaze was slow and appraising. He took in every detail of her exquisite face.

Her expressive gaze showed her surprise at the fierce flash of heat that came to his own eyes. Before he could gain control, she lowered her gaze. The dusky pink was back to highlight her high cheek bones. He wanted to reach out and touch the soft, clear skin. Trace her full lips with his finger. Cover her mouth with his own.

He clenched his jaw and focused on the pain he felt inside at the touch of her hand and felt his ardor cool to a more manageable level. His concentration strained as the internal battle raged within. The new light inside was straining to absorb the light emanating from her, and the dark was repulsing it with violent force.

He released her hand and gestured for her to move forward. "Shall we?" His voice came out a deeper baritone than normal. She nodded once and stepped forward. As she drew even with him, he placed his hand on her back to guide her in the right direction. His fingers twitched at the pain, but he kept his hand where it was. The pleasure/pain he received from the feel of only a silken sheen of hair between his palm and her warm skin was worth the risk to his dark soul.

"Is that Fergie or an impressive impersonator?" Shara's voice interrupted his musing.

"It is her. Would you like to be introduced later?" He led their small group into the full, but spacious room. Rather than a typical dance club atmosphere, this room looked more like something from a regency-era ballroom, but with low lighting and instead of an orchestra playing on the platform, a famous rock star took command. The understated elegance was testimony of the wealth involved.

"Wow!" Shara exhaled, her undecided gaze sliding between the famous singer and Andrade. "No, I'm a fan, but don't need to meet her. Hearing her live is fun though. You've got some impressive friends, boss."

"I've had the opportunity to meet many people in my lifetime. Some have been impressive, some have not."

Fergie began to sing "Clumsy" and Andrade escorted Miranda the remaining short distance to the dance floor. The music was loud and made conversation difficult, but he didn't mind. It was a good excuse to use body language.

He watched her. She laughed as Shara involved her in some silly dance steps. He could tell Miranda had no formal training, but her natural grace allowed her to follow the rhythm of the music with ease. She was enjoying herself. Her smile lightened her countenance and the white in the air gathered to her as if pulled by a magnet.

There was a decided lack of people absorbing the light in the room—most of the clubs patrons were the type to repel it—this made the energy around her strong. She was beyond anything earthly he had seen is his lifetime. He allowed the dance to move him a step further away from her.

As the night progressed, Andrade fought irritation. He didn't mind the men watching her eat, he almost enjoyed the attention she had unknowingly acquired, but the awareness her tasteful, yet sexy outfit and graceful undulations of her body to the music were attracting now, annoyed him. Her ability to physically interest the men in the club was strong, but her light was drawing the darkness in the men like moths to the flame. These particular moths would snuff her light out. Permanently. He knew this better than anyone.

He wouldn't examine why this bothered him so much. She was for the General and that was all he needed to admit to.

As the music shifted once again, this time to a slow song, Andrade gathered her into his arms.

"Are you enjoying yourself?" The beauty in his arms asked him when she looked up at him with her big silvery eyes.

"Very much so." His voice was rough. He had spent too much time in her presence tonight and the pain inside his chest intensified with each passing moment.

She gave him a hard stare. "Are you all right?"

He focused inward and pushed hard against the light threatening to engulf him. He heard her gasp when the light around her scattered.

He tightened his grip on her waist and twirled her around and around until she laughed.

"I am better now." His smile was wolfish. He leaned down and kissed her cheek before dipping her backward until she almost touched the ground. "You are a very beautiful woman," he whispered before slowly raising her upright again.

Her body was now touching his from the length of her slender arms wrapped around his neck, down to their legs entwined for balance. Her eyes were wide with desire and he saw the question in them just before the long, coal-black lashes fluttered down and hid the emotion from his view.

The hungry flash of need that stole over his body nearly pushed the pain aside. He was tempted. Severely tempted. He may be a warrior, but he was unused to denying his baser instincts.

He forced himself to move with her again. Keeping her tight against him, he danced his way toward an empty alcove. Screw the plan. For tonight, she belonged to him.

Chapter Twenty-Seven

Braedan gasped and felt the muscles in his entire body clench. He forced a slow and steady exhale and one by one, relaxed each muscle.

He was sitting cross legged in the center of his small apartment's living room floor. He trained ruthlessly for three full hours, his body was exhausted, but his mind was not.

He long ago stripped to nothing but his training pants, the air conditioning was down low, yet still his body glistened, slick with sweat.

One eye slit open to see the clock on the wall. It was three-thirty in the morning and she hadn't returned yet. Without conscious command, his body surged upward until he stood and paced again. He was not yet capable of the serenity his mind sought.

He took advantage of the bond between them to monitor her and feel if she were in danger. At first, he felt her feelings of insecurity, then a slight fear—which had energized him into strengthening the bond and deepening the connection. The clear link to her had caused him to feel the thick beat of awareness in her blood.

He knew that feeling well. He had been fighting it for the past five days. It was a losing battle.

His fist slammed into the punching bag he had erected on a stand in his small bedroom. He felt anger. A trainer was not supposed to cater to emotions. They were to keep the balance. He slammed the punching bag again...once, twice, three times in rapid succession. Then repeated it again. And again.

He could not help himself and kept checking the bond. This last time, he felt the intense heat of desire as it coursed through her veins.

He turned away from the bag in disgust. The white in the room swirled and jumped as though confused. He was upsetting the light with his anger.

He strode the length of the apartment and reached the end too quickly. He turned and retraced his steps. He looked around in disgust. He was going to get dizzy pacing in such a small area. He wrenched the door open and, barefoot and shirtless, headed down the hall and out of the building.

He ignored the desert night heat. He sprinted across the grass and through the trees that separated the apartment complex from the street. The sidewalk was empty when he reached it and he continued his pace for over a mile. He knew he was pushing himself hard enough to reach record setting race times with his run, but continued on.

When he reached the park with the jogging trail he had taken Miranda to a few nights before, he slowed his pace to a jog. He remembered the look on her face when she asked him if she had killed the jogger with her energy blast. The amusing memory calmed him enough to think. If he could connect with her, enough to feel her desire for her date, could he connect with her enough to make her feel caution for her date?

What did she know about this man she went out with? What if he was dangerous? What if he was from the dark side? What if he was just a normal man and she found that desirable?

Braedan stopped jogging. Breathing hard, he sat on the grass next to the trail. He could smell the rich earthy scent of damp grass and flowering trees. He could hear the chattering of insects in the grass. He was alone in the darkness, illuminated only by the stars. His connection to nature complete. The white energy here was strong. He could feel it gathering around him almost as strong as it would have been if she were next to him. He could not, in all fairness to her agency, force her feelings one way or the other. But he could give her a reminder of her duty to mankind.

Of why her concentration needed to stay focused, without the complications of an affair. He could remind her of their bond and the passion she shared with him, and only him.

He felt with his mind for the web of ties connecting them. It was still strong. He used powers he hadn't previously possessed to strengthen the links until he could feel what she felt. A spike of heat caught him low in the gut. His nostrils flared and he felt a vein in his temple throb. A low animal growl slipped through his lips. He reached deep for discipline and clamped his emotions down.

Everything he believed in and everything he had become was based upon pure truth and a rigid set of laws. He'd already compromised this with his one deception. He had misguided her with the energy drains to serve his own selfish desires. He would not compromise who he was. Rules existed for a reason.

This was her choice, not his. He would not interfere.

Chapter Twenty-Eight

Her head was spinning. Her pulse was pounding. She was experiencing the kind of night that only happened in her romance novels on her bookshelves.

The man holding her tight in his arms as they danced was the stuff that dreams were made of. He was rich. He was powerful. He was gorgeous. He was attracted to her. He was a gentleman.

He spun her around again and she looked up at him through her mascara enhanced lashes. There was a heat in his eyes that scared and thrilled her. The feeling that radiated from him to her was intense desire, mixed with...anger? She closed her eyes and allowed the feeling to wash over her. Yes, it was anger. He was incensed that he couldn't control the desire he felt for her. She reached further still in fascination and felt...pain?

"Miranda," his voice was sharp, snapping her out of her revelation.

"Yes?"

"Don't...do...that."

Her eyes widened.

He reached a hand up and smoothed a wayward strand of long hair back from her face. His hand stayed at her cheek, his palm cupping her cheek. His eyes searched hers. He backed her into the waist-high railing.

She noted with surprise they were no longer on the dance floor, but in a deserted niche with tall potted trees creating shadowed recesses that hid them from the dancing couples on the dance floor.

The movement of their bodies to the music stopped, but he didn't back away. They were still intimately entwined, the silk of her dress a poor barrier between them.

She lowered her arms from around his neck, but when he didn't release her, she allowed them to rest on his well-muscled arms.

"Miranda."

"Yes?" Her voice was not much more than a light whisper of air.

"I want you."

She inhaled the scent of warm spice and male heat. She tried to think. Like that was going to happen. Her brain refused to function properly.

"Don't think."

She couldn't.

He took her free hand and placed it on his chest. A strong heavy heartbeat thumped at an accelerated pace against her fingertips. His skin was warm through his shirt. Suddenly, the white was everywhere. She jerked and would have pulled away if she hadn't been trapped between him and the railing.

"Don't think. Feel." He moved his hand that was covering hers to slip beneath the curtain of her hair until he touched the bare skin of her back.

She shook her head the panic building within her, but he stopped her movement cradling her cheek in his other hand, forcing her to look up at him. His eyes bore into hers and she could feel his pain increase as the white dispersed.

She blinked, fumbling for an answer to what she had just experienced. "Andrade?"

He was silent. His breathing shallow. His heart rate greatly increased.

"Andrade?"

An angry look of pain passed over his features so quickly, she thought she may have imagined it. He released his breath and a slow, seductive smile crossed his lips. "I may need resuscitation. Care to assist?"

The white was almost back to normal. How? She hadn't

been the one to disperse it. In fact, in the past few moments, her center had been far from her thoughts. Braedan. Where was he? What was she doing here? This was her boss. This was crazy. Her brain couldn't formulate an answer.

"Don't analyze. Enjoy the moment." He was looking at her as if nothing else in the world mattered at the moment. He tipped her head up and slowly lowered his mouth to hers.

The kiss was feather light, soft, unhurried.

It was romantic. It was noninvasive. It didn't resemble their first passionate kiss shared on the beach. It didn't bear any resemblance to the kisses she shared with Braedan. It was barely even a kiss, more a sharing of breath as they anticipated the kiss to come.

She felt him stiffen right before he growled soft and low in his throat. She felt him pull away both physically and mentally. He released her, breaking all contact between them. He turned his back on her and ran his hands through his hair in agitation.

She waited, but he remained quiet. "Andrade?"

His response was slow. "Yes?" he responded without turning back.

Something wasn't right. She sensed pain, although she couldn't imagine why. He looked very healthy—in fact, he looked so good she was wondering if she should check her chin for drool. No, this was an internal anguish. Perhaps a remembrance of a past lost love? Maybe a recent break-up? Or most likely, he remembered she was nothing more than a waitress who worked for him. Surely that wouldn't cause him an actual feeling of physical distress?

She took a step forward and reached a hand out to touch him gently on the sleeve. He flinched and she dropped her hand back to her side. "Are you all right?"

"Yes." His response was curt.

She had a gift of light. Maybe she could ease his suffering with a small offering of the white energy. She took a deep breath and gathered a small amount of the light to her. She was much, much stronger than she used to be. She would focus this time and not overwhelm him as she had the poor jogger she had inadvertently blasted off the trail at the park.

She would need her center to control the white. Braedan. Thoughts of him, while with another man, confused her. She closed her eyes and allowed herself to feel his strength.

Their bond was strong tonight. Her eyes popped open as she felt his tension along the shimmering ties that linked them. She turned her mind inward and reached deep to feel the source of his distress. He was troubled, but as she pushed further, his thoughts became resolute, then calm, centered.

As Braedan focused, so could she. With great control, she directed the light to Andrade.

As the light surrounded him, his body went rigid. The white was accepted in. After the space of several heartbeats he contracted as if someone had sucker-punched him in the stomach.

"Andrade?" Had she done it wrong again?

Slowly, he straightened his spine and without even a backward glance at her, he strode forward and disappeared into the crowd.

Chapter Twenty-Nine

She was exhausted. She couldn't even keep her eyes open for the ride home. Miranda could hear Shara and Kevin murmuring in the seats across from her, probably wondering about her disappearing date. She was too tired to care if Andrade's vanishing act made her look pathetic. She would deal with it tomorrow...or maybe never.

She was grateful he was gentleman enough to arrange a ride home for them. In style even—his limo driver had found her still standing in shock in the alcove and informed her that Mr. Andrade had been called away on an emergency and had instructed him to escort the party home whenever they desired.

She had desired immediately. Exhaustion threatened to consume her. After all, it was late. Without any further explanation than what the chauffer had given her, she apologized to Shara and Kevin and asked if they were ready to leave. She felt horrible to ask them to go, but it was four in the morning—not exactly an early night. They had graciously agreed.

Their voices slurred and the nothingness of deep slumber crept in around the edges of her consciousness. Her last thought was of Braedan and how very different his passionate kisses compared to Andrade's tender one.

She was near. Their bond hadn't allowed him to follow her progress home. Something had happened to weaken their link and he lost contact with her. He had only been able to sense her for the past mile. This was not good. Braedan's steps quickened until he emerged from the trees next to the parking lot just as the limo pulled up to the front door of their apartment building. A large, impeccably dressed chauffer opened the back passenger door of the car and Shara was the first one to step out. Braedan continued his brisk approach and a second man exited the car to stand next to Shara.

"It's okay, I'll carry her in. Can you find her keys?" the unknown man offered.

Shara's top half disappeared back into the car and her muffled voice floated out. "They should be in her purse."

Braedan stepped forward. Miranda's energy signature was very low. It was weaker than he had yet sensed it. He reached the car about the same time the two men realized he was there. "Step aside. I will take her."

"Who are you?" the first man demanded.

The second man, the chauffer, doubled as a body guard, but only watched him with a defensive stance. Smart man. Braedan was itching to expel more energy and a good fight would've helped tremendously.

Shara reappeared from inside the car and her eyes widened. She took in his state of dress...or lack thereof. "It's okay, Kevin. This is Miranda's, um, neighbor."

Kevin did the typical male sizing up thing and stepped aside. "I can help."

"No."

"Well, okay then." Kevin sounded rather annoyed at his briskness.

Braedan ignored him and nodded toward the car. "What happened?" Her signature was so low, she had to be sleeping. It felt like the exhausted slumber of an energy drain. He felt no further injury to her through their bond.

Shara grinned. "Yeah, guess Cinderella stayed out too late."

Braedan leaned into the long car and stopped. Even in slumber, she was breathtaking. He scooped her into his arms, tucked her close to his chest, and easily straightened back to a standing position. She was very light, perhaps a small amount of this was due to her skimpy clothing. He was both disgusted at the lack of fabric and yet appreciated that he was feeling so much skin. He was surprised she owned something like this. He hadn't thought that was her style.

Shara held up Miranda's keys triumphantly. "Found them. I'll walk up with you and get the door since your hands are full."

Braedan said nothing and headed for the apartment. Miranda didn't stir.

At the door, Shara looked him in the eye, before inserting the key into the lock. "Miranda is my best friend. She's innocent and defenseless. Don't take advantage of her, or you will answer to me."

His look was grave as he responded to the inconsequential threat. "I would never touch a female without her permission."

"I wasn't talking about just tonight."

He nodded once. "Agreed."

She unlocked the door and stepped aside as he entered.

"The man downstairs?" he asked as he passed her.

"He's mine."

He stood in the middle of the room, holding Miranda to him with ease. "What happened to her date?"

Shara shrugged one shoulder. "Disappeared. Some kind of an emergency."

"Any trouble tonight?"

"None, except her date had to leave early."

Braedan studied her face. There was no deception in her countenance. "Who was he?"

Shara paused. "You know, I think I'll let Miranda tell you all about it tomorrow when you have your *training* session. For now, let's get Sleeping Beauty tucked into bed."

Braedan felt along the web of ties that connected him to Miranda. He was certain she experienced an energy drain. Therefore, he wouldn't be leaving her alone tonight. He looked at her small bed and then down at the hard floor and made his decision. Without a word, he walked past Shara and back out Miranda's front door.

"Where are you going?" Shara followed right on his heels.

He opened his apartment door and crossed to his bedroom. He tenderly laid Miranda down on his oversized bed. As soon as her head hit his pillow, she sighed and rolled to her side pulling the top cover with her. His lip twitched at the destruction she caused to his bed.

Shara stood in the doorway. "I think I'll be going now, but please, she's special. Take good care of her."

He heard Shara pull his door closed behind her, then close and lock Miranda's door before she left down the hallway.

He stood watching the beautiful woman in his bed, slumbering, for a long time.

He had tried very hard not to feel so much for this protégé of his, but his feelings couldn't be suppressed. Tonight had proven that to him. The thought of her in another man's arms was enough to make him break the rules.

Typically, the General frowned upon relations between teacher and student, but his father had encouraged this relationship. He said what they shared was momentous, not just between them as a couple, but what they could accomplish together in this war. They were destined to be together.

The feelings of desire she felt toward this unknown man tonight could stand in the way of their attainment of the ultimate goal.

Forget the ultimate goal. He wouldn't be the same man if he lost her.

"Damn," he muttered. Perhaps it was time. Time to bend his own personal rules and fight for what *he* wanted.

Chapter Thirty

The balance was shifting. Andrade moaned aloud in pain. He was still on the floor in his entryway. He barely got the door closed behind him before falling to the ground and writhing in pain on the cold, hard tiles.

The additional white light he absorbed tonight, had been too much. The internal war was now raging full force again. The dark had been slowly winning before, now it was a close battle yet again. The pain was excruciating.

Were he in any position to think logically, he would remove himself from this particular battle. His soul identity had been compromised.

The pain that spread throughout his chest, now exploded inside his skull as well. He gripped the sides of his head and staggered to his feet. He would not, could not, lose himself, and all he had become. He worked too hard to get where he was.

He stumbled his way across the living room until he reached the glass windows. He could not see her, but he could feel her. His hands pounded at the glass in anger at the injustice of it all. He was beyond attraction for the one woman—the one thing in the entire world—that could destroy him. She alone could tear down all he had done, all he had worked toward. She could take it all away.

Was he as powerless as the men in the club whose darkness was drawn to her light?

"No." The word was weak and pathetic.

"No!" It came as a ferocious growl.

"No!" The power built within him and the word thundered at the darkness beyond the glass.

She was exquisite—there were many beauties in this world.

She was extraordinarily desirable—he coveted many priceless possessions.

She was powerful—he was the most favored warrior of the Dark General and would one day rule even her.

Was she truly exceptional enough to transform the part inside of him that was the very blackest? The part that should have been immune to change?

The pain was rapidly becoming more than he could think past. It would be far simpler to let go of the darkness and let the white consume him. It was tempting.

No. He had no desire to change. He had many more pleasures left to experience and mankind to rule before he was done. He would fight the light and remain the General's most favored one. Even if it nearly killed him in the process.

Chapter Thirty-One

Her eyelids felt weighted down. Her senses explored what her sight was too tired to do. Miranda felt the softness of a bed beneath her. She felt a hardness beneath her cheek. She heard the steady thump of a strong heart in her ear. Her eyes flew open.

She recognized Braedan's bedroom. She was lying in his bed. Her head was using his bare chest for a pillow.

"How...what?" She placed a hand on the muscled skin near her cheek and pushed herself up. She was shooting for a sitting position, but felt weak and only managed to lift her head enough to look up at his face. He was awake.

"Good morning, *Love*."

"What time is it?" She blinked her eyes and tried to focus her vision.

"Ten. I expected you to sleep much longer after such a complete drain."

"Drain?" He lost her again. "I, uh…" She cleared her throat and stared at his chest. It was bare and beautiful. Her eyes traveled down its expanse and she was relieved to see his exercise pants were on. Her clothing was in place as well. At least she hadn't missed anything good. "Um, how did I get here?"

"What do you remember?"

She blinked again and raised her eyes back to his. Better that way. She could think, at least a little. She couldn't seem to think at all when looking at his body. "I was on a date. No, I was on my way home from my date."

"With whom?"

"My date, except he wasn't with me anymore. He left unexpectedly." She was too tired to hold her head up, but managed to shift until she lay next to him, instead of on top of him.

"And who was this date?"

Her stomach rumbled. She was hungrier than usual, which was saying a lot. "Food?"

"As soon as I get some answers."

She turned her head and looked at him with a glower. "You are going to deprive me of *nourishment* just to have your curiosity appeased? These better be some pretty big questions to threaten me that way."

"No threat intended. Leverage. What happened last night?"

She groaned and covered her eyes. "You want a play-by-play of my *date*?" When he remained silent, she uncovered her eyes and looked at him. "You're kidding, right?"

"No."

"Oh, come on! You can't be serious."

He turned on his side, supported his head on his palm and looked down at her. "What happened to drain your energy?"

"An energy drain? Is that why I'm so tired?"

He raised one brow. "I am waiting."

She shook her head. "I have no idea."

"How can you not know? Were you threatened? Did someone try to harm you?" The anger in his voice said he was losing patience.

"No one threatened me. I didn't do anything. Not one energy storm. Except ..."

"Except what?"

"Well, when, um, my date and I were dancing I think I created a little white blizzard, but it didn't get out of hand."

He had an eye tick she hadn't noticed before.

"You were able to find your center and control it?"

"Kinda." Her stomach growled again. "Food?"

"Explain."

She huffed. "I didn't find my center, but it went away. No harm, no foul. All is good. Satisfied?"

"No. What else?"

She rolled her eyes. "He was upset and I tried to send him a little of the white energy."

"And?"

She frowned. "I didn't blast him out of the building, if that's what you're thinking. But I might have used a little too much."

"Why do you think that?"

"He acted like he was in pain and then he left without a word." There, she embarrassed herself and he heard all about it. "Happy now? How about that food?"

He didn't look happy. In fact, he still looked kind of upset.

"What?" she said propping herself up on her elbows.

His expression shuttered, the irritation hidden, and his eyes took on a decided gleam. "Nice dress."

"Huh?" Her brain was foggy. "Oh." She looked down. She was still wearing her clothing from last night. It was a little twisted and had ridden a little high on her legs, but was still basically salvageable for having been slept in.

"Where are my heels?" She sat up looking around the room.

"She rises for shoes," he muttered to himself, before pointing down the side of the bed to the floor.

She leaned over the edge to make sure they were there. "Good." She sighed in relief and flattened back out on the bed.

His grin was reluctant as he lay back on the pillow with his arms crossed behind his head. "I am worried for your safety, and you fear for your shoes."

"They're very nice shoes." She couldn't help the defensive note that crept into her voice.

"So tell me who this date was with. Who did you cause pain with your lack of control?"

"I didn't hurt him. At least, I don't think I did."

"Miranda, who was your date with?" His voice was no nonsense.

She glared at him. It was none of his business.

"It is my business. I am to keep you safe and something happened last night that threatens your health. Who was your date?"

"Fine, Danny. My date was with my boss."

He raised one brow—she didn't know if it was at the hated nickname or at the man she told him she went out with.

"The one who sends you gifts?"

She nodded.

"He is one of Shara's castoffs?"

She looked away.

"Andy?"

"Andrade."

"Hmm. So I am Danny, but he is only Andrade?"

"Grrr. Food. Got any?"

He smiled now.

Big mistake. "Danny, feed me or I will find a way to torture you beyond belief."

"Too late," he muttered under his breath. The many muscles covering his abdomen contracted and he sat up. "I will get you food, but you will answer all of my questions as you eat. Agreed?"

"Yes. Just give me food!"

He left the bed, but was back in record time. The food evidently already prepared and waiting.

"Oh, yeah!" She struggled to a sitting position. The plate he held in his hands was stacked high with sandwiches that looked more delectable than anything Subway had to offer. They were going to disappear fast.

"How badly did you hurt poor Andy?"

"Hey—" she defended with a mouth full of food—"That's not fair. I think he was already in pain. That's why I tried to help him."

"What was causing his pain?"

"I have no idea. Old love lost?" It was a wild guess. She didn't know.

"Did you make him feed you? Maybe late night indigestion? He has a weak constitution? Not everyone can eat as we do."

Miranda studied him in irritation and took another bite of her sandwich.

"How did your energy get depleted?"

She shook her head and took another huge bite. If her mouth

was full, she could avoid answering questions she didn't have the answers to.

"Enjoying your food?" he asked.

She nodded and realized the sandwiches were good. Better than that, they were unbelievable. Ham, turkey, cheese, onions, olives, lettuce, mayo, mustard, and was that pepperoni she tasted? Amazing. She tried not to change expressions, but the food tasted so fantastic, how could she not?

"I take that to mean yes." He shifted positions on the bed until they faced each other. "An energy drain can only happen one of two ways. One, your trainer can drain it to help you control it. Two, you expend a tremendous amount of energy. This typically occurs only during battles. You have multiple times, during training, expended remarkable amounts of energy without feeling the after effects of a drain. While this is unusual for other warriors, it appears to be normal for you. This leads me to believe that you are not telling me everything that happened."

She grabbed a second sandwich from the plate. "I seriously don't know what to tell you. No bad guys jumped out at me. No brawling on the dance floor. I'm totally baffled."

A strange look crossed his face. "Only your activator should be able to drain your energy. You were activated by an unknown source. Is it possible someone—your missing activator—could have drained your energy last night?"

"No one kissed me like you do. I woulda noticed that." No, Andrade's kiss had been nothing like the passionate ones Braedan had to use in order to drain her power and it had been only mere seconds long.

A look of confusion flitted across his face, only to be replaced with resolve. He waited until she had taken a big bite before speaking. "Miranda, an energy drain can happen with nothing more than a touch."

She chewed for a moment longer, then stilled. Her eyes searched his. Finally, she slowly finished chewing.

"Did anyone touch you last night to drain your energy?"

She swallowed. "Does that mean...do you mean..." Words were once again evading her. "All of those kisses...were unnecessary?"

"I wouldn't say that."

Her mind was spinning. "You could've drained my power without kissing me?"

His nod was brisk.

She scooted to the edge of the bed and stood. She faced him. She knew there were logical questions she should ask, but was unable to think of what they might be.

They stared at each other in silence.

What could she say? Sometimes, it is better to think before you say something you cannot take back later. Without a word, she headed out the door. Halfway there, she turned and retraced her steps. She stopped at the edge of the bed and with a defiant look grabbed the plate of sandwiches, then left with her head held high.

Chapter Thirty-Two

"You have nothing to say, *Love*?"

She looked at Braedan. He merged his powerful car into traffic from the onramp. What could she say? She still had no idea what to think. He never actually lied to her about it. He only *implied* he had to kiss her to drain the excess energy away. Was it possible she had been too eager to accept the choice he offered, without questioning it?

Why on earth would he do such a thing? He wasn't a ladies' man like his brother, although he certainly had the looks and body to be one—just not the temperament. He occasionally acted like he was attracted to her, but the man had more control over his emotions than anyone she'd ever met. She didn't believe for one moment that he was unable to restrain himself where she was concerned.

She looked away from him. She couldn't quite convince herself that he was toying with her either. He was too straight-laced, too serious, to bother playing games like that. So why?

Regardless of the reason, she felt hurt. Betrayed. Used.

Shara had once told her, "If a man makes you cry once, it's good, because it means you care. If he makes you cry twice, shame on him. If you let him make you cry three times, shame on you."

This had been once.

She cleared her throat and looked out the side window at the passing city. "Thanks for returning my heels." An hour after she stormed out, he showed up at her door, her new shoes dangling from his index finger. He simply informed her that they would skip the training and the bonding session today because her energy was too low to accomplish either. He suggested she be ready to leave to see her family in one hour and left without waiting for her to speak.

"You are welcome." He changed lanes to bypass a slower moving car.

They were on their way to Overton. Her home town. Her family. How on earth was she going to explain this man to them? She had never really brought a man home before and this was a *family* function...Mother's Day. They were going to think he was her boyfriend. A possible *significant* other in her life. Why else would she bring a man to meet them all?

His eyes still on the heavy traffic, he answered her silent question as if he could read her mind. "I think it might be best if we act like lovers for your family's sake. They may not be ready to hear the truth at this time."

Her jaw dropped and her head swiveled until she stared at his hard profile. "Oh, no. No. Not lovers. My brothers wouldn't understand that one. You'd probably get hurt." She looked at his heavily muscled arms in his short sleeved polo shirt and felt the waves of power that radiated from his body. No, her brothers would be the ones to get hurt. Even three against one.

"Boyfriend and girlfriend then?"

She sighed. "Yeah, I suppose so. We could try for the whole trainer thing, but they won't believe it."

His eyes left the road and focused on her. "Do not worry. I believe, *Love*, that we can convince them that we belong together."

Chapter Thirty-Three

"Oh, ye of little faith."

"What?" Miranda turned to face him.

Braedan looked pointedly at the finger nail between her lips and she dropped her hand back into her lap. She had twisted a lock of hair for nearly forty-five minutes while they traveled the freeway. As they took the exit to Overton, she chewed on her nails.

"Trust me. All will be fine with your family."

Her big eyes looked unconvinced.

"You have had a rough week—"

She snorted.

"—and the time with nature and family will be good for you. It will help you to find your balance."

When she only snorted again, he took a left off the main road and slowed as the asphalt turned to dirt and wound its way uphill.

"Why are we going to the reservoir?"

Braedan remained silent until he found what he was looking for. He pulled the car to the side of the road and cut the engine. "You need to connect with nature. Now. Before you see your family."

He had expected the warrior within her to be upset with him for misleading her, but he also hoped the woman inside would understand the chemistry between them. As of yet, the attraction hadn't won her inner battle. The fact she left her precious shoes behind in his apartment led him to believe she was much more upset than he'd imagined she would be.

She exited the car before he could help her. Together they walked down the hill to the small, deserted beach.

They neared the clear blue water and Miranda stopped and watched the lazy waves lap at the shore.

Braedan stood at her side, close, but not touching. "What has you so concerned?"

She lifted one delicate shoulder and let it drop again.

"You do not know?"

She shook her head.

"If you are worried for your family's safety, I will protect them."

She continued to stare at the water.

He took a deep breath. "Are you upset over the way I have drained your energy?"

She did look at him now. Her beautiful eyes wide and searching.

"I apologize for leading you to believe that is how it had to be done, but I do not regret the intimacies we have shared."

The eyes that looked up at him in confusion reflected the clear blue of the water.

He reached a hand out and touched her cheek. The white particles around them swirled and jumped as if excited. "It was wrong of me. I should not have taken advantage of you in such away. You should always have a choice. However, I will continue to drain your energy in the same manner as I have always done. So, if you choose not to have my kisses, you must use your center. You have been forewarned. The choice is now yours."

He watched her eyes widen imperceptibly and heard her slight intake of breath as he leaned down and brushed his lips lightly against hers. He didn't need to feel through the bond that connected them to know she was confused. He didn't need the bond to know she desired him. He didn't need the bond to be certain what they had *was* worth fighting for.

Now he'd done it. He went and confused her to the point

she didn't know which way was up. He'd admitted to being deceitful—even apologized for it—then told her he was going to continue doing it and had even followed up on the threat with the most gentle, heartfelt kiss she had ever experienced.

Men.

Miranda sat down in the soft, warm, white sand and crossed her legs. She closed her eyes—knowing he wouldn't approve—and reached out with her senses. She needed to clear her mind. To find a balance. She needed peace.

She felt the warmth of the early afternoon sun as it caressed her face and body. She listened to the waves gently lapping at the shore. She reached into her mind and found the silken ties that linked her to Braedan.

She marveled at the beauty of the connection. The white was brilliant, sparkling, and many faceted like a diamond in the sunlight. Never had she seen anything so beautiful—except, perhaps, the man it connected her to.

She allowed herself to feel along the ties until she could join with his thoughts. She inhaled sharply and pulled back as she felt not the peace she had expected from him, but turmoil. She tentatively stretched forward again and focused on all of his emotions. She sensed tension, desire, regret, longing, and...hope?

She squinted one eye open and stared at his back. He stood five feet in front of her facing the water, legs wide and arms folded—a defensive stance. She cracked a small grin. She realized he was protecting her since she had chosen to meditate with her eyes closed.

"You are not done yet. Find your balance."

"Yes, oh Great Master." She closed her eye and focused again.

This time, she ignored the bond and concentrated on the man himself. Although the two were connected, she opted not to feel his inner thoughts. Her mind flashed through scenes of the two of them creating white energy when they first met, the way he diffused the excess energy. The first training session where she found her center. Strawberries in sweet red syrup. Of the time when she had first seen the link between them. Sculpted abs. The kisses they shared to diffuse her energy. Fluffy whipped cream.

"Are you finding your balance with nature, or letting nature overtake you?"

Miranda wondered from the odd tone of his voice, if he had been feeling her emotions through their bond. She determinedly pushed all thoughts of yummy desserts and a shirtless trainer to the side.

Clearing her mind again, she focused on the sounds around her. She dug her hands into the sand at her sides and let the small grains sift through her fingers. She inhaled deep, noticing how the wet smell of water in a desert is purely unique. She could feel herself calming. The balance with nature almost complete.

With her body centered, she exhaled through her nose. Her mind found something she glimpsed once before. She concentrated on this unknown light and realized what once was only a thin, unidentified thread, was now thick and strong. She followed along this unknown link with her mind and felt a sharp pain. She gasped before crying out.

"Miranda!" Braedan rushed to her side.

She ignored Braedan and again tried to follow this new tie. Where had it come from and who did it bond her too? Once again the pain was sudden and exploded both in her head and her chest. It was the most excruciating agony she had felt in her entire life. Her body swayed and grabbing her head with both hands, she abandoned the tie and opened her eyes.

"What happened?" Braedan's strong arms were already around her. He gathered her close to his body.

Even though the pain was gone as suddenly as it had begun, she couldn't form any words. Whether from the lingering remembrance of anguish or lack of how to explain, she wasn't certain.

"Miranda?" Braedan picked her up and cradled her in his arms.

"I'm okay." Her voice sounded weak and shaky, even to her.

"What happened, *Love*?"

"I have no idea."

His arms tightened around her. He headed back toward the car. His face grim, his eyes searched the surrounding terrain.

"I don't think we're in any danger," she assured him. Though she still felt weak, she was getting stronger by the second. She watched the white gathered around the two of them. She realized Braedan was infusing her with his strength. Interesting, she hadn't realized he could do that.

"How do you know?"

"Because—" she paused—"I think it came from inside of me."

His eyes cut to hers. "Are you ill?"

"No."

They reached the car and he stopped, but continued to hold her close to him in his protective embrace. "Then what was it? I felt great pain."

She looked up at him. How could she possibly explain? "So did I, but it wasn't mine."

Chapter Thirty-Four

It was awkward. For her, but not for him. Braedan quite enjoyed Miranda's relations. The loving family of his protégé reminded him of his own.

When he proved to be well mannered and respectful toward Miranda, they accepted him—with some small reservation.

"So, Braedan—" her mother, Susan, asked at lunch—"How did you and Miranda meet?"

He felt Miranda tense in her chair next to him, but he answered with ease. "I was a guest at one of her tables at the *Cheri*."

"Wow!" Tracey, the youngest of five siblings, at fourteen years of age, asked, "You can afford to eat there?"

"Tracey, mind your manners," Susan said.

Braedan smiled at the teenager. "I'll let you in on a secret, I knew your sister was there and requested to be seated in her section. I wanted to meet her."

"Cool! But that's not much of a secret with the whole family hearing it. You owe me a better one than that." The girl wore an impish grin.

"I'll see what I can come up with for you."

"Right on!"

He looked at Miranda. She had been quiet since their arrival, but in the chaos of the large family, no one seemed to notice. Her color was back to normal and her energy pattern was rebuilding from the unknown drain the night before. The unexplained pain from their time at the reservoir was gone—he checked along the bond constantly for any sign of it returning. He was clueless as to what had caused it and she either didn't know herself, or wasn't telling.

"So, what do you do for a living?" Miranda's oldest brother asked.

A small frown slipped across Miranda's face. "Lay off, Tyler. This isn't going to turn into an inquisition. Braedan's just a friend, no need to give him the third degree."

"Hey, you started it, Sis, by bringing him home to meet the family. Besides, nothing wrong with finding out what a man does for a living. Is there, Braedan?"

Tyler's question was almost a challenge. Braedan was assured this family loved his Miranda. Should he be unable to care for her, they would do their best. Their attempt wouldn't be enough against the dark side, but it was a comfort none-the-less. "I am an international business man. I travel, but am currently based in Las Vegas. I plan to make Nevada my home for a while."

"You talk funny. Where are you from?" Tracey said, piping in.

Braedan looked across and up the table to her. "Europe. I do not talk funny. You do," he said with a wink.

Tracey giggled.

This family was large by today's standards, but his was bigger. Her father, Dave, sat at the head of the table. Susan, her mother, next to him. The children were seated by descending order around the table. Tyler, the oldest next to his mother, then himself, and Miranda on the end. Eric, Brad, and last, but not least, Tracey, who sat next to her father.

"Do you intend to return home when your work in the city is done?" her father asked while buttering a slice of bread.

"Yes, sir. For a visit. I have not yet decided where I would like to settle for the long run. I believe when my work is completed, I will have the ability to choose where I would like to stay."

"Do you think you'd like to stay near here?" Tracey asked, her big eyes bouncing back and forth between himself and Miranda.

Braedan liked this young girl who was so full of energy and life. He imagined Miranda had been very similar to her at the same age. He wondered if she would also become a White Warrior. "I think I might like that."

"Nice!" She reached across the table with a smile at her mother and grabbed a handful of carrot sticks from the tray in front of her.

Braedan looked at Miranda. She remained quiet, but her appetite was good. She had an incredible recovery rate.

"What do you like to do for fun?" Eric asked.

"I work most of the time, but in my spare time I like to train... and spend time with your sister."

Eric ignored the sister part and jumped on the training. "What do you train for? You play sports?"

"I enjoy sports, but mostly I train in martial arts."

"You do any competitions?" Brad leaned forward in excitement.

"No. Where I lived growing up, it was something we competed in daily, but not in the way your system does it."

"What do you mean?" Brad questioned.

"I guess you could compare it to the movie version of what the monks do. It was a part of our daily lessons to learn the skills of defense and battle. We all practiced and competed amongst ourselves, but never in a formal setting."

Eric leaned forward too, almost into his plate. "Did you ever have to fight? Like in a war?"

"There are battles all around us that we all participate in, whether we know it or not. But no, I have never shot a gun at anyone." It was the closest to the truth he could come up with and still put her parents' minds at ease. He had found out many years ago it was easiest to tell as much of the truth as he could and simply leave out the parts others shouldn't know about. This appeased his conscience and kept him from getting caught up in lies.

"Were you raised by monks?" Tracey asked wide-eyed.

He grinned. "No."

"Hey, maybe you could show us some moves later?" Brad's expression was hopeful.

"Sure. If you will show me what a sandrail is? I have heard your sister mention this once."

Tyler grinned. "I'd be happy to take you for a ride later."

"You own one of these?"

"Yeah, I got a pretty nice one. Built it myself."

Braedan heard the pride in Tyler's voice. "Then I would be honored to ride with you."

"Oh, boy," Miranda said under her breath.

Braedan turned to face her. "You do not agree?"

"Only if you have a death wish," she replied. "He drives like a wild-man."

Braedan looked between Miranda and Tyler, then at Tracey. "Have you ever ridden in this sandrail?"

Tracey rolled her eyes. "Yes. It's a blast!"

Braedan grinned. "Then, I think I may enjoy it."

Chapter Thirty-Five

He felt her. She discovered their bond and searched along it. This was good. He knew she recoiled at the pain and yet, returned again. Their tie was strong and growing stronger.

Andrade rolled over with a loud groan and forced himself to his hands and knees. For ten hours he lay on the cold tiles inside his front door when the heat inside his body had become unbearable. The battle had been vicious and every muscle and bone ached beyond belief. He panted from the exertion of rising only this far and he tried to clear his mind. He would not think of what was changing inside him.

He was what he was. He was the most favored warrior of the Arbiter General. It didn't matter that some of the dark had been pushed aside by her light. He hadn't become the favorite by being good. Many sins blackened his soul. It wouldn't take long and his dark deeds would push the light back out. He was what he was.

The heavy metal song blaring from his pocket jerked him back to his present position on the floor and he forced himself to stand before answering the custom ringtone he'd programmed for the Dark General.

"My General." His words were strong, though his body felt weak.

"Report."

Always short and to the point. He did like the General. "She is coming around nicely."

"How long?"

"As I explained before, this one has great power and many obstacles for us to overcome as we seduce her to our side. I do not believe it wise to rush this one."

"How long?" the General demanded again.

The pain in his head started to throb. "I do not know."

"Are you certain she can be turned?"

"Most definitely. She only requires special handling. Trust me, I can bring this one into the fold."

"I am not a patient man. Do not make me wait long."

The pain was spreading from his head to his chest again. "No, General. I will change her, but you must understand her power is incredible and to push too quickly might cause a loss we would not easily overcome."

There was a pause. "Should I continue to wait, do I run the risk of losing my most favored warrior to the other side?"

The General was perceptive, but there was no way he could know of the extent of the battle raging inside of him. "No, General. As always, you have my complete loyalty. I will stand by your side when the light falls and help you to rule eternity."

"Well done, my warrior. Do not make me wait longer than necessary."

The line went dead.

"Of course not." Andrade staggered to the nearest piece of furniture. Luckily it was a couch and he collapsed onto it. It was much softer than the hard tiled floor, but not as cool to his burning skin. The war inside was fierce enough to cause a noticeable change to his outside. He hoped when the battle was over, he would still look the same.

It had always pleased the General that he looked so wholesome and good as it was deceiving to the unwary and masked the darkness within. This opened doors for him that might otherwise remain closed.

He pushed at the light threading like tentacles through the blackness inside of him and the fiery pain intensified. He returned his thoughts to Miranda to help dull the crushing force in his skull. The General wouldn't wait long before taking matters to another favorite. The thought of another warrior touching

Miranda's light, or her exquisite body, caused him to fist his hands. He would not share her with another, or watch as another extinguished her light. Not until he was done with her. If he won her to their side, the General would owe him that much.

Who was he kidding? The General was indebted to no one, he did whatever pleased him. Only if it pleased the General would he allow for him and Miranda to work as a team, destroying the light together.

Andrade ground his teeth. Never had any battle he fought caused him so much effort and pain. Never had any battle caused him so much pleasure either. When his internal battle was over and her light no longer caused him suffering, he would find a way for their union to please the General.

Chapter Thirty-Six

"So, are you sleeping with him?"

"Tracey!" Miranda exclaimed.

Tracey shrugged before flopping down on Miranda's bed. "I'm not a baby anymore and that guy is...wow!"

Miranda paused in brushing her hair and looked at her little sister's reflection in the vanity mirror. She didn't look any more grown up than she had a month ago. She was still small and thin. Not very curvy. She would probably follow in her big sister's footsteps. Poor thing. "And just how grown up are you now?"

Tracey shuddered. "I am *not* having the *talk* with you. Bad enough to have gotten it from mom, but no way am I gonna have it with you too. All I'm saying is, the man is gorgeous and he's obviously got the hots for you. Just curious what's going on. So tell your little sis all about him."

Miranda couldn't help but smile. "Skipping any sex talk, what do you want to know?"

"Oh, sure. Leave out the good stuff." Tracey flipped over onto her back and watched Miranda pull her hair up into a ponytail. "Tell me everything. Did Shara set you up with him? Are you guys getting serious? Are you gonna marry him? Are there more like him?"

Miranda laughed. "One question at a time. No, he's not one of Shara's cast-offs—"

"—That reminds me, how did your blind date turn out? The one you told me Shara was going to make you go on? Was it with Braedan?"

Miranda grinned and swiveled on the vanity stool to face her little sister. The girl had a very short attention span, which was a definite plus, because how could she possibly explain Braedan?

"No, the date ended up being with my new boss. And yes, he is also very handsome."

"As gorgeous as Braedan?"

"Uh, yeah. I guess so, but in a different way." She could see Tracey getting ready to rattle off a whole new batch of questions and held her hand up to stop her. "Yes, it was fun. No, we probably won't be going out again."

"Oh, man. Why not? Is it cuz of Braedan?" Too excited to hold still, Tracey rolled back onto her stomach and propped her chin in her hands.

"No. The man is my boss, not a good idea to date the man who controls your paychecks."

Tracey blew at her bangs, which had shifted over one eye. "If you had fun, what does it matter?"

"Hmmm. It's just not a good idea. Besides, he had to leave early and I'm not certain he enjoyed our date." She enjoyed it. She enjoyed it very much. But she didn't belong in a lifestyle such as he led and besides, she had a confusing trainer and a war to be thinking about. There really wasn't time for her to concentrate on a new boyfriend and she really didn't want to find a new job when he decided she wasn't sophisticated enough for him. It'd be better to just keep the fantastic memories and cut the relationship short before future failure could destroy her past fantasies.

Tracey snorted. "Course he did!"

Miranda smiled halfheartedly at her sister's loyalty, but didn't want to continue this line of discussion, so she redirected her. "So, are you gonna come hiking with us in Valley of Fire?"

Tracey sat up. "Who's us?"

"I thought I'd take Braedan for a short hike when he comes back from his ride on the sandrail. He's never been out this way, so I thought I'd show him around a little."

Tracey rolled her eyes. "A little is right. Take you all of two minutes to show him around town and that's if traffic is heavy."

Miranda threw a pillow at her. "I happen to like living in a small town. It's comfortable. Safe."

"Everyone knows everyone's business. I can't sneeze and not have mom find out about it sixty seconds later," Tracey said, complaining.

"It's not that bad." Miranda chuckled at her sister's exasperation.

"Is too. If you like it so much, why'd you leave?"

Because she had to in order to protect her family. She shouldn't even be here now. "Cuz I'm old and shouldn't be living at home anymore and Shara hooked me up with a great paying job."

"Which is where you met your new boyfriend."

Miranda had almost denied the boyfriend part, but couldn't. There was no other good explanation to give her family. She was stuck with the deception for now...kinda like how Braedan had deceived her with his kisses? She groaned inside. Life was just too complicated.

"So how old is he? He looks great, but seems old. You know what I mean?"

Miranda paused. She had no idea how old he was. And yes, she knew exactly what Tracey meant. The man had an ageless wisdom in his eyes. As if he'd seen and done everything there was to do, and—being Braedan—had learned from it.

Tracey was taking a breath to fire off another question, when their mother knocked on the bedroom door.

"Hi, girls." She entered the room and closed the door behind her.

Miranda smiled. She had missed her family. She'd only been gone a short time, but so much had happened, it felt like years.

Her mother sat on the bed next to Tracey before she, too, started in with the questions. "I like your new man. How long have you known him?"

"I've only been gone three weeks, so not really all that long," Miranda said, hedging.

"It must be going pretty well if you're bringing him home so soon after meeting him." Her mother had a way about her that let her probe gently into other people's business without offending them.

"Uh, yeah. I guess it is." She saw the hopeful look in her mother's eyes and clarified. "We're great friends and he helps me a lot, but we aren't like...ready to get married or anything like that."

Her mother's look was speculative. "So, just what does an international business man do, and why is he interested in my little girl?"

"You don't think he should like me?" Miranda avoided the first question, and was not offended by the second, because she had been asking herself the same thing.

"Of course he should. You're young, beautiful, full of life. But handsome, wealthy men rarely appreciate the more wholesome things in life. Not when they could have their pick of so many."

Miranda turned away on the pretext of straightening her vanity top. "Braedan is different, I guess."

When her mother stood, Miranda looked up at her reflection in the mirror. Her mother came forward and wrapped her arms around her, giving a big squeeze. "He certainly is. He's smart enough to fall in love with you."

Miranda started. "He's not in love with me. We're just, um, dating."

"Of course you are." Her mother's arms tightened once more before letting go and heading for the bedroom door. Before she left the room, she added, "You two seem to have something special, just don't give up what you really want in life for what you want right now. Remember who you are."

Miranda hated it when her mother guilted her into responsibility.

Chapter Thirty-Seven

"Don't work up too much of an appetite, sis, we're all hungry too." Brad snickered passing her on the trail.

"Not listening," she said. There was no end to her brothers teasing, and if she responded, they could keep it up forever.

Brad looked over his shoulder with a grin. "You don't have to. He is." He indicated Braedan with a lift of his chin.

Miranda, in front of Braedan on the trail, stuck her tongue out at her little—but taller—brother.

Brad grabbed his heart. "I'm shocked and appalled at your childish behavior. Did you see that Braedan?" Without waiting for an answer he took off with a chuckle to catch Tracey and the rest of her brothers further on up the trail.

Miranda felt a chill race down her spine and looked around in confusion. It was hot out here. Not the take your breath away, you can't breathe kind of hot they got here in July and August, but it was in the mid to high eighties. They were hiking, she should be sweating—in fact, she had been up until a few minutes ago.

She looked back at Braedan. His pace was slow and measured. Her family was ahead of them on the trail. She thought with all of the training they did, he would have them at the front of the pack, leading the way. Not falling behind.

A wave of uneasiness washed over her and she looked around at the surrounding hills again. They were peaceful, beautiful. Wasn't nature supposed to help her relax?

She took a deep breath and exhaled slowly. Nope. Still felt

tense.

"Braedan?"

"Yes, *Love*?"

I feel strange. "Never mind." Not something she felt like explaining to him just now.

"We will rest up there." Braedan pointed to a large rock a short distance ahead where the trail opened up into a little sandy meadow set in the middle of tall, odd shaped rock formations.

She didn't feel like resting. In fact, she wanted to turn around and go home. Right now. Reaching the designated rock, she decided it would be a good time to suggest it. She looked over her shoulder at him, but his attention was on the rocks around him. Who could blame him? They were magnificent.

When she turned back around, the steel on the blade of the knife in front of her gleamed wickedly in the evening light, but it was nothing compared to the wild-eyed look of the man who held it not more than thirty feet in front of her.

"Braedan?" Miranda whispered and she scooted closer to his side.

"Do not worry, *Love*." His tone was casual and relaxed. He stepped slightly in front of her to protect her with his own body.

Miranda looked around her. The red sand and white hills on this particular trail were so beautiful and tranquil she never would've imagined something like this could happen out here.

"What is it you want?" Braedan sounded bored.

The man twisted the long jagged-edged knife as if ready to attack, but said nothing.

"We want your woman," said a new voice, making Miranda jump and turn to face the new threat that had materialized out of nowhere.

Braedan shifted until he stood in the middle of the two threats, watching both and forcing Miranda behind him still.

Miranda felt the power radiate off Braedan in waves only she could see. She took a deep fortifying breath and stretched out her hand to touch his back, the connection starting her own whirlwind of white. She was a warrior. Warrior's didn't cower and hide behind another.

"That's my girl," Braedan said, though he turned again to more fully protect her with his own body.

For once, she left her eyes open while she forced herself to concentrate on her center. This was the real thing. Whether these men were from the dark side or just hoodlums, the weapons they held were absolutely genuine. There were two men and only one of Braedan. She was needed to even the odds.

Make that three. Miranda let out a little squeak as a third man stepped out from behind the large rocks not more than fifteen feet in front of her. She shifted until she was back to back with Braedan and could watch two of them. Braedan would only be able to see two at a time, not all three. Her heart rate accelerated. She realized she truly was going to have to help. In the back of her mind, she knew Braedan could easily handle two, probably even three, if they weren't armed. But they all had knives and he couldn't possibly fight three at once.

The new man spoke. "Let her come with us and no one will get hurt."

Miranda swallowed and gathered the white closer around her and Braedan like a shield. "He's lying." She could see it in the darkness around the man.

"Yes, *Love*, he is. You will stay with me." There was a hard edge to his voice she had never heard before. It sent a chill up her spine, but helped her to relax—a little—because he was on her side.

The man in front of Miranda laughed. It was an ugly, evil sound. "Last chance, *White One*. If you want to live, you will join us now."

"Braedan?" Hoping they were just plain, old thugs, she kept sending small bursts of light toward the two men she could see. The shadows around the men repelled the light. That, combined with his offer of joining them, told her they were from the dark side, but she still needed to hear confirmation from Braedan.

"Yes, *Love*."

"Oh, great." Just what she needed. Half of her family were just ahead of them on the trail and should they wander back to check—chaperone—her and Braedan, they would be caught right in the middle of a small war.

"Yes, *Love*—" Braedan answered her unspoken thought—"I suggest we end this quickly."

She sighed. "Let's get this over with." To the two men within her vision, she said, "Fair warning, you leave now and no one gets hurt."

All three men chuckled. Without warning, the man closest to Miranda started forward with a lunge, the arm that held his knife extended.

Miranda centered and lifted her arm, sending a blast of energy at the man that hurtled him backward—with much more force than the jogger had received—and slammed him into the rocks he had appeared out of just moments ago.

Before the first man hit the ground the two remaining men attacked. Braedan sent the first one to reach them flying with a mighty kick to his chest and knocked the second to the ground with a chopping motion to the man's neck. These were moves Miranda had seen in action movies, but Braedan performed them faster, smoother, and with inhuman deadly force.

To Miranda's surprise, all three men rose quickly to their feet. The closest one to Braedan received a quick jab to his nose. Miranda guessed it broke from the sickening bone crunch she heared. Braedan continued with three powerful body shots that backed the man up.

Miranda watched the other two move forward. She reached deep inside and felt along the bond to Braedan, using his presence to increase her powers. Every day she spent with him she became stronger and more able to focus the energy. She inhaled and focused all her might, so she could accurately direct the discharges of energy and not harm Braedan in the process.

The white swirled around her with such force that it kicked up sand.

The men paused, watching her cautiously. "She is powerful," one said to the other.

"Buddy, you have no idea," she told them. "If I were you, I'd get, while the gettin' is good."

They grinned as if enjoying the fight and moved forward to attack.

She centered, and discharged the white at them with enough force to fling them through the air as if they were nothing more than pesky flies.

Braedan had incapacitated the first one and watched her handle the second two. She knew from his wary stance he would let her fight this battle unless one of them got too close to her, then he would step in and finish up.

Wanting to show Braedan how well she could do, she waited for the men to scramble to their feet again. Were they too stupid to know they couldn't win? She reached deep inside once more. She grew in power and felt a new hum of strength from the oddly shimmering smaller bond. Confused, but enticed by this additional force, Miranda drew from it. Her eyes widened as she felt the white around her shift to reflect this new change.

Every cell in her body tingled. She could hear the hum of power in her ears and felt the vibrations radiate deep from the core of her body.

"Easy, *Love,*" Braedan cautioned near her ear. "You have called on more power than is needed to win this battle." He put his hands on her shoulders and she felt the strange shimmering light filter into him as well. He was trying to help her disperse the excess energy.

The men had regained their feet and were staring in awe at Miranda. They started to edge away until, in unison, the three men turned to run.

"Oh, no you don't." Miranda spoke in a voice so serene it surprised even her. Using Braedan's touch to control the intensity, she sent the men enough light to threaten the darkness inside of them. They collapsed to the ground and with their hands gripping their heads they writhed in agony.

Braedan's voice had deepened with the exertion he was using to control the energy. "You cannot force them to accept the light."

Her voice, too, was low and beautifully modulated, even to her own ears. "They would have forced me to accept their darkness or die."

"We are different than they are. Better."

"I am simply infusing them with light."

"Against their will."

"Once the darkness is removed, they still have the option as to whether they remain with the light or return to the darkness. Their agency is intact. I doubt the dark side gave them as much of a choice when they recruited them."

"How do you know they were turned and not from the original one-third who chose the dark in the above?"

Miranda cocked her head to the side as she studied the men on the ground. "I could feel where the light was once inside of them."

Braedan was silent for a time as he worked to disperse the surplus power still flowing thick around them. When he spoke again, the words were softly spoken, but with an underlying steel to them. "I believe, *Love,* you have just changed the rules of the game."

Chapter Thirty-Eight

He made her a promise, and he was going to keep it. Braedan picked Miranda up and carried her around the bend in the trail, away from sight or sound of the dark ones struggling on the rocky ground.

He kept a tight rein on the shield he erected to contain the shimmering light. He was not assured that without her help he could restrain the white. This was more than he suspected even the White General had ever, in all his extended years, dealt with from a single student. Regardless, his pledge to her must be fulfilled.

Braedan slowly lowered Miranda down onto a rock until she was standing eye-level with him, but didn't release her. "I promised you I would continue to drain your power as we have always done, *Love,* and it does need draining."

Her eyes were still silvery from the white flowing through her and the soft laughter that tinkled on the warm evening breeze welcomed his kiss.

"Ah-hemm," Tracey cleared her throat loudly. "Oh, geeze. Figures this is why they made me come back to look for you."

Braedan smiled ending the kiss. His senses told him the white in the air was still tremendous, but he studied Miranda and knew she could control it. Of course, he would be by her side at all times and could certainly give her any additional help should she be in need of it.

He watched her eyes lose their glow before stepping to the side so she could see her sister.

"Are you guys coming, or what?" Tracey turned and marched back up the trail. They could see the bounce in her step and hear her whistling as she moved farther ahead of them. The white was contagious.

"Yes, we are," Miranda called to her retreating back.

Braedan grabbed Miranda's hand and helped her step down off the rock. He threaded his fingers through hers and together they followed Tracey.

"How do you feel?" He tried to keep his eyes locked on her face, but they drifted over her body anyway.

"I feel great." Her smile confirmed her statement.

"Yes, you do. However, I am referring to your stamina and not the way your body fits with mine. Are you feeling tired as the energy is draining away?"

"Oh." Her eyes widened, but the flirtatious look she gave him only made him want her more. "Not yet. Guess that could be a problem since we're on a hike, huh?"

Braedan squeezed her hand gently. "No. Should you get too tired, I will carry you."

Miranda rolled her eyes. "My brothers would love that. I'd never hear the end of it."

He chuckled.

Her voice dropped a purposeful octave. "Are they safe? My family?"

"Yes, *Love*."

"How did you know they were waiting to attack?"

"Could you not feel the men before they approached us?"

Miranda looked up at him. "You know, I did. I just didn't know what was making me feel so very uncomfortable."

"That is why we slowed and let your family move on ahead."

Miranda tossed her hair over her shoulder with a flick of her free hand. "So you knew there were three of them?"

"Yes."

"You weren't worried?"

"No."

"Are there any more of them?"

"Do you sense any more darkness?"

Her steps slowed as she concentrated. "No."

"You are correct."

She stopped. "I don't even sense the three we left behind."

"Search harder."

She stared back at him, her expression thoughtful. "They are changing. The darkness inside of them is almost erased."

He tugged her hand and they started walking again. "You did well. Extremely well."

The look in her big blue eyes as she stared up at him was enough to give him pause. His praise had pleased her. "Should we...move them? So no one will see them on the trail?"

"Not necessary, they are already leaving."

"Where will they go? Will they follow us?"

He almost wished they would. "No. They should go back and report. However, perhaps this time they will not return to the Dark General. It is conceivable that given the light now inside of them, they will choose their own path."

"Will it always be so easy?"

"No. Not always." He maneuvered her down some natural looking rock steps set in the trail. "Although, they don't always send so many for just one warrior."

"Hm, guess I should feel special," she said.

"They know you are exceptional. I believe they were just testing your strength tonight. The Arbiters will learn from this battle. Subsequent encounters will be more difficult."

"What do we do if they attack in public next time?"

"They, like us, find it easier to accomplish what we do if the general population does not know what's happening. The fallen rarely attack in public places. However, they do change the rules to suit their needs, so always be on the watch for them."

She nodded and the white particles nearby became livelier, as her emotions transferred to the energy.

The air was steadily clearing little by little, although the light gathered closest to the two of them was still thick and shimmery. The shield wouldn't be needed for much longer. "Miranda, *Love,* the white you called on tonight was different. How is this?"

She looked away. "What do you mean? How was it different?"

She knew. She was aware it was unlike the power she had used before. Why was she refusing to explain to him?

"It was stronger." She gave him a sidelong glance with her answer. "Isn't that what we've been training for?"

He guided her around a rather large rock on the trail before answering. "Yes. Your strength and control have greatly increased."

She tucked a few errant strands of hair behind her ear. "People come from all over the world to hike these trails. It's beautiful out here, isn't it?"

She was done discussing it. He had been right that first night in the restaurant. She was going to teach the teacher. Patience. He looked back down at her. The majestic red and white rocks and cliffs couldn't compare to the magnificent woman strolling next to him. "Yes, *Love,* it most certainly is."

Chapter Thirty-Nine

Her eyes were heavy. The drain had taken its toll.

"Here you go, honey." Miranda's mother handed her a heaping plate of food, then sat in the chair next to her.

"Mmmm. Thanks, Mom. I'm starved." Miranda straightened from her lounging position in the wicker rocking chair on the back porch and dug into the steaming plate of spaghetti, corn, and garlic bread.

"How many times have I told ya, Mom, forget the plate and just hand her the pot," Tyler said striding past her and loping down the steps into the tree shaded back yard to check out what Braedan was teaching their younger brothers about training.

"Shut up," she said, calling after him, but without any heat. It was a long standing family joke that skinny Miranda could out eat any of them. At least now she knew why.

"Sure is good to have you home." Her mother smiled. "Just not the same without all of you here to pick on one another."

Miranda paused with a forkful of spaghetti in front of her lips. "I haven't missed the teasing, but I have missed your cooking."

Her mother looked at her in concern. "Are you eating enough? You look thin."

Miranda rolled her eyes and the fork disappeared into her mouth. "Yes, Mom. Appetite is bigger than ever."

Her mother looked like she wanted to pick her up and cuddle her. "And you look so tired. Honey, are you getting enough sleep? That job of yours has you working nights. You need to get more sleep. You even have dark circles under your eyes."

Miranda wondered just how bad she looked. It had been a pretty powerful energy drain to diffuse the extra light she hadn't needed. "Gee thanks, Mom. You look great, too."

"Oh, Miranda, you know I didn't mean it like that. I'm just worried about you. Maybe you should move back home? I'm sure you could get your old job back at the grocery store and you wouldn't have to work late anymore."

Her dad stepped out onto the porch carrying his own plate of food just in time to hear her mother's last comment. "Come on, Susan. She's twenty. You have to let them have their own lives sometime." He sat on the opposite side of Miranda from her mother and looked at her closely. "Course, you can come back anytime you want to. We haven't let Eric touch your room in case you decide to come back."

The spaghetti was divine. She broke off a piece of the garlic bread and used it to swipe at the red sauce that was heavy with oregano. "Thanks, Mom and Dad."

"Hey, Dad," Brad called from across the yard. "Check this out!" He demonstrated a move he just learned that ended with his older brother lying flat on his back. "Cool, huh?"

Her dad stood and set his plate on the patio table. "Guess I'd better go see what they're up to, before they learn how to get the better of me. Susan, don't let Miranda eat my food!" he said with a wink before heading down the stairs.

"Good grief. You'd think I never left any food for them." A weary chuckle escaped her lips.

"I made extra, so go ahead and eat until you're full."

"Did I ever tell you, I love you?" Her mom was the greatest. If it wasn't for the war, she'd be tempted to come back.

Her mom smiled. "Yeah, you say that, right up until I make you do the dishes."

Miranda groaned.

"Hey, sis! Come on out here. Let's see if you've learned any of these moves from your new boyfriend." Eric was waving an arm at her.

Miranda sighed. She would dearly love to show them some of

the moves Braedan had been teaching her during their training. His sessions included physical exercise, defensive martial arts, and then, the dreaded mind control. But she was so tired she could barely chew. "Gonna have to kick your sister's butt another day. I'm too tired."

"Yeah, sure. You just don't want to get embarrassed in front of Braedan." He gave up and turned back to learn more.

If only he knew how often Braedan had seen—and heard—her at her worst. "Yep, that's it."

Her eyes were drawn back to Braedan's gorgeous body and she paused with the fork in front of her lips. The man was impressive. No matter how many times she looked at him, he always seemed to look better than the last.

She felt along the bond and he turned to smile at her. Her breath caught in her throat at the look in his eyes. Even from across the yard, she sensed his desire—not just the physical attraction, but his need to be with her. She placed the waiting forkful of food into her mouth and leaned back in her chair. Life just didn't get any better than this.

Strong, familiar, arms stole around her body. They lifted her into the air until she was cradled against a hard chest. Miranda's eye lids were too heavy to lift, so she snuggled in closer, her sleeping body knowing the man who held her was safe.

"Goodnight, *Love*."

And the warmth was gone, replaced by the soft bed now beneath her.

Throughout the night, she tossed and turned while dreams flitted through her mind.

She found herself standing alone in the middle of what seemed like a warm, shimmering snow storm. The white so thick, she couldn't see anything beyond it. It felt peaceful, comforting—as if she were being hugged by someone with great love for her. The light curled around her—the shimmers multifaceted and beautiful—then sporadic and agitated.

She felt the darkness creeping stealthily toward her through the white. The light resisted, but was steadily pushed back.

Miranda stepped backward with the white. Every fiber of her being wanted the light to stay thick around her. She moved away, the air before her churning thick and black. Mesmerized, she was unable to turn from the oncoming darkness.

The white was nearly gone and confusing jumbles of feelings—anger, horror, and despair—darted through her dream consciousness. The bleakness of the emotions so strong, she wanted to cry. She desperately tried to gather the last of the vanishing light around her, but it dimmed and the black overtook it, swallowing the last of the radiance.

The murky shadows hung all around her now. There was no way to avoid it. She stood helpless. The darkness crawled down her throat and choked off her air supply. She panicked and tried to summon the white back to her, but the dark was too strong. Again, she tried to step away, to run until she found the light, but dark tendrils snaked forward and wrapped around her legs and body, pulling her deeper still into their inky blackness.

She couldn't get away. She felt the darkness pushing the light out of her very core. The two sides battled within her causing agonizing pain.

Darkness obliterated the goodness inside of her and she felt the physical change of it. The light faded away, the pain easing, creating room for a new sensation. Her new energy craved more power. She reached out with her mind and drew more of the blackness to her, but still she hungered for more. The light in her soul was almost gone. Her powers increased approaching the point that a mortal body could no longer contain them. It was an ecstasy she had never experienced.

Through the darkness, she saw a strange white shimmer moving toward her. The shadows retreated and the darkness made way for the new comer. With each step he took, she felt her powers increasing. It was like a drug addiction—multiplied by one hundred. She laughed—a full throaty sound that reflected the growing power inside.

Miranda's eyes opened wide and she lay in her bed staring at her bedroom ceiling, her breathing labored, her body chilled. The darkness from her nightmare was gone. She missed it. Her body still hungered for the power she experienced in her dream. She must have called the darkness to her while she slept, because the white was dim and she could feel a small amount of power coming from the darkness in the shadows of her room. She desperately wanted to call it to her. She lay there trembling. The physical need for power fought with her ingrained goodness.

She didn't jump when her door opened. She knew he was coming.

Braedan crossed the room with silent steps and slipped into her small bed with her. He gathered her shaking body to his and held her while infusing his own light with hers.

His warmth and strength soon calmed her enough to call the light to herself. She relaxed her tense muscles and let the white soak into her body, pushing the last of the darkness away.

She lay against Braedan, his steady heartbeat in her ear comforted her, his strong arms tight around her. He must have sensed her need for peace, because he didn't question her. Still, the questions ran through her own mind. What had caused such a dream as this? Was she supposed to learn something from it? Or was the dark side simply trying to sway her to their side while her defenses were down?

She didn't know the answers. But something nagged at the edges of her memory. She had seen him. She closed her eyes and forced herself to remember. He was important. He was a major part of all of this. She was connected to him, but for the life of her, she couldn't recall the face from her dream.

Chapter Forty

"Food?"

"Shh." Braedan warned her with a grin she never saw. She wasn't even awake yet. "Yes, *Love*. I have breakfast for you."

He watched her shift and struggle to open her eyes.

"Food?" she asked again.

He opened the lid of the Styrofoam container and held it closer to her nose, letting the tempting aroma waft toward her.

Her eyes snapped open. "Food." She purred, energized into sitting up against the headboard and reaching for the square white box in his hands.

He watched her dig into the large, cheesy Denver Omelet he ordered from one of the town's few restaurants. Understanding her need for nourishment, he let her eat in silence. He opened another take-out box from the stack of four sitting on her nightstand. He took a bite and was surprised at how good it was. For a small town, the food was truly superb.

For the hundredth time, Braedan felt along the ties that bound them together. The white was fully restored. He stared at her while his mind tried to process what had happened to her last night. The Dark Side had tried to sway her through her dreams. This was unheard of. This was cheating on a whole new level.

He had felt her change in his sleep. He woke instantly, warrior instincts on alert, but there was no one to fight. When he felt her glory in the new powers, he sensed some of the darkness in himself too. It was difficult to push it away. The desire could compete with the highest addiction. He had to call on years of training to find the strength to push so much power and darkness away, not only from himself, but from her as well.

Miranda was on her second container before she even looked at him. "I think I love you." She shoveled a big bite of chicken fried steak into her mouth. "I've never been so hungry in my whole life."

She appeared none the worse for her late-night trauma. "She loves me for my ability to provide nourishment—" he said to no one in particular—"I guess that is acceptable." He shifted until he sat next to her, his back against the tall, oak colored, wooden headboard.

Her cheeks were already rosy from sleep, but they turned a darker shade at his words. Embarrassed or not, she didn't stop eating.

"After such an extreme energy drain as you experienced yesterday, I knew you would be more hungry than you would be able to explain to your family. So I took the liberty of sneaking out early and getting food so that you may be able to eat a normal amount at the breakfast table."

Her look of appreciation was enough to make him lean against the wood and take a deep breath. He looked at her from the corner of his eyes. She was once again totally absorbed in her food. No other human enjoyed the simple act of eating as much as she did. He was sure of it.

"What time is it?" She was polishing off the Eggs Benedict.

"Six-thirty. You may go back to sleep until your family wakes if you wish."

She paused in her eating—this was a good sign, her hunger was getting controlled—and looked at him. "How did you get the food so early? The restaurant doesn't even open until seven."

He shrugged. "It was a simple matter. I simply asked the cook as she exited her car if she could possibly do a special order for me. She complied."

"Yeah, I'll just bet *she* did," Miranda muttered, as she took another bite of the perfectly cooked eggs.

"You are not pleased to have the food?"

"Yes. Just that if I had asked a woman to do the same thing for me, she would of told me to come back when the door was opened. Must be nice to be so handsome that you can have anything you want."

He turned until he could look directly at her. "Anything?"

Seeing him, she stopped chewing.

"Will you give me anything I want? Because, *Love*, there are many things I want from you." He was pretty sure she quit breathing, so he lifted his free hand to stroke the skin of her neck exposed by the simple cotton t-shirt she wore. Her pulse was steady, if a little fast. He came close to losing her last night. This scared him more than any battle he had ever fought. How could he fight against something he couldn't even touch? He raised his hand to trace her jaw with his index finger, following the strong line up and tucking a strand of hair behind her ear.

Leaning forward, he kissed the corner of her mouth. While lying in bed with her, holding her while she slept, he had realized he would never be the same again if he lost her. "There are many, many, things I want from you, *Love*."

With wide eyes she swallowed hard.

It was time for him to make her realize she would not be the same without him either. "But I am afraid they will have to wait. I fear your family is waking and I do not wish for us to be interrupted."

That broke the spell. "Oh, crap!" She jumped from the bed, grabbed the empty cartons and turned in two complete circles before realizing she had nowhere to hide them.

Braedan stood as well. "Give them to me, *Love*."

She thrust the evidence at him.

He stepped close to her and as he took the empty boxes, he leaned forward and touched his lips to the sensitive spot in her neck.

A shiver wracked her.

He winked and left her standing in the middle of the room. He disappeared out her open bedroom window with the proof of their early morning tryst.

Chapter Forty-One

"So are you gonna marry the guy or what?" Shara demanded when Miranda stepped into the break room at work.

"What?" Her mind was still back in Overton on the great lunch shared with her family right before returning to Las Vegas to come to work.

"You took the man *home* to meet your family. That's serious stuff." Shara crossed her arms over her chest.

Then she shared a totally enjoyable ride home with Braedan. They hadn't discussed the dream. Which was good, because she didn't want to. Not yet. "Yeah, well, I would've taken you home instead, but you had other plans." Miranda kept her face straight.

"Ha-ha," Shara said, but Miranda saw her lips twitch. "So how serious is it?"

Miranda tossed her purse into her locker. She didn't know the answer to that particular question. "How did you even know he went with me?"

"I called Tracey."

"Oh, that is low."

Shara closed her own locker and waited for Miranda to finish with hers. "Hey, a girl's gotta do what a girl's gotta do when her best friend doesn't give her the low down."

"There's nothing to tell, or I would." Miranda walked toward the door. It was time to get ready for the Mother's Day dinner crowd.

"Ah-hem." Shara stopped her from leaving.

Miranda looked over her shoulder at the hold-up and Shara

pointed to the table. There sat a large vase of pastel flowers. Miranda wrinkled her brow. "Mine?

Shara nodded.

Miranda hesitated, then stepped forward. After inhaling the sweet scent, she opened the envelope. There was only one word. 'Unforgettable' was written neat and bold across the small white card.

"So, do I hear bells?" Shara prompted.

Miranda shook her head at the bouquet. "They aren't from him."

Shara whistled low and crossed her arms again. "Okay, spill it all."

She wished she could tell Shara everything. She desperately wanted to talk to someone. Until two years ago, she never kept secrets from Shara, but some things just couldn't be told.

Shara refused to budge. "Oh, no you don't. We've been friends for too long for you to shut me out now. I wanna know how serious this really is."

A male voice echoed her sentiment. "Yes, just how serious is it?" Andrade entered the room, his muscular body making the room seem much smaller.

Shara, who faced Miranda, pulled an exaggerated comical face at having been caught discussing men by the boss, before turning and replying, "Miranda was just about to tell me how serious a penalty it is to drive without your seatbelt in the state of Nevada." To Miranda, she said, "We'll definitely have to finish this discussion later. I do feel it's *very* important you tell me all about your *serious* driving skills." Shara grabbed her apron and gave Miranda a look that assured her they weren't done. She left the room.

Andrade raised one brow. He didn't appear to buy Shara's lame explanation.

"Hi." Miranda wondered just how much he had heard? The spot on the wall behind his shoulder seemed fascinating. Her hands were just hung there. Shouldn't she be doing something with them? Why wasn't he saying anything? She took a fortifying breath and snuck a peak.

"Hi." He had been waiting for her to make eye contact.

It took a huge strength of will not to look back at the spot on the wall.

"How was your visit to your family?" He leaned one muscled shoulder against the wall, blocking her view of the spot she so desperately wanted to look at again.

How had he known she went home? "Good." She cleared her throat. Should she say anything about his ditching her on their date and thank him for the flowers, or just try to resume the boss/employee relationship?

"I missed you while you were gone."

She swallowed. *Definitely the boss/employee relation-ship. Right?*

Miranda jumped as the back door slammed and two of the evening shifts servers entered the break room. Both Katherine and Stephanie smiled at Andrade and passed closer than necessary to him.

Andrade ignored their very existence, though he seemed irritated at the interruption. He straightened from the wall and his eyes sought out Miranda's for a few brief seconds, before he turned and left the room.

Miranda let out a pent up breath and realized her hands were shaking. The desire to call on the darkness for power was just at the edge of her mind. Why would the dream addiction come back while she was at work? Was this going to be a constant threat to overcome? Should she be finding some kind of an AA meeting to go to?

"I'm gonna get me some of that," Katherine vowed looking at the empty spot where Andrade had been standing.

Stephanie disagreed. "Get in line, honey."

Miranda rolled her eyes and headed for the door before she could get caught in the middle of the female showdown.

"How bout it, Miranda?" Katherine asked, her voice dripping with cattiness. "You gonna make a play for him, too?"

"Like she would have a chance," Stephanie responded cruelly.

Miranda was surprised at their rudeness, while she had never been more than a pleasant coworker to them; they had never shown open hostility to her. She funneled some white at them both and was surprised to see it hesitate before absorbing in.

"He's the boss. Probably we should all avoid getting involved with him if we want to keep our jobs," she suggested, then headed out to work before the women could say anything more.

It was going to be a long night.

"Miranda, can I see you in my office, please?" It was more of a command than a question and Andrade didn't wait for her answer before leaving.

"Uh-oh," Shara said under her breath from next to her. "Want me to wait?"

Miranda looked at the empty doorway where Andrade had stood, then closed her locker door. "No. Braedan's already outside. Would you mind telling him I'm gonna be a few more minutes?"

Shara grinned and tucked her purse strap onto her shoulder. "Wish I had your problems. Call me."

Miranda watched her leave and, gathering her courage, headed for the office. Her stomach had butterflies. She knew it was a bad idea to get involved with her boss, but technically, wasn't she already involved? For crying out loud, she kissed the guy. Twice.

She knocked softly.

"Come in," came the authoritive voice from the other side.

Miranda hesitated, then opened the door wide.

From across the small room, Andrade stood and walked around to the front of the desk, where he leaned casually against the edge and crossed his long legs. "Please, close the door."

She was tempted to close it...while remaining in the hallway. She wasn't positive she knew what the meaning of this meeting was about, but she was pretty sure she didn't want to find out.

Andrade smiled. "Please, come in first."

She could feel the heat in her cheeks. She stepped inside and closed the door.

He motioned for her to sit in one of the two chairs in front of the desk. It would put her very near him. She looked around the room as she walked forward to take a seat. Of course she had been in here before. This was John's office, too—although, John was nowhere to be seen at the moment. The room was comfortably furnished with dark, moderately expensive furniture. There was a desk, three chairs, one file cabinet, and two book shelves. A couple of paintings adorned the walls with a few official documents in frames above the desk. It was typical for an office. That's all there was to see, except for the gorgeous man waiting for her to look at him.

His voice was deep and pleasant. "How are you?"

Her eyes traveled up to his. "Good. Is this work related? Have I done something wrong?"

Andrade placed his hands deep into his pockets, assuming a very casual, nonthreatening, stance. "No. I apologize for speaking to you of private matters on business time, but I have an apology that needs to be extended and I didn't feel it could wait."

Miranda stared at him wide eyed. A man of his standing, requesting forgiveness? "Don't worry about it. Apology accepted." When he said nothing for a moment, she continued. "It's all good. Thanks for arranging the ride home for us. It was unnecessary, but thoughtful—"

"Miranda, I am sincere when I say that I am sorry for leaving you without explanation. It was hugely my loss. I wasn't feeling well and had to leave before I embarrassed myself in front of you. I would be honored if you'd give me the opportunity to make it up to you." He reached for an envelope sitting on his desk and offered it to her.

She stared at the envelope.

"Please." He extended it further.

She looked at the innocent cream colored envelope. It was embossed, expensive, yet simple. Somehow, she knew if she took it, life wouldn't be quite the same.

Her eyes lifted to his and she saw the sincerity—and the hope?—that proved beyond a doubt that it was imperative to him, she accept his offering. As she stared, debating, she could've sworn his eyes became darker just before haunting shadows flashed across them. His gaze burned into her and she saw the pain.

She blinked and both the shadows and pain were gone. She blinked again. She had *not* just imagined that. She stared hard at him, willing herself to see more than he was showing her. The air around him crystallized into the same strange shimmer she had seen and used when she was under attack in the Valley of Fire.

It was the same strange shimmer she saw in her nightmare last night. Why was she experiencing the different white now? In John's office?

"Miranda, please accept." His voice was low, sexy, compelling.

It felt as though he were extending much more than just an apology by way of an envelope. The image from her dream of the darkness parting to make room for the strange shimmering light jumped into her mind. She rubbed her eyes with her fingertips. When she opened them again, the shimmer was gone.

"The tickets are nonrefundable. Please?" he begged, with a boyish grin.

Still she hesitated. Braedan's face flashed through her mind. She thought of him with her family—teasing Tracey, teaching her brothers, complimenting her mother. If she thought hard about it, she could still feel his arms around her when he held her and infused his own energy into her last night when she needed him so desperately.

Andrade leaned forward and placed the elegant envelope in her hand. "Just look."

She shouldn't be going down this road with Andrade. Her head knew this, but some other source was drawing her toward him. With nervous fingers, she turned the envelope over and opened the flap. She slid two tickets out and had to read them twice to understand what they were. "A ball?"

"Yes, a charity ball. Will you join me?"

She read the tickets again and her jaw dropped. "I've heard of this ball. These are the $10,000.00 a plate tickets. Am I right?"

"Guilty," he said with an easy smile.

"I...I can't accept something like this." She couldn't imagine herself in a place like that. A $10,000.00 date for her ticket alone? Good grief. He should be taking a socialite or an actress, or a famous singer to a dinner like that, not a small-town nobody like her.

Andrade knelt on the carpet in front of her and looked her in the eye. "I have never been so rude to a date as I was by leaving you. The money goes to charity. The tickets are nonrefundable.

Please, please go with me and give me the opportunity to make a better impression on you?"

Miranda relaxed back into the chair, trying to put more distance between them. "I can't. I really can't."

"Why not?" His eyes regarded her, but didn't show the least bit of acceptance toward defeat.

"Because it's too much."

"Not if it's for a good cause."

"I...I wouldn't have anything to wear."

He gave her a lopsided grin and set a second envelope she hadn't noticed on top of her hands.

She was afraid to look inside. "What's in it?"

His eyes danced.

She reluctantly opened the envelope and withdrew an appointment card. "I have a prepaid appointment at the spa on Saturday?"

"Yes. Massage, hair, make-up, manicure. The works."

Her mind reeled. "I still wouldn't have anything to wear. I don't have the kind of income to buy the appropriate kind of clothing for an event like that."

He set a third envelope in her hand.

She looked cautiously inside. "We have an appointment for a dress fitting on Thursday?"

He nodded. "You don't work on Thursday. We shall shop to your heart's content, then eat."

"This is very kind of you, but I can't accept something like this."

His smile never faltered. "Yes, you can."

"You're my boss. It wouldn't be right."

"Miranda, I have never been just your boss. I promise you, it will be okay."

"Even if you weren't my boss, it wouldn't be right. It's just too much."

He looked deep into her eyes. "I have more money than I know what to do with. Please allow me to enjoy myself in the way that I wish to do so. For one night, you'll be the belle of the ball. If you choose to never see me again, at least you'll have one fantastic memory to tell to your grandchildren someday."

What a story that would be. "I'm not the kind of girl you should be dating." She thrust the envelopes toward his chest before she could change her mind. "You should find someone more of your social class. I'd only embarrass you. I'm sorry, but you'll have to ask someone else to go."

He looked at the envelopes, but made no move to take them. "Miranda, you are the one I want to take."

She shook her head. "I'm your employee."

He looked her straight in the eye. "If you're worried about your job, I would be happy to have my lawyers draw up a contract securing your job for as long as you want it. I have other investments and should our relationship not work out, I would absent myself from the *Cheri* so that you could work in peace."

She looked at the tickets again. A real Cinderella ball? "But it's for this Saturday."

"Yes, it is."

"I have to work." Kind of a lame excuse, but the last one she could come up with.

"You can easily be removed from Saturday's schedule. Paula requested a few extra hours due to a new orthodontic bill for her teenager and I would be happy to put her in your place for this one shift. You would be helping her out. What do you say? Can I have my driver pick you up Thursday at seven?"

She ran out of excuses. Andrade was determined to spend time with her and although Braedan was still kissing her, he never placed any kind of a claim on her. There was no reason she couldn't go to a real 'Cinderella ball' and create some great memories to tell her future descendants about. She looked up at Andrade, her mind forming the words to accept, and a strong feeling of unease settled over her.

Andrade stiffened. Had he felt her unease?

"Tell you what—" he stroked the corners of his mouth, the stiffness seeming to magically leave his body—"It's been a long night. You're tired. Accept the apology and the tickets, and if you should have second thoughts throughout the week, simply tell me and I'd be happy to convince you—again—to go with me."

She almost choked on a laugh. Probably would have, if she

didn't feel so apprehensive.

He rose to his feet. "How about letting me give you a ride home? It's late and everyone has left."

She jumped to her feet. Braedan had been waiting a long time. Maybe that was why she felt anxious? "Oh, no, that's okay. A friend is waiting for me."

Andrade's head tipped to the side, he seemed to be listening for something, or perhaps just thinking. "Let me walk you to the door then."

Miranda nodded and spun around toward the door. The unease was increasing and she didn't know why.

Andrade reached it before she did and paused with his hand on the knob. He seemed to be pondering something, then, apparently satisfied, opened the door and stepped out into the hallway, motioning her to precede him.

When they reached the back door, he opened this one for her as well. "Is that your friend waiting for you?" He inclined his chin toward Braedan who was striding across the parking lot toward them.

"Yes." She was uncertain how to introduce Braedan to Andrade.

Andrade looked preoccupied. "Have a wonderful night, Sweetheart," he said before closing the heavy door on her heels.

Just like that, he was gone. No awkward goodbye in front of Braedan. No uncomfortable declarations of affection. This was good. She didn't know what her relationship with Braedan was anymore, but somehow, she was pretty sure he wouldn't like her dating Andrade.

Her gaze traveled to Braedan. She walked toward him. Even without benefit of their bond, it was obvious he was very, very unhappy.

Chapter Forty-Two

"So the General became impatient, did he?" Andrade said to the empty hallway.

The lights were off in the kitchen, but one shadow detached itself from the rest. "If you were as great a warrior as you think you are, he would not have felt it necessary to send me," the deep voice taunted.

"Oh, but I am the best. That's why I am the most favored. You are a poor second, sent to speed things along." Andrade wanted to provoke Daimon into a fight. He needed to release some of the darkness building inside. The energy flowing through him was causing internal pain—and he hadn't even touched her today. Not once.

"We shall see. When this war is over, it will be interesting to see who is left standing by the General's side," Daimon sneered, and moved toward Andrade with the confident deadly swagger of a man who believed himself to have no equal.

Andrade held his ground waiting for the man to draw near enough to engage the fight. It was a show of dominance and control that he made Daimon come to him.

Andrade flexed his fingers. It would have been a simple matter to use their powers, but there was a sense of male pride in destroying another using only your fists. Also, much more satisfaction when your blood ran hot, as his did tonight.

"I hear this new power is not only strong, but very beautiful," Daimon said, taunting Andrade.

"If you are trying to provoke me, there is no need. I am

looking forward to this battle." The darkness inside Andrade pulsed, writhing, and demanding to be released. It was almost a separate entity from his mortal body—separated by the light. Andrade felt a feral grin split his lips and waited the few seconds it took Daimon to reach him. It was unfortunate for Daimon that he didn't know about the changes taking place inside of Andrade. The poor warrior who used to be nearly as powerful as himself, was now nothing more than a welcomed nuisance to release his savage irritation upon.

Chapter Forty-Three

"Get in the car, now." Braedan held the door for her.

Miranda took one look at his face and didn't argue.

They were almost to their apartment complex before he spoke again. "What happened at work?"

"What do you mean?"

"I felt darkness."

"You did?" Is that what made her feel so uncomfortable each time she talked with Andrade?

His nostrils flared and his jaw clentched. "Did you not feel it? The darkness was strong."

"I did feel it. I think." His eyes left the road, briefly, to give her a disbelieving look. "I'm not certain. I was distracted."

"Distracted by what?"

Open mouth, insert foot. "Work?"

He raised one thick brow.

"I don't know what to tell you. I did feel something. But I didn't see any Fallen Ones. No one attacked me. I thought it was just the situation making me uncomfortable."

"What situation?"

Insert other foot. "Um, I had a meeting."

"With the boss you dated?"

Not ready to recount her encounter with Andrade and resulting pending date, she went for distraction. "If you felt the darkness, why didn't you come rescue me?"

"I was on my way. I had just sensed the darkness when you exited the building." His eyes left the road again. "And are you going to go out again?"

Good grief. She hoped to have a day or two to figure out what to say. "I guess so."

"You are not certain?"

His eyes were on the road again and she pulled a face at the mess she was in. "I am, um, going to the benefit ball with him next Saturday."

He turned the corner to their apartment a little fast, and Miranda grabbed the seat to keep from sliding.

"This is why you had a meeting after work tonight?" His voice was low, but controlled.

His tone worried her, but not as much as the tires squealing into the last corner before he hit the brakes hard to come to a perfect stop in front of their building.

Braedan exited the car and opened her door. She looked up at him in trepidation. Just what was their relationship anyway?

Miranda squared her shoulders and left the relative safety of the car. As she stood, Braedan moved forward trapping her between his body and the car.

"Perhaps, *Love*, I have not made myself clear?"

He was very close. "Clear?" She always had a difficult time thinking when he was so near.

"Yes." He rested his hands on the car behind her blocking her more fully. He leaned in closer and stared at her, the gleam in his eyes made her heart flutter.

"We are bonded." He dipped his head until his lips rested next to her ear, giving her goosebumps. "Together. As no others have ever been connected before." He moved his mouth down an inch and breathed warm air on her neck.

Her breath caught in her throat.

"I experience what you feel." He touched his lips to her neck.

She turned her head to give him better access.

"We are meant to be together." His late-night whiskers rubbed against her sensitive skin. She moaned so low that he couldn't hear. She hoped.

"It is fated." His lips traced a path toward her mouth.

She shifted to meet him halfway.

A car door slammed and Miranda jumped, but Braedan didn't step back. "Have I made myself clear?"

Miranda looked past him to the couple walking up the sidewalk. "I, uh, yes. I think."

"You are not certain?" he inquired, leaning his body further into hers.

"Yes. Yes," she said. The couple passing them, turned their heads to watch.

Braedan smiled and ignoring the pair on the sidewalk, leaned in and gave her a kiss to rival all of the kisses he previously used to drain her energy.

Her knees went weak and her mind went blank. The passing couple no longer mattered.

His lips moved to the corner of hers. "If I am clear, there is no need for you to continue dating anyone else. Tomorrow night, we will go out together. Agreed?"

She would agree to anything if he would just kiss her again. "Yes."

Braedan's lips brushed hers again. "No training."

"Uh, huh," she murmured, trying to convince him to increase the pressure.

His tongue licked her top lip. "It will be a date. I wish to court you."

Her mind went blank as his lips traveled down her neck again. She couldn't think of a response, so she simply opened her mind to the emotions his words and touch created.

"We are destined for one another."

The fog his words and actions had created, lifted a little.

"You will cancel your date with your boss."

Yes. No. A $20,000.00 dollar date—nonrefundable—plus spa and dress costs. Two dates that would cost almost half of what she hoped to make this year. How could she possibly cancel? She couldn't. She wouldn't. Why? She looked at the need blazing in Braedan's eyes. *Because* he *desired* her. He'd said they were *meant* to be together. They were *fated*. They were *destined*. He never once said anything about love.

Chapter Forty-Four

Miranda was reserved. He had hoped that once he clarified his intentions toward her, she would've been happy. Instead, she insisted on keeping her date—some nonsense about the cost—and had gone to her apartment, closing the door in his face.

Perhaps she didn't feel the same connection that he did? How could she not?

He had spent the night training, trying to physically exhaust the confusion from his mind. All it had accomplished was to make his bad mood match hers.

"Boy, you two are a barrel of laughs today," Trenton muttered to Braedan. They surfed the internet to locate the closest trainers to Las Vegas. Miranda and Kelsy were visible through the doorway as they chatted in the kitchen. The four had trained together today, giving Kelsy the opportunity to see what potential she might possess. Who was to say that Miranda's strength couldn't be locked inside of them all and they just didn't know how to release it?

"Leave it alone," Braedan warned.

"Why? What's happened?"

Braedan had already filled Trenton in on all the happenings of the weekend, except the personal ones. He looked through the doorway at Miranda. Time with Kelsy had improved her mood, but not his. "None of your business."

"Have you decided yet if you want her for more than physical pleasure?"

Braedan glared at him.

"Look, big brother, I know you don't have problems attracting women. Especially short term. But when it comes to the real thing, you have to look at it from the woman's point of view. Females are very different from men. They're a whole other species. They don't think the same and sometimes you have to loosen up a little. Get romantic."

"She is dating her boss," he said in a growl.

Trenton looked at Miranda in the kitchen, then back at Braedan. "You're kidding?"

"No."

Trenton's serious gaze returned to Miranda and he smirked. "You have to fight for her. There is too much at stake."

More than Trenton knew. He wanted this woman, wanted her for much more than just physical pleasure. Wanted her enough to break his own personal rules. He wanted her enough that she could be used as a weapon against him if the Arbiters discovered his weakness. Yet, he didn't care, he wanted her anyway.

"What are you going to do?" Trenton asked.

Braedan willed her to look at him, and she did. The silent message he sent her, had her blushing and looking away. "I am going to a ball," he answered, his eyes never leaving the dark haired beauty.

"A what?" The confusion in his brother's voice was almost comical.

Braedan stared hard at Miranda. "I will do as you suggest and fight for her. I am going to play the part of a knight for her. I will follow the damsel to the ball and sweep her off her feet, I will protect her, and I will take care of everything for her. I will... leisurely romance...her, until she becomes mine."

"So, what's the deal with you two?" Kelsy snapped her gum.

Miranda looked across the corner of Braedan's kitchen table where they were seated and shrugged. No use pretending with Kelsy, the girl knew most of her secrets and had seen her and Braedan together. She just didn't *know* how to answer.

"Oh, come on. You both got the hots for each other, but you are like, miles apart. What's the problem?"

Kelsy had lost her belligerence since Trenton first brought her, but she was still outspoken. Miranda missed her the last few days. Even though they were a couple years apart in age, they had the potential of becoming great friends, so she tried to answer her honestly. "We are supposed to be together. So we are. Kind of."

Kelsy rolled her eyes and blew a bubble.

Miranda fumbled forward. "It's not right to be together just because we were 'preordained' to be, you know?"

Kelsy turned her head to check out the two men in the den behind her. She inhaled deeply and swallowed her gum. Turning back, she coughed a few times before she was able to respond. "Girl, you're not that much older than me. There is no way you can't see what I do. That man has got it bad for you—no predestined anything about it. Besides, a man like that, he doesn't do something just because he's supposed to. He *only* does it because he *wants* to. Know what I mean?"

Miranda's eyes were drawn to Braedan. He was watching her. It was such a long searing look that she could almost feel the heat sizzling in the air between them. His eyes held the promise of absolute pleasure and...devotion? She looked away.

"See?" Kelsy said.

Miranda didn't know if she did or not. Forcing herself to breathe deep and not hyperventilate, she tried to look objectively at her so called love life.

Braedan? Andrade? Did either of them really want her? Or were they both 'meant' to be with her?

She was hesitant to look inside and find out just what Andrade truly was to her. She had a sneaking suspicion who she might find on the other end of the second bond she was linked to. But she was afraid to find out. So she didn't.

Her head ached. She was tired. She didn't want a man who didn't truly want her, for herself, and not because they were supposed to be with her. Men like Braedan and Andrade, wouldn't want her for any other reason than they had no choice. Men like that were not for women like her.

She rubbed her temples and when she looked up at Kelsy, she changed the subject. "How are things with Trenton?"

Kelsy drummed her fingers on the table. She had intelligence in her young eyes, but wisdom as well, and let Miranda change the subject. "The man's an egomaniac and a tough slave driver, but he is feeding me and I have a warm bed to myself at night."

Miranda peered at Kelsy. It hadn't even been a full week, but the girl was changing. Her face was fuller, her eyes bright, her hair and skin had a healthy look to them. Her body seemed to have filled in, or possibly out, a tiny bit. Food, sleep, and lack of stress appeared to be very beneficial to Kelsy's appearance. "You look fantastic!"

Kelsy grinned shyly at the compliment. "You think so?"

Miranda smiled in return. "Oh, yeah. It's a wonder what good food can do for you, huh?"

Kelsy looked over her shoulder and then back at Miranda. "So if I'm looking so great, how come *he* doesn't notice it?"

Miranda looked at Trenton before answering. "I don't know how he could possibly miss it, especially since he's training you, but I think there's some kind of rule that they aren't supposed to get involved with their protégé. Kinda like at school with teachers and students."

"Doesn't seem to be stopping his big brother."

"I know, but—" Miranda paused, but decided to say it anyway—"don't you think Trenton's a little old for you?"

Kelsy's eyes took on a look way beyond her short years. "Could be. But you know, sometimes, I wonder if Trenton might be a little old for any of us."

Chapter Forty-Five

He had a plan. It was a great plan. But he couldn't implement it until Saturday, five and a half days from now. Three days he would have to share her with his competition—her boss. Two full days, he would have her to himself. Today was one of them.

"Come with me." He softened the order by extending his hand to her.

Miranda, sitting at the kitchen table with Kelsy, looked at her young friend and shrugged one shoulder before placing her hand in his.

As always the energy in the air was excited when they touched. He had to forcibly modulate it to keep it from growing too powerful. He looked forward to the time when they would be able to release it full force. He didn't doubt that day would be in the very near future. They were warriors and the Fallen would not rest until she showed them what she was truly capable of. With a grin, he pulled her to her feet, and not releasing her hand, tugged her through the house behind him until they reached his car in the garage.

Miranda looked back at the door leading into the house. "Where are we going? I'm hungry."

"Of course you are," he said as he held the car door for her. "Trust me."

They drove a few short minutes before he pulled into a rear parking lot of a restaurant and an attractive Italian woman wearing a chef's apron stepped out the back door holding a large white bag.

"Thanks. I owe you." He smiled, slipped money into the woman's hand and took the package that smelled of garlic and oregano.

"Yes, you do," the woman's voice was suggestive, even to his own ears.

Miranda stiffened beside him. Jealousy was a good sign. If she was in love with her boss, she wouldn't be envious of any female attention he received.

He placed the heavy, warm package onto Miranda's lap and pulled back into traffic. He heard her sniff. From the corner of his eye, he saw her reach toward the bag.

"No peeking."

She looked at him in disbelief.

"We will be there soon. Then you can eat."

Other than during training, he had never made her wait for food. Hopefully, it would heighten the anticipation. Of course, they ate immediately after their session, so she wouldn't suffer anything more than the temptation of it being so close, yet untouchable.

Two minutes later, he pulled into another parking lot, this time to a city park. "Ready?" he asked, climbing out his side of the car.

He opened her door, and she inquired, "Aren't we done training for the day?"

Her despondent attitude today worried him. This outing would be good for her. He took the package from her lap and grabbed her hand, helping her to stand. He then got a blanket from the trunk and motioned with his head for her to follow him.

One of the nice things about Vegas was the large number of outdoor recreational areas available. This particular park was lucky enough to have tall shade trees and lots of space. It was well populated for a Monday, but this he had anticipated.

He found a shady spot and spread the blanket. He sat down and motioned for her to do the same. Reaching into the large bag, he pulled steaming containers out and placed them on the blanket.

"Ooh, manicotti!" she said, joining him.

He was glad to see some animation come back into her spirit. From the bottom of the bag he extracted two plates and silverware. Instead of letting her dig in, he served her. The look of appreciation and anticipation in her eyes was worth the effort.

"Thank you," she said, taking her plate and waiting for him to serve himself before beginning.

Together they ate in silence, watching the varied people around them.

"This is excellent," she said. "But, why are we here?"

Braedan gave them both another large scoop from each container before answering. "Because the white energy is much stronger when we are in balance with nature. Every day we should leave the pavement and feel the energy from the earth herself."

"Makes sense. So we aren't here to train?"

One side of his lips lifted in a crooked smile. "No. But we should always be spreading the light wherever we go. Now that you can control it, we should begin our share of the battle."

He saw the distress on her face and knew she was thinking of the jogger. He couldn't stop the smile as he thought of him too. "Do not worry. You had control in the last battle." When she didn't relax, he continued. "This is the fun part. You get to make people feel good. You will also get pleasure from the joy you spread to others. I think you may enjoy it almost as much as you do food."

At his reference to food, she narrowed one eye.

"Think of it as a game." She was still giving him a skeptical look. "For instance, look at the young mother over there chasing her children and scolding them. Try to guess her story."

When Miranda just stared at him, he did it for her. "The woman has dark circles under her eyes and looks exhausted. I believe her to be a single mom, working the night-shift at an all-night convenience store. The neighbor sleeps on her couch so she doesn't have to pay a babysitter, which she can't afford. She works all night, and tries to be both a mother and a father during the day. The children are naughty because they are young and lack constant supervision. She has to catch a little sleep when she can. She loves them, would do anything for them, but can't get them to do as she instructs. This causes her to lose her temper with them and then feel frustrated for what she perceives as failing to be a good mother." He looked back at Miranda who was watching the woman in question with sympathy. "Do you not think it would be fun to take the darkness out of her day, even just for a little while? Wouldn't it be beautiful to see someone trying so hard in life to smile and laugh?"

She nodded. He felt the electricity in the air and the energy gathering around them. He smiled in approval. She carefully sent a small amount of the pure white to the agitated mother and to each of her children. It was accepted into them and before long they were all laughing and playing like the happy families you see in the movies.

"How do you feel?" he asked Miranda.

Her lips tipped into a true, genuine smile that lit her eyes. "Fantastic."

He pointed to a couple arguing on the sidewalk seventy feet away from them. "What do you think their story is?"

This time, she participated in his game. "She thinks he's cheating on her." She paused and studied the man. "I don't think he did, but he's been considering it with a girl from work." She tipped her head to the side and narrowed her eyes a little. "He loves her, but the other girl has been pushing and he is tempted. If something doesn't change, he's going to do it."

Again Braedan felt the change in the air. The arguing between the couple softened to discussion, the man's face became apologetic. Miranda sent a little more light and the couple smiled at each other.

"Care to play again?" Braedan asked her.

"Not yet," she said in a hushed voice, still watching the couple. The man embraced the woman and the woman's eyes filled with happy tears. The man bent his head and tenderly kissed the woman. Miranda sighed, turning to him, eyes sparkling. "Okay. Again."

Braedan pointed at two teenage boys who looked like they were about to break into a fist fight.

Miranda didn't even guess, just sent the white to the boys to prevent the brawl. The light bounced off them, without penetrating in. She sent a little more. It recoiled. The first boy made a fist and pulled his arm back. She sent a small blast that knocked the boy back a step, but not off his feet. Some of the light penetrated. The second boy followed the first boy's backward movement, so intent on beginning the fight he didn't notice the other boy's forced retreat. Miranda sent this boy a hard blast as well. Both teenagers appeared to be in some discomfort. Miranda watched them and said, "They both liked the same girl and she made her choice for one of them."

Braedan shrugged. "I would have guessed a drug deal gone bad, but female problems are plausible."

Miranda scowled at him, but not for long. The boys were in good health again and clapping each other on the back. They seemed to be the best of friends.

"Do you see the difference we can make?"

She nodded.

"Do you not feel the pleasure that pushing back the darkness in humanity can bring?"

Miranda smiled. "Yes."

"Does it still seem like work?"

She shook her head. "No," she said, sounding surprised.

"This is my favorite part." He observed the happy people near them.

She turned to face him. "Can you do that, too?"

"Yes."

Her eyes were wide. "Can all trainers do it?"

"Yes."

"Then what makes you trainers, rather than warriors?"

"Only a trainer can activate a protégé. Only a trainer can modulate someone else's energy. Trainers can only be born from one blood line. Warriors are born with the ability to fight because of the choices they made before they came to earth."

Her eyes sharpened at the new information. "The blood line? Your father and mother?"

Braedan nodded.

"So all trainers have the same powers as warriors?"

"Yes. In varying degrees."

"Why didn't you tell me this?" She leaned toward him from the waist, her body tense. "All this time, I thought I was the one powering the white, but it was you contributing that made me so strong." Her expression bordered between anger and bleakness. The tension left her body and she slumped. "There's nothing special about me."

He sought her hand and twined his fingers with hers. "It was you. Combined, we are a very powerful team, but as of yet, the only power I have contributed has been to modulate yours and to shield it. I have never added my power to your own. I think should we try to do so, before you learn full control, we may destroy the entire state of Nevada."

The anger left her expression.

"You are most definitely something special."

The bleakness left her expression.

"You are special not only to the war, but to me as well."

He could feel her probing his emotions through the bond. He could sense when she found he spoke the truth.

Her body calmed, she found comfort in this new knowledge. "But you can all drain energy from warriors?"

"Typically, this is only from the protégé predestined to work with the one trainer. We know that someone, a rogue trainer, has been activating students that do not belong to him."

"More than once, you've said you thought someone has been draining my power. Do you think this trainer has been draining power from me without me knowing it?"

"It is possible."

"Who?"

"I do not know yet. There is much about you that we must still learn. You are not as the others before you, therefore, there could simply be times when the power is so overloaded that your own body takes control and drains itself."

"Really? Do you believe this?"

He shrugged his powerful shoulders. "I do not see how it is possible a Fallen One could get close enough to you without you sensing their darkness and realizing they are draining your power. It would be much easier to protect you always if you would move in with me and train full time." Then he could protect her from her boss and from the darkness that was searching for her. He had not slept well last night, worrying she would be attacked through her dreams again.

She held up a hand. "Don't even go there. We've already been through this and it's not going to happen." When he started to speak again, she cut him off. "See that old man sitting on the bench over there?"

"The homeless man conversing with himself?"

"Yes. Let's see you tell his story and then send him some happiness." She was great at changing the subject when she didn't want to talk about something.

"All right." He would let her have her way, for now. "The man was married to a woman who had absolutely no faith in him. She constantly argued with him and never listened to him. He chose to be homeless rather than live with such a shrew. He is normally very happy with his chosen life, except when he allows himself to think of her, then he becomes nearly insane with anger and argues with her even though she is not there."

Miranda snorted.

Braedan ignored her and sent the light to him. The homeless man easily accepted the light and was soon off the bench, dancing a happy waltz to music only he could hear. The man was in complete peace with the world, at least, the world as he saw it.

Miranda laughed. "I like this game."

Braedan looked at the radiance shining from her beautiful face. "I have always enjoyed playing it, but I believe I find it much more enjoyable in your company."

Her long lashes veiled her expressive eyes as she looked down at their entwined fingers.

Using the hold he already had on her hand, he pulled her to him until he had her settled—sitting in front of him—her back to his chest. Resting his chin lightly on top of her head, his arms around her, their hands linked, he issued a challenge, "We shall take turns spreading the light. The one to come up with the most outrageous story...wins."

She laughed and relaxed into his embrace. "And what does the winner get?"

"You decide."

"Okay," she answered. "Loser has to make dinner!"

He chuckled and his arms tightened around her. "Figures."

Chapter Forty-Six

Andrade stood with his arms folded in front of his large glass window, watching the lights turn on in the city below him, one by one. This was his favorite time of day—when the darkness swept over the land. Tonight, he found it entertained him to see the lights turning on, trying to push the shadows away.

The Dark General's ring tone sounded and Andrade ignored it. He had never done so before, but tonight, he didn't wish to be disturbed just yet. He continued to stare at the lights and revel in the power flowing through him. His body had changed, morphed into something different than it had been one short week ago. Outwardly, he looked the same. Inside, he was nearly unrecognizable.

She had done this to him. Her light had melded with his dark. Neither side won the painful battle that raged for days. Back in control, the choice was his once again. He could go either way—light or dark.

He rubbed his jaw, the sound of his evening whisker growth bringing to mind the contrast of her silky soft skin. Was it worth it to give up all he had worked for? The power, wealth, respect, control? He would lose it all if he chose the girl and the light. If he chose the darkness, he would rein more powerful than any other save the General. He would have it all—everything...except for the girl. Now that her light was a part of him, he was no longer confident he could change her. There was too much good inside of her.

There was too much dark inside of him. What could the girl

possibly give him that was greater than the darkness offered? He could have many women—as many as he wanted—if he chose the path that came most natural to him. But none of the women got under his skin like Miranda did. No other would have the power to do so.

He ran his hand through his hair in agitation, the motion spiking his short cropped hair. He could have any other woman. Yet, she was the only one he wanted. She was the only one as powerful as he. He felt the anger building. She came at too high a price.

He turned from the window and with one sweep of his hand his couch flew across the room slamming against the opposite wall. He didn't even feel the slightest drain to his energy. He was more powerful now than any of the Dark General's warriors. With this new strength he *would* sway her to his side. He would turn the girl and request from the General that he receive her for his reward. He was no longer easily replaceable. He was a greater asset than ever before. The General would be a fool to deny him such a simple request.

Winning her over was the only option. The light had no true power and wealth to offer him. Changing to her light just for the added power would profit him nothing. The light General would never let him rule. He knew this personally. Besides, if he couldn't turn her, she wouldn't accept him once she discovered what he truly was. His sins were many. After all, he was the most favored warrior of the Dark General and this had come at a price…his eternal soul. No amount of white inside could wipe out his past.

His grin, reflecting on the window, wasn't pleasant. He would turn her. It was his destiny. He hadn't been born to merely exist in this world, he was born to conquer it. The two of them together could do just that.

His phone rang again. He let it ring four times before answering. "Yes, my General."

"Ahh, my favored warrior. How is your mission progressing?"

Andrade's smile felt almost savage. "It would progress faster if you would not send incompetent warriors to interfere."

"They were only meant to speed things along."

"It did not help."

"Daimon has not reported back in." The General didn't ask.

Andrade didn't tell. "Sending those with lesser skills will not convince the girl to change sides."

"I sense a difference in you. You are much stronger." Again, the General didn't inquire, simply stated, as he already knew the answer. "Your bond to this new power has caused your strength to grow. I believe the two of you combined will be unstoppable. Almost." The General didn't need to point out his power would still be greater. This was a given.

"You will continue with your assignment," the General ordered. "Bring her to me as soon as she consents. If she does not see it your way soon, bring her anyway. I will convince her myself."

The phone line went dead.

Andrade continued to watch the lights. The General irritated him. He let the calming effect of the lights take hold. The General admitted that Daimon was in fact sent by him. Andrade knew of her battle on Saturday when she had drawn power through him. Those fools had been sent by the General as well. How many others had the General sent or would he be sending? He heard the almost imperceptible excitement in the General's voice. The General was hoping to magnify his own strength using Miranda.

This would not happen. The bond he shared with her would not extend to the General. She was useless to the General, unless she was with him—her activator. And no one...*no one*...was going to touch what belonged to him.

Chapter Forty-Seven

"Wow, you called. I'm feelin' honored."

Miranda smiled. "Come on, Shara. Cut me some slack. Life's been crazy lately."

Shara's laughter came through the phone. "Wish I had your problems. Two gorgeous guys fighting over me."

"They aren't fighting."

"They will," Shara assured her. "Give it time."

Miranda shook her head even though she knew Shara couldn't see it. "No. No fighting."

Shara laughed harder. "Girl, you can't stop it. It's inevitable."

"Grrr. Men." Time for a subject change. "You still wanna come over and eat?"

"You mean, you don't have a date?"

Miranda pulled a face. "Not until nine."

She could hear the amusement in Shara's voice. "With which one?"

"Braedan."

"Ooh. I like him. Good choice," Shara said. "I'll be right over. I wanna hear everything before our time is up. Bye."

Miranda stood in the middle of her living room floor staring at her phone. What could she possibly tell Shara? She would have to figure out a way to avoid questions for three and a half hours. Gee, how fun.

The doorbell rang and she about jumped out of her skin. Was Shara sitting in the parking lot waiting for her call?

Miranda walked the few steps required to reach the door and

paused with her hand outstretched. It wasn't Shara on the other side of the door. She could feel the energy. It was white energy. But not Braedan. This one had the strange shimmer to it. She could feel the tug on the unexplained bond.

She shook her head and backed up two steps. If she opened the door, her fears would be confirmed. She would know who the person on the other end of the link was.

The bell rang again. If she was quiet, he wouldn't know she was there.

"Miranda, I know you are there. Open the door, *Sweetheart*."

The air froze in her lungs. It was *him*. She suspected it was, but didn't want it confirmed. Now what? Did she continue to pretend she didn't know about the tie they shared? Would he continue to pretend he wasn't a part of this war?

She gasped. It was the kiss. The incredible kiss they shared two years ago at Lake Mead. Andrade activated her with the kiss and the white sparkles began. Did he not know he was the one to activate her? Was he the rogue activator wreaking havoc on all the poor warriors? Or had the energy between them simply drawn him to her until he couldn't resist the kiss, not knowing what he was causing?

Her knees felt weak. She needed to sit down.

"Miranda, are you all right?"

Would he bust the door down if she didn't let him in?

"Miranda?"

She inched forward, unlocked, and opened the door. "Andrade," she said through lips that felt numb.

He looked like the warm sun after a cold winter's day. He was blond, healthy, and wholesome. He didn't look like some kind of dark demon. When he smiled at her, he looked like a sexy angel. How could this be?

"I was worried about you when you didn't answer." His concerned look encompassed her whole body. His gaze took on a new light as he did another inspection.

She felt self-conscious in her low cost, well worn, blue jeans and simple white tank top. She had only been expecting Shara, she wasn't dressed for the likes of him. His expensive, but casual clothing looked great on him, but out of place next to her.

"May I come in?"

"Oh, um, yes." She stepped back to allow him entry.

He walked into the middle of the room and lifted two sacks she hadn't even noticed he was carrying. "I should've called, but—" he gave her a boyish grin, "I was afraid if I gave you the opportunity, you might say no."

Still dazed, she just looked at him.

His grin turned into a smile that held great promise. He stepped forward and switched both bags to one hand, reaching past her to close the door with the other. His eyes never leaving hers, he touched her hair, just a light stroke down the silky length. "Have I told you how much I love your hair?"

She shook her head. There were no words in her brain at the given moment.

His hand rose up and he tipped her chin up with his index finger. "I missed you today."

She would definitely have to sit down.

His lips were very close to hers. "I hope I'm not interrupting your plans?"

Was he the good guy, or the bad guy?

The doorbell rang.

Miranda jumped and Andrade narrowly missed getting his nose bumped by her head. Energized into action, Miranda opened the door.

Shara's grin widened when she saw Andrade. "Thought you didn't have plans until later..." Too late, Shara realized her mistake.

Andrade turned to Miranda. "You have other commitments tonight?"

"Yes. Yes, I do." She sounded dimwitted even to her own ears. If her brain would only function. "I...uh, Shara..."

Andrade smiled. "Perhaps I can convince you to change your plans?"

Miranda looked at Shara's fallen face and shook her head.

He caved gracefully. "I will go, but first—" he held up the bags she had forgotten about— "I brought you a small gift."

She took the offered bags and looked inside. "Ohh, ice cream with toppings!"

"And movies," he pointed out. "There are three. Action, horror, and romance. Didn't know which you might be in the mood for tonight. But since you already have plans with Shara...I suppose I will have to wait my turn."

She didn't correct his assumption that Shara was the only one she had plans with tonight. "We have a date for Thursday."

His eyes were intense, but his smile light. "Thursday is too far away. Breakfast tomorrow?"

Miranda shook her head. She had training.

"Wednesday?"

It was on the tip of her tongue to say no, when she felt the swirl of energy around her. Her eyes widened—he was using her own light against her to influence her to say yes—that was cheating!

His grin said he knew, that she knew, what he was doing. "Please?"

Shara elbowed her in the ribs. "Tell the guy yes already before the ice cream melts."

Again, she couldn't. She shook her head.

"Perhaps it is a good thing our date has already been planned for Thursday," he said with a wink at Shara.

Shara shrugged. "She's a busy girl."

"Perhaps I am working her too hard? Not enough time for play?"

Shara grinned and looked at Miranda.

"Perhaps she just needs someone to show her how to play?" Andrade placed his hand on Miranda's back and guided her to the door where he leaned down and brushed a light kiss across her lips. "We will work on this problem. I'll see you at the *Cheri* tomorrow." To Shara, he smiled. "Have a good night, ladies."

Miranda stood and stared at the door for a long moment after he was gone. She could hear Shara's vocal appreciation of the different flavored ice creams and toppings as she dug through the bag, it wasn't until she said something about whip cream that Miranda snapped out of the daze she was in.

Whip cream, strawberry syrup, naked chests. Braedan. Oh crap, what was she doing?

"Cheer up, honey! We have enough sugar here to wipe out any bad mood." Shara chuckled at her own joke and reached into the sack containing movies. "We have just enough time for you to tell me all about your man problems, overindulge on expensive ice cream, and watch a movie before your date with Braedan. What a perfect night!"

A perfect nightmare was more like it. Andrade was from the dark side? He was a Fallen One? How could that be? She never sensed darkness from him like she did from the men who had attacked on the hike. He was good, he was light, he was happy. She was attracted to him. She wouldn't be attracted to evil. Would she?

And what about Braedan? She just spent one of the most enjoyable afternoons of her whole life with him. Even though he only said they were *destined* to be together, he certainly acted like he *wanted* to be with her today. She had a date with him in three hours. A date. Not training, but a date.

She was so confused.

Shara handed her a bowl of chunky chocolate-chip ice-cream, covered in strawberries and hot fudge, topped with fluffy whip cream. "Come on, honey." Shara added a cherry to the top of the white cream. "Let's go forget your sorrows in the traditional way."

Miranda sighed. Strawberries and whip cream were not going to help her forget anything. She looked at the sweet red syrup running down the side of the small mountain of frozen chocolate and an image of that same sticky syrup running down the muscled abs of her trainer flashed into her mind. Nope, not going to help at all.

Chapter Forty-Eight

"Stay with me," she pleaded to Shara.

Surprised laughter rang out. "What?"

Miranda looked at her friend. "I'm nervous," she said by way of explanation. She had butterflies in her stomach, and thought she was going to be sick.

"Girl, you've got it bad." Shara shook her head.

Miranda scowled. "No. It's just that, well, I don't want to tell him I have a date with Andrade on Thursday."

"So, don't tell him," Shara said.

"He'll find out. He lives next door." And, she continued to herself, he knows everything I do because we're either together, or he can spy on me through the bond.

"A little jealousy is a good thing. Let him see he's got competition, and girl, Andrade is competition even for the likes of Braedan." Shara grabbed her purse. "Besides, you look hot. He won't be able to resist you tonight. Forget about Thursday and enjoy tonight."

Miranda looked down at her clothes. She had no idea where they were going, or if they were going anywhere—he was supposed to cook dinner for her tonight—so she opted for casual. A nice blousy top with fashionably worn-out jeans and heeled boots. It didn't really matter what she wore. No amount of glamour was going to help her find peace at this time.

"At least wait until he gets here?" Miranda said, begging. It was bad enough to wait, but if she had to be alone with herself, she'd go crazy. Because then she might force herself to think about the bond with Andrade. She had done her best all through the movie to push those thoughts aside. Really, she tried. But her mind kept returning to the strange shimmer she saw. And felt.

She was afraid to explore it. She didn't want to encounter the awful pain she experienced last time she tried out at the reservoir. What could have possibly caused Andrade so much pain?

Braedan's knock was heavy and bold. She jumped and almost fell out of her chair.

Shara chuckled. "Relax. He's just a guy. If things don't work out with him, you've always got Andrade."

Miranda nodded, not believing a word she said. Braedan was not *just* a guy, and she didn't really have Andrade.

Shara shook her head at Miranda's strange behavior and answered the door. "Hi, Braedan. I was just leaving. Have a great night!"

Braedan entered the room and closed the door. "Are you ready, *Love*?"

"Yes." Miranda's voice was a little too loud for the quiet room and she jumped to her feet in the ensuing silence.

Braedan looked at her closely. "Is everything all right?"

Miranda swallowed and took a slow breath. "Of course. Everything is great. Why wouldn't it be? I wasn't really sure what to wear, because I didn't know where we were going. So, I opted to go with casual. Is it all right? I could change? Of course, we don't really have to go anywhere—"

"Miranda, *Love*, take a deep breath. You are rambling again." He stepped closer and raised a hand to her cheek. "Do I make you nervous tonight?"

She bit her lip and nodded. "I guess it's because we've never really been out on a date before. I mean, we've trained a lot, and spent a lot of time together, but this is different—"

"You are doing it again." He rubbed his thumb across her high cheekbone. His gaze dropped to her lips.

"I am sorry. It's a habit. I—"

His mouth cut off the rest of her words.

The kiss was gentle, lazy, sweet. No pressure. No groping. Just...romantic, and like all of the kisses she received from him, it was over too quickly, but it had done the trick. She was no longer a babbling idiot. She was speechless.

"We have dinner reservations. Shall we go?"

She nodded.

His hand slid from her cheek, down her arm, and enclosed her hand in his. There was a smile in his voice when he spoke again. "If only you had been this agreeable the first night we met, we would be much further along in our relationship."

The restaurant wasn't at all what Miranda had expected. It was a tiny old building, tucked between two much larger buildings until it was almost invisible. The small oriental woman who greeted them, in Chinese—which Braedan responded back to in her native tongue—was of an indeterminable age. She could have been forty or eighty. Miranda hoped she would age as gracefully as this woman.

Although Miranda couldn't understand the words, she knew the woman was happy to see Braedan and from the looks and smiles, the woman also flirted with him. Was there a woman alive immune to this man? Doubtful.

The hostess seated them near the back in a quiet, dark corner. There was a single candle in the center of the table which gave off a romantic glow and created a bubble just for her and Braedan. It was as if the rest of the world didn't exist.

"The Mandarin Chicken here is better than any I have ever tasted. I believe you would enjoy the Cashew Mushroom Chicken as well. The Beef and Broccoli would be an excellent choice also. What do you prefer?"

Miranda looked at the menu, it was written in Chinese. This was not an American restaurant, this was for the Orientals. "Any of the three sounds great."

Braedan spoke to the woman and she left with a dreamy smile.

"What did you order?" Miranda asked.

"All three. I believe we will not waste them."

Miranda fiddled with her napkin. "I didn't know you could speak Chinese."

"I can speak several languages. I have lived in many places."

Impressive. "What other languages can you speak?"

"A few."

Not helpful. "How many places have you lived?"

"Too many to count."

A warning bell went off in her head. "How many continents have you lived on?"

He looked slightly uncomfortable, but didn't shift his position. "At one time or another...all of them."

She swallowed. Hard. "Braedan, how old are you?"

The eyes that looked into hers briefly appeared as if they were older than the world itself. Not the man, but the knowledge and wisdom reflected in his gaze. "I am older than you."

"That's not what I asked."

He sighed. "This is not a subject a trainer is supposed to talk about. However, I believe I am much more than just your trainer, so I will share with you. Are you certain you wish to know?"

For a minute she was frightened. She knew she was about to find out something that would make her question life as she knew it. She had already discovered the white energy, and the quietly raging war. Did she really want to know anymore? "Yes."

"Trainers are direct descendants from one blood line—this you already know. Because of the amount of training involved to become a teacher to a warrior, and the lack of trainers available to the number of warriors, trainers age slower than normal humans."

"How much slower?"

His eyes bore into hers. "Much, much slower."

She cleared her throat. "Are you immortal?"

He smiled briefly. "No."

"Are we talking by tens or hundreds?"

His stare was steady. "The latter."

"Oh, my," she breathed. "How?"

"We can choose to pause the aging, slow it considerably, or let it run its course—to a certain point—and start over."

"Start...over?" she questioned, trying to still the frantic pace of her mind. Under the table, her hands twisted the cloth napkin into a wrinkled and knotted mess.

"Yes, we can choose to go back to our most powerful and healthy point at any time. We cannot go back further than that stage as it is our most productive."

"But you can age if you choose?"

He nodded once. "To a certain point. We are allowed to age to fit in with society, but it would not be productive to reach the point where our bodies can no longer function properly. The oldest trainer—physically—that I have encountered was near the age of fifty, but it was a very healthy fifty."

"Is that why you move around so much? So that people don't catch on to the fact that you aren't aging enough?"

"Yes."

Wow. "How can a trainer possibly have a family when you can't grow old with someone?"

"We do not. It is forbidden."

She was shocked. "That's harsh."

He shook his head. "No. We all understand the rules. To break the rule would only cause heart ache to both the man and the woman."

"Is that because the man would have to disappear before he got old?"

"Yes. Fifty appears to be the maximum amount of time we would have with a family. One could claim he is still aging past that time, but his body would not. This would only work for a few years, not indefinitely."

"Oh." What a very sad existence. "But, what happens if a trainer falls in love? You can't always control the heart."

"This has been known to happen. Then the rules are broken."

"Is there a punishment?"

Braedan relaxed and settled into his high-backed chair. "Yes. A trainer is stripped of his powers until the union with the mortal woman is over. Then the power is reinstated."

"That's it? No further punishment?"

Braedan picked up his chopsticks and fiddled with them. "This is a severe penalty for a trainer. For many years he has to watch as the darkness creeps across the earth and threatens his family. There is nothing he can do but watch and hope."

"That doesn't seem fair. What about agency?" she asked. She watched him play with his utensils. Braedan was not the kind to nervously move things around. Something was bothering him. What?

He was tapping the wooden chopstick, end to end, on the table top. "We all made our choices in the pre-existence. It was our choice to become trainers and continue to fight in the battle for the light. We knew the consequences and accepted them."

"Have you ever chosen to have a family?"

"No."

"You must have been so lonely." She felt sorrow for his loss of never experiencing such a precious gift as your own child. She hoped to someday be able to have a family of her own. Her gaze flew to his. He had said they were destined to be together. She gasped. She would never be able to have a family with him.

"It is not so bad," Braedan assured her, but he continued to tap the chopstick on the table top. "My family is very large. I have never felt incomplete or deprived of the opportunity for a family of my own." The chopstick came to a sudden halt. "Until now."

Chapter Forty-Nine

She understood. He could tell the exact moment when she caught on because she lost all color in her face when she did.

"Do not let it distress you." He placed his hand over hers. He allowed a little of the energy to swirl around them. She needed the comfort it would bring.

"How can you say that?" she whispered. "If we are truly destined to be together, it would be a disaster."

"No. It would not. I have spoken with my father of this. He believes we are meant to be together."

She looked at him in disbelief. "But we could never grow old together. We couldn't have a family together." Her eyes widened and she pulled her hand from his. "You would have to stop being a trainer."

"Miranda, *Love*, you have taught me more than anyone that the rules can bend and be changed." He reached for her hand again and when she tried to pull away, he linked his fingers with hers. "The General has sanctioned this union. Both he and I believe that perhaps things would be different for us."

He could see the wheels spinning in her head.

"The General...The *General* is your father?"

"Yes."

"Your *father* is the General?"

"Yes."

Her eyes were round. "Oh, wow. The leader of the light, *for all of mankind*, is your father."

He remained silent while she absorbed this information.

"Geeze. Talk about pressure."

He smiled. She could handle it.

"How could he agree to a union that is against the rules?" she wondered aloud.

"The Generals were each allowed to choose a wife who would then age as they did. They bore sons and daughters. The creator has a plan for us all. Perhaps the rule will extend to us."

"What makes you think we would be so special?"

"Because you are. It would not make sense to create a warrior who is powerful enough to change the course of the battle, to increase her strength with the combination of her trainer, only to shut it all down when they joined together."

Their food arrived and in the confusion of the dishes being set out on the table, he heard her whisper, "I don't know if I'm ready for this."

Through the bond that linked them so completely, he answered her, "Yes, *Love*, you are."

He was feeling more and more uneasy. Something was happening in the city. Braedan opened his senses and felt the shift in power taking place. It appeared his plans for the rest of the evening were going to change.

They ate in relative silence. He allowed her to process the new information. She was struggling to take it all in. He couldn't blame her. He couldn't even promise her if they continued what they were doing it wasn't going to hasten the downfall of mankind. But he didn't believe it would. His father would not sanction their union if it would destroy the world. His father had told him to open his heart and his mind to Miranda. He had said she could teach him much if he would just let her. He was willing to let her.

"This is very good." Her voice was quiet.

"I thought you might appreciate authentic Chinese cuisine. American Chinese is not the same as what the Orientals actually eat."

She chewed for a moment longer, before asking, "Can you feel it?"

"To what are you referring?"

She motioned around them with her chopsticks. "I can feel the balance shifting. Can you?"

He felt pride in her. She was becoming more sensitive to the light. "Yes."

"What do we do?"

"Would you care to help me set it straight?"

She thought about it for a minute. "We don't really have a choice do we?"

"Yes."

She frowned. "No. This is bad. I can feel it growing by the second. What's happened?"

He shrugged. "I do not know. But your analysis is correct. Are you ready to leave?"

She looked longingly at the unfinished food, but responded quickly. "Yes."

As they left the building, they could hear sirens in the distance. "It's spreading rapidly isn't it?" she asked him.

"Yes. We shall go to the heart of the darkness. Tonight, I believe that to be Fremont Street. We will walk down the center and push the darkness back. Are you with me?"

"Yes."

By the time they reached the strip, the darkness was thick in the air. They parked in a covered parking garage several blocks from Freemont Street and headed for the sidewalk.

Before leaving the shelter of the multilevel garage, they were accosted by a man holding a gun.

"Give me your wallet," the angry man demanded.

Miranda sent him a little of the white. It bounced off of him, nothing absorbed in. Before she could send a stronger blast, Braedan cautioned her. "No, should he experience pain, he might pull the trigger."

"Shut up and hand over your wallet," the man hissed.

"Okay, okay. I am going to reach into my back pocket and hand it to you," Braedan told the man and then did just as he requested.

With his wallet held in front of him, Braedan opened it and showed the man the thick wad of green inside the black leather.

The man lunged forward to grab it and Braedan unarmed the man in blur of motion. The man was unconscious before Miranda could even blink.

"*Now* you may force the light into him," Braedan said calmly.

"Whew. Okay." She proceeded to do just that.

They left the man lying on the ground and headed for the streets. There was anger and shouting, drinking and loud music, fighting and looting, people making out in all of the available corners.

"I understand the anger and drinking, but the kissing? How is that part of the darkness?" she asked Braedan. They walked along, leaving a trail of bent over people in their wake. The amount of light it was taking to push the darkness back was incredible. It was no test of their true power, but was causing actual physical pain to the bodies as the darkness fought to hang on.

Braedan looked at a couple in a doorway who was far past the point of simply making out and said sadly, "A union between a man and a woman in love is a beautiful thing—a gift of light. Sex for self-gratification only—is dark. It is a misuse of the procreational powers given to man. It is one of the Dark General's greatest tools."

Miranda nodded and continued walking down the center of the street. Further ahead of them, fights were breaking out, glass was shattering, and sirens were heard in the distance, but directly in front of them, to the sides of them, and behind them, there was the beginning of laughter and light. The darkness was being pushed back where it belonged.

Chapter Fifty

He was on a rampage. Through the ties that connected them, Andrade felt her desire for another man. The unsuspecting City of Sin was the perfect place to unload his anger, and so he did.

He simply walked the streets and left darkness and mayhem in his wake. In the not so distant past, to do this for any length of time would have been a severe drain on his power. This was no longer the case. He walked the most crowded streets in the city—reining destruction of vast magnitude—without receiving the sought for reprieve from his anger.

He tried to reach her through the bond, but she shut him out. He could feel her, but she wouldn't listen to him.

She desired him, she was bonded to him. How could she yearn for him and still want another man?

Enraged, Andrade sent a strong blast of darkness to a particularly happy couple walking down the street toward him. Before they passed by him, they were arguing. The woman turned her head and gave Andrade a long appraising look. Her husband said something about it and the woman slapped him. Andrade smiled when the man slapped her back.

He would find this man who caused her longing and destroy him. No one would touch what was his.

Like a pedestrian passing the scene of a terrible accident and not being able to look away, Andrade searched the bond again. The desire she experienced was gone, in its place, a huge burst of light. He felt the energy travel to him through the bond and the darkness enveloping him turned to the shimmery white light. Instead of spreading darkness through the streets, he was suddenly sharing the wholesome goodness of the light.

He stopped and looked around him. The people near him were smiling and laughing, not yelling and fighting. It was inconceivable. Through the link, his dormant light inside had been activated. He turned in a circle and surveyed the crowd. Unbelievable. The darkness was gone. He shook his head. He smiled, then laughed. Only one woman on earth could possibly do this to him, and he was not about to lose her to another man.

Chapter Fifty-One

Her body felt as if it weighed a thousand pounds. She didn't want to move. She wasn't sure she could move. Her bed felt like the softest, most comfortable place in all the world. Except... without opening her eyes, she felt the sheets with her fingers—it wasn't her bed. These sheets were satin and the ones on her bed were fleece.

She smelled the bacon and smiled in bliss. She was in Braedan's house and he was about to give her the life affirming gift of scrumptious food.

The bed dipped as he sat down next to her. With food nearby, she smiled.

"You are awake." It was not a question, it was a statement.

"Mmm," she said by way of confirmation.

"Then open your eyes and eat."

"Do I have to?"

She heard him chuckle. "Only if you want nourishment."

Her stomach growled.

"Whether you are ready or not, it appears your body needs it."

"Yes," she sighed and she forced her eyes to open. Food. This man knew the way to her heart.

There was a smile on his face. He fed her a bite of cantaloupe with his fingers.

She closed her eyes and chewed. If he would keep feeding her, she might possibly be able to eat and sleep at the same time.

A piece of sliced banana nudged her lips and she opened

them willingly. This was heaven.

She heard his low chuckle again. "Come on, *Love,* you must wake up before you eat."

She groaned. "Too tired." She tried to roll away, but the covers got in her way. She settled for pulling the extra pillow over her face.

She heard the sound of the plate being set on the nightstand next to the bed before the pillow lifted from her head. She couldn't even tense her muscles as he lifted her and scooted her over. He lay down next to her. He was warm and she snuggled in next to him. The last thing she was conscious of was the sound of his even breathing as he too went back to sleep.

This time the white stayed strong around her. Miranda was tempted by the darkness, but refused to let even a tiny tendril get near her. It was as if a glass wall separated the two—the light from the dark.

She watched the darkness part down the center. Shimmering white proceeded him.

His smile flashed white against the shadows and he held out his hand to her, the darkness clearing a path for him.

Andrade beckoned her to him, his golden looks, muscled body, and welcoming smile tempting her to join him.

Something tickled her nose. Miranda raised a heavy hand to swat at it. It didn't go away.

"Mph," she mumbled when it happened again.

"Good morning, *Love,*" came a deep rumble that started in the firm chest she lay on and ended somewhere above her head.

Her eyes snapped open and surveyed what stood in the line of her vision. Bare muscled chest, bedding that didn't belong on her bed, cream colored walls. She was in Braedan's bed with Braedan half way under her. When was she going to quit waking up in places she couldn't remember going to bed in?

"Morning," she mumbled, but continued to lie just where she was. She should move and put a decent space between herself and his naked chest, and she would. Just as soon as she felt like it. Which might be never.

"Did the dream return again last night?"

She just might feel like moving now. "Sort of."

He was waiting for her to clarify.

She knew this, but didn't know how to explain. Where should she start? How about, 'By the way, Braedan, my boss is a Fallen One and I am bonded with him.' Somehow, she didn't think this would go over well. "Uh, yeah, but this time I didn't let the dark push the white back."

"That's my girl." He tightened the arm that was wrapped around her, pulling her closer against his body.

My girl? Oh, wow. What would he call her if he knew what she was connected to?

"Hungry?"

"Always," she said with a sigh.

He chuckled. "Then I shall feed you. After you are fed, Trenton has brought four women and four trainers that need to be bonded together. Are you feeling up to it?"

She yawned. "Yeah." No rest for the wicked. Was she wicked if she was bonded to the dark side? Was that why she craved the darkness now that she experienced it once?

"Are you certain, *Love*?" She heard the concern in his voice.

She cleared her throat and tried for a more convincing tone of voice. "Yes." At least he couldn't see her face from this angle. Her eyes roamed over the muscled pecs and abs within her view. He was truly magnificent.

His hand rose and gently tipped her chin until her head left his warm chest and he could see her face. "This could wait until tonight when you are better rested."

She looked away from the tenderness in his eyes. "I have to work tonight."

"Do you not think it is time to quit your job and focus on saving the world?" His tone was patient.

She looked back at him. Would she save it, or destroy it? "I can't."

He sighed and released her chin, but made no effort to move away from her. "Call in sick."

She was so confused. She laid her head back down on his

comfortable body. She had helped to save the city last night. She easily—or had it only seemed easy because Braedan was with her and she had used his strength as well?—repelled the darkness in her dream last night. The white liked her. This all meant she was the good guy. Right?

According to Braedan, she was destined to be with him. But according to those same rules, would that mean since she was bonded to Andrade as well, she was destined to be with him, too?

She closed her eyes. "Maybe, I will."

How could she bond with two men?

One dark, one light. One determined to preserve the light, one set on destroying it.

Chapter Fifty-Two

"She has done well," Trenton congratulated Braedan leaning over his shoulder to better see the computer screen.

Braedan looked up from the computer, through the open doorway and into the kitchen, where Miranda and Kelsy fixed dinner. "Yes, she has."

"The bonds she formed are strong. She has saved lives today."

"Yes."

"So, why are you both so somber?"

Braedan ran a hand through his hair. He wished he knew the answer to that. Since he didn't, he ignored Trenton and went back to typing.

Trenton wasn't easily put off. "How did your day go yesterday?"

Braedan continued his search on the computer. "I already told you about the shift of darkness last night."

"So you did. I was referring to your time with Miranda. Things getting any better?"

Braedan abandoned the computer and leaned back in his chair. "I do not know. Sometimes, things are as they should be. Sometimes, she pulls away. I do not understand her reluctance to our union."

"Well, it's not a physical problem—that much is obvious. Which leaves emotional. Far be it for me to tell you what to do, big brother, but this is important, so listen up. Have you told her how you feel about her?"

"Of course." He fought the urge to fiddle with a pencil. This was not a conversation he cared to have.

"What, exactly, did you tell her?"

He looked at Miranda once more before answering. "I told her we were meant to be together, that we were destined for each other."

Trenton nodded. "Nice. Did you happen to mention love in there anywhere?"

Braedan scowled at him.

Trenton held up his hands. "Come on, bro. This might be the modern world, but that woman is a throw-back. She likes all the mushy stuff."

He was right. Braedan narrowed one eye. "How do you know?"

Trenton grinned. "This is me you're talking to. I know women."

Braedan couldn't argue with that.

Trenton shifted and sat on the edge of the desk. "Trust me on this. This woman needs romance like she needs air. This is not bad. In fact, it's great. You may find you enjoy it."

Braedan was quiet as he watched the woman in question from his chair. His mood lightened as he thought of her romance novels on her shelves. The strong men…and most importantly, the half-naked women who were so very appreciative of being rescued. Yes, as a matter of fact, his brother could be right, he just might enjoy it.

Chapter Fifty-Three

Miranda shoved her purse into her locker and shut the door. She looked around wondering if the other waitresses knew she had played hooky yesterday. Shara would. Guess it was just as well Shara had tonight off.

"Miranda? My office please."

She jumped and turned to the doorway, only to find it empty.

Seated at the table, Katherine looked her up and down in a condescending manner. "What could he possibly see in you?"

Miranda ignored the jibe and left the break room. She hesitated outside of Andrade's office door, but it opened. He was waiting.

"Come in," he said pleasantly. "I do hope you are feeling better."

She stepped inside and he closed the door behind her. Before she knew what was happening, Andrade grabbed her arm, spun her around and planted a heated kiss on her lips. It happened so fast, she wasn't really certain whether or not she had actively participated. It was the kind of kiss where it didn't really matter if she did or not, he was so passionate that her response wasn't necessary.

"Did you miss me yesterday?" he asked, when he released her. He backed her against the wall by the door during the kiss and although he was no longer touching her, his body stood even with hers and his hands were planted on the wall above her head. He was still very close.

"Um...I, uh, wasn't feeling well." She needed to read more from her romance library to learn some witty comebacks like the heroines in her books used, because her extent of clever conversation was limited to monosyllables.

"Did the soup help?"

She had ended up staying the night at Braedan's—in one of his guest rooms—after a fun, late night of cards with Braedan, Trenton, and Kelsy. When she returned home this afternoon, after training, she found a lovely basket in her doorway. Of course, the soup was no longer any good by then. "Yes, it did."

"I'm glad. I made it for you myself."

"You did?" she asked in surprise.

He grinned. "No. I hate to cook. But I did order the older cook here to make it for you. He seems skilled in the culinary arts."

"Chris. Yes, he's amazing."

Andrade wasn't interested in Chris. "Not as amazing as you are, *Sweetheart*."

His head started to lower, just as John opened the door. Miranda ducked under Andrade's arm and darted out the door. "Gotta get to work, see you both later," she called dashing down the hallway. She didn't breathe again until she was in the middle of the other servers bustling around in the serving station. Good grief, what was she going to do?

Several times during her shift, Miranda felt Andrade *and* Braedan checking on her through their bonds. This was such an invasion of her privacy. She blocked them as best as she could. She had no idea how successful this was. She had no way to monitor it other than their looks of frustration. Judging from that, it must be working.

She did her best to keep contact with both of them light and public. She had no idea how to handle the situation. She was a small town girl, her experience with the opposite sex, limited.

She needed help, to talk with Shara and get her advice—this wasn't an option. She needed to have her head examined—out of her budget. She needed to connect with nature and calm herself—this must wait until after work.

Miranda tucked a stray lock of hair back into her ponytail and totaled her evening's tickets. She would not be the last one out and left alone with Andrade again. She would be the first one out that back door. She needed to clear her head before she trained with Braedan in the morning and her date with Andrade tomorrow night.

She tucked her tips into her pocket—her income increasing with Braedan's heavy tipping—and hurried down the hall. She paused halfway down and realized she didn't know if John was alone in the office. She tentatively searched Andrade's link and knew he was in the room. She retreated from the bond before he sensed she was there. She waited until Katherine passed her in the hallway, then followed on her heels. Better not to be caught alone with him again.

As Katherine was doing her best to flirt with Andrade, who wasn't giving her the time of day, Miranda slipped her tickets on his desk and headed for the door.

"Miranda?"

The voice held a ring of authority and she stopped, but didn't turn around. "Yes?"

He didn't speak until she turned to look. When she did, Katherine, standing next to him gave her a frigid look. Miranda ignored her and focused on Andrade, hoping he wouldn't say anything Katherine would use later for gossip.

"Tomorrow."

"Yes?"

"I am looking forward to it," he said with a boyish grin.

She stared hard at him. He looked so damn wholesome. How could he possibly be evil?

Because evil cheats. The words hit her hard, almost as though someone had yelled them at her. But no one had. No one had said anything.

She nodded once and almost ran the rest of the way out of the room.

She kept up her brisk pace until she stood in front of the door to Braedan's car. She was so preoccupied, she hadn't noticed the single red rose he held out to her until he lifted it to her nose for her to smell.

"Oh." She blinked in surprise. There she went with that witty repertoire again. But Braedan giving her a flower? She took it and raised her eyes to his. His glittered in a way that warmed her chilled body. "Thank you."

His smile was slow, full of joy, absolutely sexy, and breathtaking. "You are welcome." He reached around her and opened her door.

This brought them close together and he placed a simple kiss on her cheek before stepping back so she could sit down.

She looked at the flower once she was seated. Roses. Weren't red roses supposed to represent love? One single red rose. Was he trying to tell her he was in love with her?

Chapter Fifty-Four

She was quiet the whole way home. She politely told him thank you, then shut her door behind her when she entered her apartment.

Perhaps she hadn't caught the significance of the color of the flower?

He was still uncertain why she had been shutting him out all day. He could feel her turmoil, but she wouldn't allow him in to see the reason why.

He took a deep breath and held it. He would be exercising for a long time tonight before he calmed enough to sleep. He exhaled and entered his own apartment to change clothes. He stripped out of his clothing and put on a pair of exercise pants when he felt her shield drop. She was going to meditate with nature.

He opened his door and leaned against the frame while he waited for her. He didn't have to wait long.

She wore a pair of dark sweat pants, a pink tank top, and running shoes when she stepped into the hall. Her hair was still pulled back and she looked young. Young and troubled.

She let out a soft, "Oh," when she saw him waiting for her.

"Lose the shoes," he instructed.

"But I'm going for a jog..."

"You will commune better with nature if you are barefoot."

She didn't argue further, simply kicked the shoes back in through the open door and closed it behind her before walking down the hallway.

"You don't have to come with me," she said.

"You are no longer afraid to go out into the city...at night?"

She looked at him sideways. "No."

"No normal human could harm you with the strength you now possess. But it would still be wise for us to travel together in case you should happen upon a Fallen One."

She stopped when she reached the outside door of the building. "Please, I need some time alone."

He searched her face. Her confusion remained so strong it was almost palpable. She did need time, but this he could not grant her. "I will simply be your bodyguard tonight. Lead the way."

She didn't even roll her eyes, just opened the door and jogged down the steps, across the parking lot and headed for the park he had first taken her to.

He followed behind her, his longer legs easily keeping up with her pace. Their training sessions had been thorough and she reached the park without slowing her speed. She jogged a short distance down the path until she reached a small grouping of trees. Here she detoured and reduced her speed to a brisk walk. She circled the stand of trees once, then went to the center and sat down, cross legged.

She looked at him before closing her eyes. He knew she did this to irritate him, but it didn't matter. He was not upset. He would happily watch over her and protect her. Always.

The run had helped eliminate a little of the extra energy she had amassed, but she was still in turmoil. She closed her eyes and did her best to block out Braedan. It was useless. He was so much a part of her now. Braedan feeding her, Braedan teaching her, Braedan as her center.

She reached down and felt the soft blades of grass. Summer had begun and although it was night, the ground was still warm. She let the smooth strands slide between her fingers, feeling their slippery texture. She inhaled, deep. She smelled the scent of recently cut grass, water, and the leaves of the trees. Nature. She could gain strength from it, but could she gain peace?

Yes. Already she could feel her body relaxing. Her mind clearing. As she calmed, she forced herself to bring her questions to the front.

Was Andrade evil?

If so, did her bond with him make her evil?

Was she destined to be with Braedan?

Would she be denied the ability to have a family if she chose to be part of this battle?

She focused back on the first question. Andrade looked wholesome, but looks could be deceiving. She never felt darkness in him, but he activated her without being her true trainer. This meant something, but what?

She was bonded to him. Did this make her a bad person? She thought of her parents, her family, the values they taught her growing up. She had always tried to be good.

She was becoming agitated again. She reached out with her spirit and felt nature's calming influence again. She would have to wait for these answers. Time would tell.

Was she destined to be with Braedan? She felt an extreme sense of peace wash over her. Nature liked this idea, but did she? He was such a part of her world, she honestly couldn't imagine life without him now.

If she chose to follow her destiny with Braedan, would she never be able to have a family? Would she never grow old with Braedan? Would she grow old and wrinkled, while he remained young and sexy?

Again, nature brought her peace. These were not things for her to worry about at this time.

With her mind cleared, she relaxed. More so than she had in days. As her body became one with the earth, one last thought entered her mind. If she was so uncertain of Andrade's side in this war, why had she never even thought to question Braedan's?

Chapter Fifty-Five

She waited until after training to inform Braedan of her date with Andrade tonight. As she expected, he wasn't pleased.

She looked through her closet with slumped shoulders. What did one wear to try on expensive dresses? Nothing she owned was high-priced enough for her to pass as a wealthy debutante.

She straightened her spine. Oh well, she warned him she wasn't his type of girl. She really shouldn't even be going, but how else was she going to understand the bond they shared if she didn't spend time with him? She closed her eyes, reached into the closet and pulled out a shirt. She opened her eyes. It was a white, sleeveless sweater with a scooped neck. It would be as good as anything else she owned. She paired it with distressed jeans and heels. She styled her hair down with an occasional spiral curl relieving the straightness. She turned in front of her long mirror in the bathroom. Not bad. Not rich, but not bad.

Andrade rang her bell at seven sharp. She answered the door and rather than invite him in, she hurried him down the hallway before Braedan could interfere. Andrade opened the door at the end of the hall for her and she felt Braedan watching her from his doorway. She didn't turn, she didn't want to see the expression on his face. She felt what he felt, and that was bad enough.

No limo tonight. Andrade held the door open for her to a top of the line sports car. It was sleek, luxurious, powerful. She was impressed. Its motor purred as they sped down the freeway.

"Where are we going?" Miranda asked.

He flashed a sexy, wicked smile. “It’s a surprise.”

She groaned. “Not another one of those. Okay, give me a hint.”

“Uh-uh. We’ll be there soon,” he said with a chuckle. “You are impatient aren’t you?”

“Sometimes.” Her eyes roamed the interior of the car. It was like nothing she had ever ridden in before. Digital gages, all the bells and whistles, comfortable in the extreme. She noticed they were effortlessly passing the other cars and she knew it was a good thing she couldn’t see the speedometer from her seat.

Before long, they were exiting the freeway and traveling down a road she was unfamiliar with. Andrade pulled the car up to the front of a classy looking building. A doorman came and opened her door.

Andrade escorted her inside where they were met by several sales women.

“Hello, Mr. Andrade.” The first woman appraised him brazenly. The second woman stood back, as though in awe.

Andrade smiled at the woman who spoke, but Miranda noticed it didn’t reach his eyes. “Hello. I need a dress for my lady to wear to the benefit ball on Saturday. One that will make all other women envious. Can you help us?”

“Of course.” The attractive woman gave Andrade one last lustful look before turning to Miranda. Her eyes skimmed Miranda’s slim figure. “Long or short?”

“Long,” Andrade replied without hesitation.

“Dark or light?”

Andrade looked at Miranda for this answer.

“Light?” Miranda responded.

Andrade studied her body almost clinically, making her feel odd. “Light pink. She favors it and it goes well with her coloring.”

“Yes, sir. Please follow me.” The woman made a motion with her hand and the second sales woman disappeared, presumably to find the specified dresses.

The sales lady led them to a private room with mirrors on all the walls, a comfortable couch, and a curtained off section for changing.

“Take those off.” The woman waved distastefully at the clothing Miranda wore.

Miranda assumed some women didn't mind changing in front of an audience, but she did, so she stepped behind the curtain and removed her outer clothing. As she stepped out of the jeans, the woman handed her a lightweight, pale pink, silky creation that didn't look like it had enough material to be a full length dress, let alone cover anything vital.

She shook her head and carefully pulled it on. The fabric slid sensuously down her body until it reached the floor where it pooled around her feet. She slipped her heels back on and the extra material on the floor disappeared. She looked down at herself. The mirrors were all out in the main room, so she couldn't see how the dress looked.

She stepped out from behind the curtain and looked at Andrade without a peek in the mirrors. He saw her instantly from his seated position on the couch. His nostrils flared and his lips curled in pure male appreciation.

"I believe it to be a perfect fit." The sales woman's words were almost unpleasant, but not quite. She was obviously warring between jealousy and the high commission she was sure to make if she pleased Andrade. "In fact, I believe the price of that one to be reduced to merely four thousand dollars because it's such a petite size, not many of our customers could fit into it."

"Leave us," Andrade said to the other woman, without even sparing her a glance. "Wait," he ordered. "We will take this one, but gather more for her to try. Now choose a variety of styles and colors." As he spoke, his eyes never left Miranda.

Miranda dared a glance in the mirror and her eyes widened at what she saw. The dress was divine. It was such a pale color, it was almost white. The light pink against her dark hair flattered her coloring. The fabric hid absolutely nothing—had she had any flab or cottage cheese to hide, it wouldn't have hidden it. It left one shoulder bare and draped snuggly down the rest of her body until it hit the top of her thighs where it flowed to the floor. The training sessions with Braedan must have worked miracles with her body if she could look good in a dress like this.

The message in Andrade's eyes said she looked more than good. Leaving his lounging position on the couch, he sauntered toward her. He moved with a lazy grace that was beautiful to behold.

"This is the dress you will wear."

"I ..." He was getting close. "It's too much."

"It is perfect." He stopped in front of her.

He was so close, she could smell his heavenly aftershave. She had to tip her head back to see his face. Did the man have no comprehension of personal space? He was definitely in hers. Question was…did she mind?

His hands gentle on her, stroked her bare arms. "I will be envied by all who attend the ball." There was a note of pride in his voice.

She looked into the mirror again. She looked good, even she had to admit it. But the only one people would envy would be her—because her date was so handsome and charismatic she would fade into the background. "It's too much money."

He trailed one finger down her bare arm. "The woman said it was on sale. Do not worry about cost." He turned his head. "We make a striking pair, you and I." He nodded toward their reflections. "Your darkness and my light are perfect compliments to each other."

She stared harder into the mirror. Was she dark inside? Was he light inside?

One of his palms slid up to rest on her bare shoulder and the other slid around to her back, anchoring her against him. "Do not analyze. Only enjoy the moment," He let the hand on her shoulder slide upward, tracing the curve of her neck.

She was tempted to. She felt along the bond that connected them. She could feel his desire, so why couldn't she feel his darkness?

"Perhaps, I am only what I appear to be," he whispered a mere breath away from her lips.

"Excuse me," the sales woman's voice said from the entrance of the room.

"Shoes. Stilettos," Andrade ordered without turning to acknowledge the interruption. Instead of backing away, he pulled her closer. The hand on her neck shifted to the back of her head and twisted in her hair until he tipped it to the perfect angle to slant his mouth across hers.

He was too much. Too much male perfection. Too much charisma. Too much authority. People jumped to do his bidding. She meekly followed his command, wherever he chose to lead.

He was skilled and she was attracted to him. She allowed the kiss to take place, knowing that it couldn't go far—they were in a public dressing room for crying out loud. The thought of being seen making out in public like the people on the street the other night was a little exciting. Wait—Miranda pushed back from the kiss. That was the power of the darkness trying to lure her in... wasn't it? Her eyes met his and searched for the answers she needed.

"We belong together. We both know it, *Sweetheart*. No use fighting it. It is destined." His voice rang with confidence.

"Here are your shoes, sir, and the other dresses you requested." The woman stood in the doorway, tapping her foot.

With one last look at Miranda, Andrade released her. "Let the fun begin," he said with a rakish smile.

The next two hours were spent trying on the most amazing outfits. Miranda oohed and laughed at the beautiful and exotic clothing. Andrade was a patient and appreciative audience. Miranda did her best to enjoy the moment and tried to forget about what destiny had planned for her.

In the end, she ended up with the pink gown and fantastic shoes to go with it. Andrade had tried to buy her several more outfits that looked amazing on her, but she adamantly refused. The cost was outrageous.

"They will deliver your packages tomorrow morning to your address," Andrade informed her. He joined her near the door where she waited. "Are you ready to eat?"

She chuckled, her mood light. "Oh, yeah."

He grinned back and walked her to his car. "Then we shall feed you. Your chariot awaits you, my lady."

He took her to a restaurant that rivaled the *Cheri*. She noticed he was well known here. The discreet nods and hello's from the occupants showed their enthusiasm and respect for him.

The food was superb and even though she recognized he

was using the white to keep their moods light, she still relaxed and enjoyed herself. Long after dessert was served, they sat and talked. Of course, neither one mentioned the bond, or the war.

Before she knew it, it was midnight. "My, how time flies." She stiffled a yawn. "I think I should ask you to take me home now."

Andrade's eyes probed hers, his look turning sensual and carnal. "Would you care to come back to my place for a nightcap?"

She couldn't help the shiver that ran down her spine. She knew exactly what he was asking and didn't want to examine whether she wanted to go with him or feared what would become of her if she did. She shook her head. "No. I have to get up early tomorrow. I'd better go home."

"Of course," he complied, but his expression promised that one day soon she would be giving him a different answer. She would become his in every sense of the word.

Miranda knew Braedan was nearby when she felt along their bond, but she didn't expect him to be in her apartment.

When she reached for her door to insert the key, it opened on its own, revealing a shirtless Braedan standing in her doorway. "Braedan," she said in surprise.

She watched him size up Andrade, who stood behind her. She hadn't planned on inviting Andrade inside, but now that really wasn't an option, because it didn't look like Braedan was planning on leaving any time soon.

She shrugged. Oh, well. "Braedan, this is my boss Andrade. Andrade, this is my neighbor Braedan."

The men continued to assess each other, shaking hands.

"Braedan," she asked with the lift of a single brow, "why are you in my apartment?"

"And without your clothing?" Andrade added to her question. The dislike in his voice was chilling.

Braedan smiled. Andrade's irritation seemed to lighten his mood. "I had been exercising and worked up an appetite. I realized I was out of eggs, so I came to borrow some from you."

"How did you get inside?" Andrade probed.

"Key," Braedan said smugly.

Miranda rolled her eyes. "Okay, glad we got that all lined out. It's time for me to go to bed, so good night you two."

They ignored her.

"How did you get a key?" Andrade asked, his expression dark.

"He's my neighbor," Miranda interrupted, not certain what the arrogant look on Braedan's face would lead him to say.

Braedan continued with his grin, looking, for all the world, like he was perfectly at home in her house—which he was. "You know how it is, neighbors being friendly and all. Right, Andy?"

Andrade folded his arms across his chest. "If you have gotten your eggs, perhaps it is time for you to leave."

Braedan leaned against the doorjamb. "Not ready to go just yet."

Miranda slipped past Braedan's bulky frame and attempted to push him forward out of the way of the door she wished to close. "I think it would be a good idea for both of you to leave — now." Braedan didn't budge. Neither did Andrade.

The men stood there appraising each other. They were both very much aware the other was his competition for Miranda and, by their exoressions, neither liked what he saw.

The energy in the air grew shift. Miranda could feel the desire to absorb the new troubled energy into her. She clenched her hands on the door and sent both men a blast of light through the shared bonds. "You will both leave now. You will go to your own homes and leave me alone for the rest of the night."

They both stared at her as if they might argue and she sent another jolt of light through the ties. She didn't know if the infusion of white would work, but they both nodded in agreement and she stood in her doorway until they both left her sight—Braedan to his apartment and Andrade left the building.

She rubbed her temples. She was too tired to deal with fighting men tonight. In fact, she thought she might be too tired to ever deal with problems like that.

Chapter Fifty-Six

"Oooh, that feels soo good," Miranda murmured. The soothing hands of the massage therapist worked their magic on all of her knotted muscles. She groaned and relaxed like an ice-cube melting into the massage table. The stress of the last few days became a thing of the past.

Yesterday was pretty much a blur. Braedan made her an incredible breakfast of rainbow trout and fried potatoes. Halfway through, her packages arrived from the dress store—including the two she had declined. She left them all packed, not wanting to take the dress out while Braedan watched. He ignored her delivery and was playful and fun right up until forcing her to train for three straight hours. Then the real work began. Trenton arrived with two more women who needed bonding to their trainers.

The bonding process went smoothly and then she went to work at the Cheri. She did her best to keep from being caught in a situation where she would be alone with Andrade, and he told her in the hallway he was aware she was avoiding him, but chuckled and told her it wouldn't do any good. They were meant for each other and she couldn't change that.

After work, she lit candles and soaked in her tub while she reread her favorite parts of the romance novel where the knight in shining armor rushed in and saved the poor woman just in the nick of time. The knight was the woman's savior—her hero. Every woman needed a hero. So why was she destined to be the hero in her own life—the one to rescue mankind? Life was so unfair.

The massage therapist was done. She felt so relaxed she could hardly move. Thoughts leading up to this moment were no longer weighing on her conscience. She was relaxed and determined to stay that way. She was going to enjoy her once-in-a-life-time opportunity to be pampered.

Spa workers appeared out of nowhere and wrapped her in a big fluffy robe. They guided her to the waiting make-up artist. ithout a word, the woman applied a red mud mask to Miranda's skin. It made her skin feel smooth and tingly—energized. Was it from the mask itself, or because it was mud—a piece of nature? Didn't matter, she was gonna hit Target first chance she got and buy some.

When the mud was gone, the still silent woman applied make-up without the benefit of mirrors. After fifteen minutes of working in silence, and not allowing Miranda to speak – the woman took a single step back to assess her skill. She viewed Miranda from every angle. It took a concentrated effort not to fidget under her scrutiny.

"Magnificent," the woman said—her one and only spoken word—and once again the workers magically appeared and guided Miranda down the wide hallway to the hairstylist. The stylist might have looked a little strange to her with the gages in his ears and his tight pants, but he was awesome with his hands. He swept her hair up and piled it high, leaving long curling tendrils that would hang over her bare shoulder and down her back.

After forty-five minutes of listening to the man speak only to himself while he worked, Miranda jumped when his face appeared just inches from her own. "Stunning!"

Miranda accepted the hand he held out for her.

He pulled her to her feet, spun her to face the mirror and said with flourish, "Wah-lah!"

Miranda stared at the woman in the mirror. It was her, yet it was not. This woman was elegance, grace, and power all rolled into one. This woman was not a small town nobody playing Cinderella for an evening. This was…the Queen. The woman who already had control. This was the kind of woman that make-up artists and stylists bowed down to and did not chit-chat with while working. She grinned. Tonight she was going to the ball—as a woman who belonged there—and she was going to enjoy every second of it.

She couldn't help but be disappointed when Braedan didn't show up to give her his usual pre-date warnings… Some small part of her hoped he would see her in all her finery. In fact, she hadn't seen him since this morning when she told him she wasn't training today. She had been training seven days a week and she wanted a break. She tried to soften the blow by promising double hours tomorrow since she was off on Sunday.

She gave a mental shrug and focused on the curving staircase that led down to the ballroom with its many chandeliers. The wide stairs made for a grand entrance for each of the elite guests whose names were announced at the top of the stairs. As beautiful as it all seemed, stairs and stilettos were always a bad combination and she did *not* want to tumble down them.

Andrade appeared at her side with his elbow out for her to take, looking spectacular in his black tux and pale pink bow tie. They looked good together.

"The spa did an excellent job. You look amazing." His eyes were a constant reminder of his appreciation. The obvious desire burning from them made her lightheaded with the power she had over this man. Having his full awareness focused on her was rather exhilarating, when there were so many beautiful women at the ball to draw his attention.

Andrade leaned close to speak directly into her ear when they reached the end of the stairs. "This is a social hour, then dinner, followed by an auction of jewelry from Tiffany's, then dancing."

"Hmm. Thank you," she replied, grateful to understand how the evening should progress.

His lips were very near her exposed ear. "Everyone is watching you, wishing they could be you. You look gorgeous. Sexy. Powerful." He ended the statement with a light kiss to the tip of her ear.

She shivered at the sensation of his warm breath on her sensitive skin and wished she felt as confident as he thought she was.

"I will purchase you anything you please from the auction." He held up his hand before she could refuse. "It is for charity," he said with a smile.

They wandered through the crowd, Andrade stopping occasionally to introduce her to prominent citizens in the community and a few famous celebrities. He had an impressive collection of friends.

Somehow she managed to make all of the appropriate responses and people appeared to accept her—she knew it was because she walked holding onto Andrade's arm and no one questioned him. They had no idea she was a lowly waitress from a restaurant he owned.

With a slight tightening of his hand on her waist, Andrade whispered in her ear as they left the circle conversing with the judge and his wife. "Keep your head high and look down on them. Don't ever let them make you feel inferior. You have more power than any of them."

She looked up at Andrade. Was he going to pick *now* to discuss their positions in this war? After all this time of pretending it didn't exist, was he going to bring it up now?

She searched his expression with his lips turning up, and then he froze mid-smile and she felt him stiffen imperceptibly. She too, was surprised to feel the wave of darkness sweeping through the crowd.

She felt the anger radiating off of Andrade. "Here? Now?" he said through clenched teeth.

"What is it?" she whispered, afraid she already knew the answer.

Andrade looked down at her. "Sorry, *Sweetheart*. We are about to have company of an unwelcome sort."

Miranda looked around with wide eyes. "Around all these people? I thought the dark side didn't attack in public?"

Andrade shrugged. "The Dark General does whatever he pleases, whenever and wherever he pleases."

"How do you know this?" The darkness she sensed was strong. She needed to know his position before this battle began.

He looked down at her, his eyes fierce with the excitement of the impending fight, but he remained silent.

She pulled at her arm on his sleeve, but he covered her hand with his own, keeping it in place.

"Miranda," he waited until she met his gaze, "I am on *your* side. We are a team."

She breathed a small sigh of relief. The darkness invading the room was formidable; she had no desire to fight it alone. Why hadn't she listened to Braedan and stayed home? She had no business being in a place like this. She didn't belong. Now she would have to pay the consequences.

Andrade tightened his hold on her arm. "We need to leave. Come with me."

"Leave?" she said. They casually threaded their way back through the throng of people. She looked at the guests they passed. These people were no match for the evil she could feel radiating from all sides of the building. "Where to?"

"Outside. Now. That or there will be many people witnessing the battle about to take place. This does not worry me overly, but with the prominent people in attendance tonight, it would be hard to negate the stories that would spread throughout the country."

People would know she was different. Innocent bystanders could get hurt. She quickened her steps.

They reached the side door and exited the building. Andrade pulled her along behind him until they reached the back of the large building. Miranda looked around and saw that this area was better than she could have hoped for if she had to do battle in public. There were only a few windows overlooking their battlefield. She stood on a large lawn surrounded by trees and a solid fence that provide visual shelter from passersby.

Andrade pulled her into the center of the lawn—difficult to walk in the grass with spiked heels sinking deeper with every step. He held her hand and stood proud and tall waiting for the fight to come to him.

Wanting to at least appear as confident as he did, Miranda took a deep, calming breath to steady her nerves. It didn't help. Her gaze swept the area again. The moon was not yet lighting the earth with its glow so the back lawn lay in darkness. Should anyone from the ball look outside, they wouldn't see much more than a few dark shadows. The white in the air was enough to allow her to see all she needed to.

"Do not worry, these minions are nothing compared to the power we wield together."

Miranda wished she had his confidence. She slanted him a quick look, but didn't dare look away from her surroundings for long. The warriors were here, she just couldn't see them yet. "How do you know this?"

His smile was somewhat cold. He was already in battle mode. "Miranda," he said, "we have fought together before, using only the bond we share. We are much stronger when physically together, like we are now. There is nothing to fear."

"What do you know of the bond between us?" Maybe now was not the best time to bring it up, but she needed to know.

"I am your activator. We are bonded together. We were meant for each other." His voice radiated his absolute belief in this fact.

Miranda shook her head. "I don't understand. Are you the one activating all of the women and leaving them without a trainer?"

Andrade sidestepped the question. "I am *your* trainer, Miranda. We are meant to be."

He was the one. *He* was the rogue activator. What else was he?

She didn't have time to question him further. The darkness became oppressive. Miranda gathered the light around her to keep the darkness from getting too close. The craving for dark power was returning. She pushed it back with her light and focused on gathering more. She was not going to give in to the darkness this time.

Andrade looked down at her and his beautifully sculpted lips curled in a cruel smile. All traces of the all-American-boy disappeared. The man before her transformed into a frightening warrior. She was glad he was on her side. At least, she hoped he was.

The first of the warriors shifted from the shadows around them. Like the men who had attacked her in the Valley of Fire, they looked wicked and deadly.

Miranda searched inward for the strength she gleaned from Andrade's unusual shimmery light. She gathered it around her and waited for someone to make the first move.

"This one is very beautiful. No wonder you wanted her for yourself," the dark one closest to them commented to Andrade. "Was she worth incurring the General's displeasure?"

Andrade looked at the warrior in disdain and ignored his question. He stepped toward the man and three more warriors materialized from the shadows. Andrade laughed. "Only six? Surely he could do better than that."

The dark warrior smiled and four more stepped forward.

Andrade grinned. "Still not enough."

Three more stepped forward.

Andrade laughed. "That's more like it."

The lead man shook his head. "You dare challenge the General?"

Andrade quit laughing. "He challenges me in sending you here. How dare he question me. This is your last chance to return to him with a message."

"And what would that message be?" the warrior asked.

"To never doubt me again." Andrade sent the man flying backward with a blast of light. Before the man hit the ground, the others all rushed in unison toward Miranda.

Miranda concentrated on Andrade and his light and attempted to send out a blast toward the oncoming danger, but nothing happened. There was no focus, no control. The white just jumped and shimmered around her. She looked at Andrade in panic.

"Focus, *Sweetheart*. Find your center." He reached into her own power through their bond to strengthened his enough to send the attacking warriors all a blast that knocked them back a good twenty feet.

Focus. Center. Not Andrade. No center with thoughts of Andrade. Braedan. Shoes off. Feel nature. Focus. Strawberries.

Whip cream. The white around her brightened and swirled strong around her. Braedan. Shirtless. Braedan holding her when she needed him. The white was so intense that it blew at her dress and tugged at the pins in her hair. Braedan always helping her. Braedan always with her.

The dark warriors regained their feet and attacked again. This time she simply placed a shield around her and Andrade. The warriors slammed against it again and again, but could not get through.

Andrade laughed. "Nicely done. But we need to finish them off and return to the ball before someone discovers our private little party out here."

Miranda hesitated. She knew they needed to end this battle before they were discovered, but the darkness pulsating just outside the shield was tempting her with its strength. It was as though it had a mind of its own and it wanted her. Even worse, she wanted it.

She was afraid to drop the shield. She needed extra strength. With a deep breath, she reached along the bond she shared with Andrade and drew from the strange shimmery strength that together they created. Feeling the added power, she dropped the shield and blasted the dark ones with light. There was so much darkness inside of them, that it took a steady blanket of white covering them before the darkness was weakened enough to let the light in. Miranda viewed the battle ground, thirteen dark warriors lay writhing on the ground in agony.

Andrade wrinkled his brow. "What did you do to them?"

Miranda was in her calm and focused center. Braedan induced. "I infused them with light."

"No. Finish them off," he said, snarling.

Miranda looked at him. "There is no need to destroy them. They are changing for the better."

Andrade spared the moaning warriors a thoughtful glance. "Perhaps. I suppose the torture you are putting them through is fitting enough."

"I am not causing them pain. If they simply release the darkness within, the white will take its place and they will find great peace."

Again, Andrade laughed. Miranda didn't share in his humor.

Miranda felt the darkness creeping up on her from behind and sent a blast of light without even looking behind her. She didn't need to. She felt them. She could feel the warriors' darkness snake forward, slicing through the white surrounding her and trying to claim her for its own. Her aim was accurate and nine more of the Dark General's men lay on the ground in excruciating pain, the white battling with their darkness.

Andrade smiled. "I am impressed. The General sent a small army to stop us. He has not amassed so many against one before. There has never been a need to do so. Too bad he didn't send more."

"Oh, but he did." Ten more came over the walls from all directions. The darkness they brought with them swirled and prodded against the white surrounding her. Miranda drew more of the shimmering light from Andrade to strengthen the barrier between her and the darkness. Andrade's light filtered through her own white energy and the darkness mingled with his light at the outer edges of her whiteness. She narrowed her eyes, watching the strange dance between the darkness and light.

"What is happening?" she asked Andrade.

"We are becoming one," he said with satisfaction.

Eyes wide, Miranda watched as the light and dark frolicked together. This was not like the battle the warriors on the ground were facing. She felt no pain. She felt only power—incredible power that flowed through her veins and filled her to the point of bursting with light. The warriors who had come over the wall paused and watched the awesome sight in front of them.

Andrade approached her, a look of possessive pride in his eyes. "You are powerful. Together, we will be unstoppable."

Miranda held up her hand to halt his approach. "Which side are you on?"

"Yours," he said, and he drew from her power to blast the ten who watched the awesome sight of their powers combining.

"But are you a Light Warrior or a Dark Warrior?"

He shrugged. "Does it matter?"

The temptation to say it no longer mattered was strong. Miranda nodded slowly. "Yes, it does."

"Why?"

These were hard questions when the darkness was so near, so very tempting. "Because the darkness cannot take control or it will destroy mankind."

"Do you really believe that?" he asked. "What could the Dark General possibly gain by destroying man? Who would he rule and what power would he control if mankind was wiped out?"

The darkness half-way infiltrated her protective circle of light, making it hard to think clearly. "There is more than one way to destroy man. Taking away our freedoms would end us just as surely as killing us."

Andrade shook his head. "Do you really think man is ready to rule themselves? Look around you. Man is destroying himself and the world as well. Would it not be better to control them until they learn how to take care of themselves?"

She was confused, and without her concentration, she was going to lose control of the white she had gathered. "Newsflash: the Dark General lies."

Andrade paused, then grinned. "Of course he does. And he cheats. But if you are one of his most favored, you receive all that you ask for."

"But are you still one of his most favored?"

Andrade lost his grin. "Perhaps not. We have destroyed more than thirty of his preferred warriors tonight. This will make him angry. Together we can appease him. With our power combined, we can rule alongside him. Join me."

He dropped his shield and Miranda saw the darkness within him for the first time, but it wasn't what she expected. He had light infused within the dark—woven together. She tipped her head and studied it. It reminded her of the gene sequences she had seen in science class—the threads entwined until inseparable. It was strangely beautiful, the white and dark mingled together. Was that what her white would soon look like?

"Can you see it?" he asked.

"Yes," she whispered, struggling to hang on to the white

around her. Her focus was becoming splintered.

"You did this to me. Your pure white is the only light powerful enough to bond with my darkness." He closed his eyes. "You have no idea how excruciatingly painful it was. But the old saying 'what does not kill you, makes you stronger' is most certainly true. I am now more powerful than any other warrior who has existed. Ever. Come. Join me." He looked at her and stretched out his hand.

Chapter Fifty-Seven

The shield of white separating her from the mingled light and dark was spiraling out of control.

Andrade sent a blast of darkness toward her, pushing the uncontrolled white away.

"No!" Miranda cried out, desperately trying to pull the light back around her. She stepped backward with the retreating white.

Andrade continued to hold out his hand. "Join me."

The darkness pushed the white away, just like in her dream. She panicked. She didn't want the dark crawling inside of her, choking off her air supply. She wanted to be good. She wanted to be light. She didn't want the darkness…Did she? She craved the power he had to offer her just as a drug addict craves the next hit. She wanted it so badly her hands shook. She shook her head. No. Darkness was bad. To claim the darkness would be painful. Not the pain. She felt that awful pain before—first from Andrade's bond, then in her dream.

Andrade's voice came to her through her confused fog, "There is no pain if you simply accept it. Accept it, Miranda."

She had to have it. She couldn't have it.

"The darkness is drawn to you. Feel the increase in strength it gives you. Embrace the power," he coaxed in a hypnotic voice. "If you don't fight it, there will be no pain. You don't have to let go of all the light. If you choose to keep it, we can have both. We need not join either side. We can become powerful enough to create our own faction. Think of it, *Sweetheart*. We need answer to no one."

The darkness beckoned her.

He sent waves of pulsing darkness toward her again. Her own scattered and out of control white barely kept it at bay.

"Together, you and I could rule the world. Feel the power. Feel the desire. Feel what has been destined for us. We were never born to serve. You and I, we were born to rule."

Miranda stopped struggling. Her eyes focused on Andrade. She opened her mind and her heart and felt along the bond they shared. She felt his power, his wants, and his desires. Her own turmoil was put to rest. She now knew the answer she had been looking for all along. Within the bond she shared with Andrade, she found the difference between Braedan and Andrade. Andrade loved power. Braedan loved her.

She knew Braedan loved her in the way he fed her, took care of her, and always came to her rescue. Braedan. He was her focus. He was her center, her trainer and her protector. And now, he had come to save her once again. When life got tough, he came to her rescue. He truly was her knight in *shining* armor.

He drew near and she felt the added power he gave her. The white secured around her once again. The darkness and temptation pushed back to a safe distance. Miranda smiled.

"Which will it be, *Love*? It is your choice," Braedan's deep, strong voice said from behind her.

Andrade glared at Braedan, but continued to hold out his hand. "Join me," he sais, demanding her answer.

She looked at Andrade. Wealth, power, control. These were the things he desired—he craved. He was incapable of true love. If he could feel love, he wouldn't be evil. Evil cannot love.

Miranda turned to see both men. They were handsome, strong, powerful. She was drawn to both of them. Bonded in a way no other human could understand.

She closed her eyes and found her center once again. When she opened her eyes a moment later, the power she felt came so strong, she knew it shined from within.

With her eyes open, she turned to Andrade. She saw his triumphant smile. She reached deep inside and released one of the strands connecting them. She no longer chose to be connected to someone who couldn't love. Not when her heart had chosen Braedan all along. Irritating, demanding, rule abiding, stiff—she loved all of it.

"What are you doing?" Andrade asked in stunned disbelief.

She released another shimmering, powerful strand.

"*Sweetheart*?" His eyes were round.

She released another.

"No!" he shouted, reaching for her.

"Hello, *brother*." Andrade's body stopped its forward movement. Braedan blasted him with his own power. "Continue, *Love*." Braedan coaxed her on.

He knew what she was doing? When had Braedan realized she was bonded to Andrade? Had he known all along?

"Focus, *Love*."

"No!" Andrade shouted again, charging forward against the white.

Braedan dropped his shield and met him halfway. They connected with a force that would have ended most mortal men. They exchanged blow for blow, punch for punch, and kick for kick.

Miranda stood by, knowing she could help end the battle, but even now she was reluctant to fight against Andrade. Besides, she knew that Braedan had a personal score to settle with one of his brothers. One of his very own had broken the rules and traded sides. Only one blood line raised activators. This meant Andrade was one of the Light General's offspring. He must have traded sides many, many years ago for Braedan not to recognize him. Depending on their ages, it was possible they had never met?

This brought up an interesting question, just how big and how old *was* Braedan's family? Considering the powerful blows being exchanged, perhaps she should wait for another time to ask these questions...

The battle was taking too long. She was impatient—only because she knew without a doubt Braedan would win. Should there be any question, she would send him some of her own energy through their bond. She watched a moment longer. Braedan got the upper hand. Andrade was strong, but Braedan was stronger, more skilled. Good would triumph over darkness once again. Miranda couldn't wait any longer, she focused and traced the threads still connecting her to Andrade, releasing yet another one of the ties that bound them together.

"No!" Andrade bellowed.

Braedan, about to initiate a stunning blow, paused looking to Miranda to see what had caused Andrade's distress.

Miranda continued and released another strand. The sooner they were separated, the better. "No!" Andrade roared, mentally reaching for her.

Too surprised to stop him, she felt him draw on her power through the remaining strands of their bond only milliseconds before he released the blast at Braedan. She watched, stunned, as Braedan's body absorbed the impact of the white woven with darkness and doubled over in pain.

"Braedan!" she screamed. Andrade sent a second and third blast into Braedan's body. She watched in horror. Braedan's powerful body slumped to the ground. Too late, she shielded Braedan's body and called on all of the light within her and surrounding her. She called on the white throughout the city. She called on nature. She called on love. Her entire body filled with light. She sent a focused blast at Andrade containing more white than she had ever released before.

Andrade slammed into the solid wall at the end of the yard—crumbling the bricks—before collapsing at its base in a heap.

Miranda rushed to Braedan's side.

"Braedan?" Her voice came in a hoarse whisper. He wasn't moving. She felt for his pulse, but her hands were shaking too hard to tell if he had one.

"Braedan?" she whispered again. Her hands continued to move over his body, searching for injuries. His chest wasn't moving. He wasn't breathing. This was her fault. Andrade had drawn on *her* power and used it to destroy Braedan.

"Braedan?" Her voice grew louder. "Braedan?" She was hysterical. This man was hers. She loved him. Weren't they destined to be together? "Braedan? Braedan? Open your eyes. Please?" she begged.

His eyes remained closed.

"Braedan?"

He wasn't responding.

She searched along the bond connecting them and felt the change. His end was losing its brightness. She watched the light that had always been Braedan grow dim. The white was leaving his body. He was not immortal. He could die. Her own energy, warped by Andrade, was killing the man she loved. She choked on a sob and closed her eyes. She couldn't lose him. Not now. Not when she finally realized how much he meant to her. She gathered the purest white she could find inside her and sent him a blast of light through the bond. Nothing. She placed one of her hands on the grass and dug into the soil, calling on the strength she could gain from nature. Braedan had taught her that. She tried again. This time she felt his body jerk, but his chest didn't rise. With tears flooding her cheeks, she refused to give up. She pulled from deep inside and called on the love she felt for him. "Please," she whispered, before she sent him another jolt. His chest heaved beneath her hands and he inhaled oxygen. Once. She opened her eyes and felt for his heartbeat. Nothing. He took a breath, which meant he wasn't dead. Right? She gathered more light and sent him another flash. His chest rose again. His heart began a slow and steady thump, but his eyes remained closed. She closed her eyes and once more drew on all that dwelt inside her and sent it to him.

"Miranda, *Love*," he whispered. "That is enough."

Her eyes flew open. "Braedan!" She cried, throwing her arms around him and infusing him with even more of her white in the process.

"Never close your eyes," he reprimanded her. Without releasing her, he sent a small blast of light at one last Arbiter who tried to sneak up on them. The dark warrior fell to the ground.

"Braedan," she said, reining kisses on his face.

"Yes, *Love*, I am going to be all right." He inhaled deeply. "In fact, I think you may have fixed me better than I was before," he said with a smile, pulling her down for a real kiss.

She participated, just as she had every time he kissed her. As always, he stopped too soon.

"Sorry, *Love*, there are things here we need to finish. Then I will take you home and show you how a proper kiss is done." His beautiful dark eyes shined, full of promise.

Miranda laughed. He helped her to her feet and she looked around at the bodies still on the ground. Half of them were already gone. The white had taken over in those warriors and they had slipped away—hopefully to seek a better way of life. The other half still writhed on the ground, their bodies doubled over in agony fighting the light.

Andrade lay on the ground, farthest away, his body motionless. "Did I kill him?" she asked Braedan.

Braedan looked at her. "Did you mean to?"

She frowned. "I'm not certain."

"Search along the bond and see for yourself."

Remaining with Braedan, Miranda hesitantly checked on the remaining strands that connected them. The blast she sent Andrade was enough to kill any dark warrior. But because he was so very powerful now, his body had not only survived, but was already healing itself. He was broken and bruised, but he would live. Unconscious, his body twitched at the pain of the new stronger white that fought for supremacy in his soul. The blast of light she sent him was more than anything he had absorbed from her. His body was fighting something more powerful than any other warrior had ever faced. She knew the white was attaching to the light already woven into his darkness, increasing its strength. His temporary inability to fight would make it easier for the white to win.

She watched with sadness. This man she had once been such a part of fought against the light even in his lifeless state. She didn't wish to see him suffer. He was evil and he nearly killed Braedan, but she had shared a bond with him and couldn't quite bring herself to hate him. With a heavy heart she carefully, and thoroughly detached each remaining link she held with him, strand by strand, until at last she was free. She breathed a sigh of relief before turning to Braedan.

"You knew I was bonded to him?"

Braedan nodded once.

"And you still liked me?"

He nodded again. "I know. Crazy, huh?"

She grinned in relief. "Yes."

Andrade moaned and his eyes fluttered open.

Braedan kept a tight hold on Miranda, and they walked across the grass to the dark warrior. Together they looked down on him and Braedan spoke. "If the white does not succeed in chasing the black from your dark soul, pass this message along to your boss...One day you may raise up one strong enough to fight the two of us combined, but until then, you will leave us in peace or we will destroy all of your followers and the darkness will end. The balance of the war has just shifted and the rules have been changed."

They turned to leave.

"Miranda...wait." Andrade's voice echoed his pain.

She turned back. "Yes?"

"How can you leave me? We are destined," he whispered above the pain.

She shook her head. "Destiny is a poor replacement for love... and you are incapable of love."

He groaned and his back arched off the ground, then dropped back. He panted, his eyes pleading. "I can accept the light in, then, the love will grow." It was more of a question, than a statement.

She shook her head.

His eyes bore into hers. "For you, I would change."

"For my power, you would change," she said, correcting him.

"No, it has already begun. You are the one to heal my heart and let me love again." His face contorted in pain and he stopped speaking.

Miranda felt sadness for him. "No, you only feel a desire for supremacy."

He raised one hand. "Help me. Join me. I will change for you."

Miranda shook her head. Even without the bond, she knew he was not capable of changing for her. "If you are so willing to change for me, why are you still fighting the light?"

His eyes bore into hers and his beautiful face twisted from a different kind of pain. "Because," he spat, "I have experienced this love you speak of and it is a weak and wasted emotion. No woman is worth the pain and misery it brings."

"I feel sorry for you." And she meant it.

Andrade let out a roar of pain. The darkness within him fought desperately against the much stronger light.

"Good luck," she whispered and turned away.

"Don't go!" He pleaded from the ground.

Braedan wrapped his arm around her waist and shared his new brighter light with her through the bond, trying to ease her sadness. They crossed the lawn. It was nearly empty of bodies now.

"Do you think he'll change?" she whispered.

"It is possible. I will hope for it, after all, he is my older brother."

"I'm so sorry," she whispered.

"Don't be. He must be very old, I have never met him before. And let's not forget, he did try to kill me. He would have destroyed you. We can hope the light will take hold, but there was much darkness inside him. He will have a long road back to the light if that is the path he choose."

As they neared the patio at the back of the building she looked back one last time at Andrade and was surprised to see he was already gone.

"Miranda, *Love*?"

"Yes?"

"Will you dance with me?" he asked, already pulling her into his arms.

"What?" She laughed, surprised. They had just fought the biggest battle of their lives and he wanted to dance?

"Listen. You can hear the music from here." He swayed with her to the soft melody. "Besides, you cannot look so breathtakingly beautiful and not chose to dance in the arms of the man you love."

Being held in his arms distracted her and it took her a moment to process his words. "Hey! You were doing so good, right up until that last little bit."

"What did I do wrong?" He raised one eyebrow.

She reached up and traced his brow with her fingertip. "Well, you started out great. You showed up at the ball just in the nick of time to rescue me—dressed the part of the dashing prince in a tuxedo—"

"Is a tuxedoed prince close enough to a knight in shining armor? Armor is difficult to come by, even in this city..."

"Don't interrupt. You saved me. You swept me into your arms. Then you told me I loved you...here's where you went wrong, *Danny*, you were supposed to tell me something I didn't already know. Like, how much *you* love *me*..."

"Miranda, *Love*, I have been telling you I love you from the very first day we met."

"Oh," there was that witty humor of hers again. "Wait...Huh?"

"Think about it, *Love*."

If her arms hadn't been wrapped around him, she would've smacked herself in the forehead. "You mean your nickname for me..."

"Yes, *Love*."

She gazed into his eyes and saw what she had been looking for all along reflected in their depths. "We missed dinner. Will you feed me?"

"Of course," he said. Stepping back, he lifted her hand, spinning her around twice before pulling her up tight against his body.

She laughed, reaching up and pulling his head down to hers. His smile was absolutely brilliant and just before their lips touched, she whispered, "My hero. My knight of light."

From the first romance I read I was hooked—thanks to author Johanna Lindsey and her perfect Uncle Tony! After that, I refused to settle for anything less than a man who could make my blood run hot and who would treat me like a "princess." A few years back I decided the best way I was going to be swept off my feet by such a man was if I got down to the business of creating this perfect hero myself. So, that's exactly what I did!

I wrote four books before *Knight of Light* (see my website www.annette-louise.com for titles). My sixth book *Knight Games,* is the sequel to *Knight of Light*. It is Andrade's story and I'm writing it now!

Knight Games

Chapter One

Thirty feet from the front door Tianna's steps slowed. The darkness radiated outward from her apartment. Twenty feet and the strength of the light pulsing through the fury of the darkness hit her. Ten feet and she nearly doubled over in pain at the suffering coming from inside. She stared at the door and the desire to turn and run overwhelmed her.

"Jackson." The word escaped as an anguished whisper. Jackson was inside. She sensed his innocent soul just beyond the haze of misery that tried to consume her. She forced her feet to take a step forward.

Her brow wrinkled in concentration as her mind sorted through the confusing signals. With every step drawing her closer to the entrance of her small apartment, the pulsing waves of the battle raging on the other side of the door assulted her. Considering the strength of the mixed emotions, she expected to hear the sound of a violent battle taking place, perhaps even see a body come crashing through the wall and land at her feet, but there was only silence—the hallway empty. The doors near her own, belonging to other tenants, remained closed and no sound came from within them. She was alone—just her, Jackson, and whatever else lay inside the place she called home.

The incoming pain numbed her. She hadn't yet been able to block it out of her system. *Jackson.* She had to face whatever horror awaited her on the other side of the wooden door because that's where he was. She inhaled through her nose and exhaled—clearing the old air out of her lungs. One more inhale, this time gathering any good energy from the air around her and using its healing strength to push the pain to the far corner of her skull. Exhaling, she reached for the silver door knob. Her fingertips rested on the cold metal circle and she wished she had a weapon of some kind. She had no idea what she would face once she turned the knob.

A fresh wave of excitement from the pure spirit inside washed over her. *Jackson.* It no longer mattered what waited for her. Jackson needed her. She raised her chin and tightened her grip, preparing to open the door, when the knob in her hand turned on its own.

"Sis!" Jackson's green eyes were wide with excitement when he flung the door wide. "Get in here!" He grabbed her arm and pulled her in, closing and locking the door behind her.

Tianna's gaze swept the small living room and found nothing out of order. No broken furniture, no blood, no signs of any battle taking place. Except the intense pain that spread through her head once again.

"I know. It hurts. Block it."

She looked up at Jackson when he spoke, startled to see his grin. The only observable sign of anything amiss was his blond hair, which normally hung just below his ears, now stood on end like he had run his hands through it.

"I don't understand," she whispered. Her eyes darted around the room once more.

Jackson's lean frame almost vibrated with excitement. "I found a man. He's unlike anything I've ever felt before. Come." He grabbed her hand, pulling her toward his bedroom. "You have *got* to see this."

Tianna resisted.

"It's safe." He tried to reassure her, pulling her forward again.

Tianna pushed the pain to the corner of her brain where it belonged—the space that allowed her to function when the feelings she picked up on were too intense.

"Ready?" Jackson opened his bedroom door and stepped inside.

Tianna wanted to close her eyes, shield herself from what

might be inside her younger brother's room, but she didn't. She was drawn forward to the form. She stepped softly across the carpet and looked at the large shape lying motionless on the too small bed. It appeared to be a man. Large. Blond.

She sucked in air through her teeth. *He's beyond beautiful – like a fallen angel.* "Explain yourself."

Jackson bounced on his heels. The excitement radiated off every inch of his six-foot frame. "I was walking home from the gym and felt *this,*" he indicated the man on the bed. "*From almost two blocks away*!"

Tianna said nothing. Her silence demanded more of an explanation than he had given her so far.

"Sis, I've never felt anything like it. *Ever.*" Her brother stared at her. "What do you make of it?" he asked.

She shook her head. She had no idea. The man on the bed was warring with *himself.* There was no visible battle taking place in Jackson's bedroom, yet there was a war raging inside of this man stronger than any she had felt the likes of before.

"There is good inside of him. I had to help him." Jackson's energy changed to signs of nervousness at her silence.

Without looking away from the man, she said, "There is also great darkness inside of him."

Jackson sighed. "I couldn't leave him there. He was all alone."

For the first time since entering the room, Tianna's eyes snapped to his. "Jackson, he is not a puppy. You do *not* bring strange men home with you as though they were a stray animal. Especially not a *rabid* puppy."

Jackson snorted and an easy grin split his face. "Puppy nothing—this man is more like a pitbull!" Realizing what he had just said wasn't helping his case, Jackson hurried to reassure her. "He won't bite us. The good inside of him is strong. I can feel it replacing the darkness. He needs help while he heals. I couldn't leave him lying in the ally. He would've been unprotected."

Now Tianna sighed, her eyes traveling back to the man who dominated the twin size bed. The bed was small for her brother, but the man lying on it reminded her of the story about Goldie Locks—if they weren't careful, he might crash the little bed to the floor.

"Come on, Sis. There is good inside of him—good that's brighter than any whiteness I've experienced before. I couldn't leave him there to die. You know we have a responsibility to help him."

Tianna tightened her lips. "No, we don't."

The man arched on the bed and at the same time a fresh wave of pain slammed into her skull. Tianna pushed the pain into the corner and closed a mental door on it. She knew Jackson did the same when he straightened back up. The man lying on the bed was not so lucky. His eyes remained closed, but there was a fine sheen of sweat on his forehead. His white button up shirt was already damp.

"See, he's fighting it. We have to help him."

Tianna took her time answering. "Yes, he is fighting it. The question is, which side is he fighting for?"

CPSIA information can be obtained
at www.ICGtesting.com
Printed in the USA
FFOW03n2055231014
8310FF

9 781934 05177